# Seahorses
## are real

For Mark

# Zillah Bethell
# Seahorses are real

seren

Seren is the book imprint of
Poetry Wales Press Ltd
57 Nolton Street, Bridgend, Wales, CF31 3AE
www.seren-books.com

ISBN: 978-1-85411-494-5

A CIP record for this title is available from the British Library.

Cover image: 'Winnie' by Rosie Irvine www.rosieirvine.com
Typesetting by Lucy Llewellyn www.lucyllew.com
Printed by Bell and Bain, Glasgow

Extract from *The Little White Horse* by Elizabeth Goudge,
published by Lion Hudson, reprinted with kind permission.

The publisher works with the financial assistance of The Welsh Books
Council.

**Mixed Sources**
Product group from well-managed
forests and other controlled sources
www.fsc.org   Cert no. TT-COC-002769
© 1996 Forest Stewardship Council

FSC

# Contents

She knew that one day, when she was a very old woman, she would dream this dream for the last time, and in this last dream of all she would see the little white horse, and he would not go away from her. He would come towards her and she would run towards him, and he would carry her upon his back away and away, she did not quite know where, but to a good place, a place where she wanted to be.

*The Little White Horse*

# Part one

# Fairies, feathers and Quality Street

# One

At the edge of the town there are tulips and pretty cottages, bright fences and small dogs, foxes and wild rabbits. There is a quarry where boys fish and herons sit hunched like old men in overcoats or open their wings and fly in slow motion. On the hills towards Farningham you can sometimes see a horse silhouetted against the sky or a tractor going up and down the fields in pyjama stripes. There were orchards long ago – before the motorway – around the woods at Farningham. Apple trees and pear trees apparently. The boys would sit beneath the trees and watch the dogfights – they didn't get much schooling. It's a cricket ground now and a model aeroplane club on Saturdays. You couldn't hear a sound in the orchards long ago.

St Margaret of Antioch rises up, like a medieval hat, into the flight path of birds and Boeings heading for Heathrow, dreams and prayers heading for God. There are many soldiers buried here and one Anna Czumak, who suffered much in this life. You can see the Dartford bridge on a clear day, straddling the Thames and the boats that have come from Gravesend, though they no longer sail for the Holy Land. At night it looks like a fairground attraction – a giant Ferris wheel or even a Christmas tree. If you followed the Darenth River to the Thames you would eventually come to the sea. If you follow the Darenth River through Sutton at Hone, past the tulips and pretty cottages, bright fences and small dogs, foxes and wild rabbits, you eventually come to the trade park where cars are dumped, like rusty old dinosaurs, for fun and for birds to make nests in. Crows' feet lead along the track beside the lake where you have to beware of Bohemia's ghost repenting poisoning her lover with agrimony and meadow saffron; of lines and mermaids' hair full of fish eyes, hooks and cut-glass confetti; trees laden with graffiti ('I like it firm and meety'); and last but not least the old Canterbury road where many pilgrims must have trailed in search of an ever-receding god. To the park where Leslie Finch sits watching the kids and waiting for a bus, though he never takes one; where Rasputin strides tall and tyrannical with his tiny pink haversack; and Pegleg Pete hops around collecting snails (He was in the war!) in plastic carrier bags. Gentlemen and old ladies congregate in the shrubbery per diem for a whiskey mac and a packet of nasturtium seeds while gardeners bend over hollyhocks, chrysanthemums, primulas and old bones and the library sits with its unkempt shelves next to the public lavatories and a memorial for the dead.

There are directions here for a Sikh temple that has never been found by its worshippers, Talk of the Town (How much can you handle, boys?), the Emmanuel Pentecostal and a Tudor church. In ancient times (mainly Tudor), so the saying goes, an old hermit sat with his back to the church and helped travellers across the ford. He was a pilgrim of a sort. He doused and sang and waited by his billabong – they must have washed their clothes in the Darenth too – and now Waltzing Matilda sits feeding the ducks and if you do not look at her too close or speak to her too long you cannot tell that she is mad. The Emmanuel Pentecostal is always full on Sundays and they park quite hazardously round the launderette on East Hill, where there was once a Peasants' Revolt in 1382 due to unfair tax and impoverished conditions; where the cemetery sits above the steeple because 'Dartford people are the

strangest people and bury their dead above the steeple';
and Marly stood with her hand on Umfreville's tomb,
wondering at what bad luck people had.

Somebody had fallen asleep in the lap of God, another
had swapped time for eternity. Two or three were
remembered in the grave while a party of six had tragically
died yachting off Greenhithe. One more, unlucky man, had
had a son die in the Darenth and another in the Tebekwe.
Blessed husband, loving son, beloved wife, precious one and
only... a jam jar upturned, two withered flowers, an
evergreen wreath and a florist's loopy card – each grave its
own universe. What a story each could tell, Marly thought,
and her fingers sought the tip of the shopping list she had
come across suddenly, unexpectedly, in her mother's coat
pocket, like an odour blown on the wind: awakening long-
forgotten memories, memories that haunt the edge of
dreams, her mother's ashes on the breeze. Milk, two bread,
orange juice, fish. They would have had cod in white sauce
for supper that night, for sure. Ivy, ever pristine. Between
Scylla and Charybdis. Between a rock and a hard place.
That's what her gravestone would have said: Ivy, ever
pristine, between Scylla and Charybdis, between a rock and
a hard place.

Marly blinked away the tears and craned her long neck
up at the horse chestnut trees. Horse chestnut trees were
trees of death, trees of death and varicose veins apparently,
of conker fights and bonfire nights, supper and ashes, seeds
and ashes. Seeds and ashes on the breeze. How beautifully,
how perfectly they popped out of their prickly lime-green
pods – a deep, rich, varnished mahogany – and yet how
quickly they were tarnished or bashed in playground fights,
hardened little warriors hot-roasting in the oven. Tough
little pipsqueaks with grey socks and cold sores. Marly
moved like an automaton along the concrete path, mentally
ticking off the register – Ruth Kemp? Here miss. Charles
Messenger? Here miss. Patience Penn? Here miss. Clara

Weaver? Here Miss – and a class of old bones grinned back at her, except for Ivy, of course. Ivy Smart? Absent miss. Absent due to death. Marly Smart? Absent miss. Absent due to her complaint. Her complaint! What a ridiculous word. What a limited dictionary those doctors had, to be sure.

She cracked her knuckles in the open air. To be sure, that was the thing. To be sure of being loving and beloved, unconditionally loving and beloved like the fairytale books of happy ever after, the childhood imaginings of tall dark handsome strangers, the fizzy sweets you sucked and read: 'Blue Eyes', 'My Heart', 'Pretty Lips'.

They had lied, of course, the fizzy sweets and the fortune fish. The fizzy sweets had lied! The fortune fish had lied! You sucked and sucked and read and read and it didn't get you anywhere. Might as well be back in the pram, her friend Helen had said; and it was true that life did not progress in a linear fashion nor was it predictable, though Marly read her stars each week and desperately tried to make them fit. You could regress way past the pram, way past birth, until you were seeing through the eyes of your father, your mother, even your grandmother. It was a horrible fact but true. Things shattered in through the wallpaper, breaking your world apart until you were on your knees, on your back, paws up and begging at the sky, like the fox she had seen on the motorway, dead and begging at the sky. It was a makeshift life, they should have said, the fizzy sweets and the fortune fish, a rickety thing built on the sands of disappointment, disillusion, even tragedy; a jumper of loose ends, knit on the needles of terror and the French Revolution with wool the cat got hold of first. Ever shrinking, ever stretching, in colour co-ordinations even Ariel couldn't fix. Lumping up like porridge when you needed it most – home-made, no treacle – porridge even the bears would have left, let alone Goldilocks. Goldilocks was an imagined fact, for children. Adults and bears got on with the burnt leftovers, the bread and scrape of days.

# Seahorses are real

It didn't really matter, Marly thought, sprawled against the cemetery wall and watching two boys playing with a large yellow ball like a dirty full moon, that your eyelids got a little creased – she could cover them with iridescent blue shadow; that your hair became a little thin – she could sweep it over to one side; that your feet were worn and calloused – she could wrap them up in thick stockings and pink stilettos (she had always wanted pink stilettos); it didn't even matter that your mind got a little strained now and again – she could dose it up with paracetamol and Oprah Winfrey shows. But when your head had left you for the body of a passing stranger, an uninhabited crow's nest, a blue violet, then you were really in trouble, she decided, watching two boys kicking an old moon about, pointing, whispering, then eventually smiling at her. She smiled back, feeling jarred, embarrassed; almost fearful. Two boys with a ball like an old moon could do that to her now. It was unthinkable. She got up, pretending to look at a bowl of roses on a fresh grave – a visiting relative perhaps – and her eyes saw her mother's body in the chapel of rest, statuesque in its white lace Edwardian dress, ice cold, frost-filagreed. One of her mother's economy drives that dress – it had lain packaged up in the cupboard for years, along with the unopened bottles of Chanel perfume she'd been given – awaiting its purpose like the pink, sequined, honeymoon dress (meant for Marly) in the glory box above the boiler. No fear! 'Damned sore. Had to lock myself in the bathroom all night.' Ivy, ever pristine, between Scylla and Charybdis... Marly twisted the daisy ring on the silver chain around her neck, too big for her twiglet fingers. He loves me, he loves me not. A ring from Topshop, David had said. What more do you want?

A vacuum bomb, she whispered, climbing over the wall when the two boys weren't looking. Hoovering stuff out and sucking stuff in. That was her complaint. Someone had opened her head with a rusty tin-opener, she was open to

the ether, and the traffic in and out was worse than the
M25, though no one paid her a quid at any tollbooth.
(Cross my palm with silver, pretty lady.) They just walked
in, wiped their feet, had a dump and went out saying thank
you very much. Things flew by, fell in, got stuck and lay
putrefying: a few twigs, an old leaf, somebody's face, a bad
day, a daffodil maybe or a dead cat, scraps of conversation,
even the shape of a tree. They all got stuck in that little
garbage can, stinking, overflowing, emptied sometimes but
always refilling. A little garbage can that ran across zebra
crossings so the cars didn't have to wait so long. Smile, smile
and the agony abides, someone had said and it was true.
Apologising almost for being there, for having to cross the
road at that particular place, impeding their speeding
progress, their mobile machines. How ridiculous! I feel like
a piece of trash, she said to David in her worst moments;
and he would put on his tender eyes and say in his wise old
Gandalf voice: 'You're a little piece of stardust if only you
could see it.' She could kick him then, for not understanding
that at that moment, ever before and ever after, she really
was a piece of trash, a piece of trash that ran across zebra
crossings so the cars didn't have to wait so long.

'No fear, not me!' sang a voice in her head as she walked
down the road to their little flat, the ring thumping against
her chest, her backbone jutting out (an abnormality
inherited from her mother) almost through the skin so that
her neck reached forward like a delicate, etiolated plant
making a bid for the sun. Lovely boy and all that. 'A real
brick,' some horsey woman in a book would have said. 'A
real brick, by Jove!' But wife didn't quite feel right. It didn't
envelop her tongue the way fiancée did. Wife was a life of
soapsuds and dishcloths, daydreams and under the thumb.
Wife was merging with the sealed-up things in the
cupboard. Put away. Done and dusted. Wife was a life
between a rock and a hard place – Ivy had taught her that.
Fiancée, on the other hand, had a pretty-sounding ring to it,

but not the heavy, dark, gold thing that made you, like Frodo, a little more invisible every day. Oh no, fiancée was flashing daisies on silver chains. Loving me, loving me not. Completing but never completed. Fiancée was promising to give yet ever withholding.

It suited Marly perfectly.

# Two

David was waiting for her in the kitchen and cooking pasta, which he did when he was worried about her or got home early. His pasta meals had developed over the years from a simple cheese and tomato affair to a gastronomic extravaganza full of bits of old vegetable he'd found in the fridge – mushrooms, peppers, courgettes, potatoes – thrown into the pan and let sizzle seemingly for hours on end while he sang and clicked his fingers to any old tune in his head, jumping onto the magic carpet, as he put it, when he got to the good bits. In response to Marly's refrain that the life was boiling out of her as well as the vegetables he would say that it was love grub, practical love – it took great time and care – and she had come to understand, as she waited for her supper in an old pink dressing-gown, that in every buttered mushroom, skinned potato and deflowered tomato there was love, painstaking love. Sometimes, however, when faced with a steaming mound of vegetable and pasta, she would have preferred a simple *I love you.*

'I love you,' he said now, in greeting, a questioning note to his voice.

'And you,' she returned, homing into his outstretched arms, her eyes avoiding his.

He sighed and kissed the top of her head. It had taken her two years to let him touch her face. She was a bottomless pit and sometimes he could shout in frustration. Sometimes he did shout in frustration.

'Guess who,' she said after a while, disentangling herself and looking at him now, almost expectantly, 'was painting the door all day in a pair of purple trousers and a little kerchief?'

'Oh no, not the purple trousers,' he joked. 'Mr Ratty?'

'Has he been out?' Marly cried in alarm, her toe nudging the porridge and peanut butter-filled trap that lay against the wall beneath the table. 'Humane Dead Cert' it had said on the box.

David shook his head. 'Not a squeak out of him. I've been dancing about on the floorboards: he thinks I'm some sort of voodoo fella! I'll put poison down when you're gone,' he added.

Marly half smiled. She was always on the point of going, leaving for a new life in the countryside, by the seaside, somewhere nice away from this hellhole, but she never did, would or could without him. It was simply a threat she used to keep him precariously balanced, on his toes, never quite settled in the relationship; and it was not for him to be telling her she was going but for her to be telling him.

'No,' almost angrily, 'Mrs M. All day she was on that stupid stepladder. I went up and down three times and in the end I thought I've got to come in for lunch. She said all the snails were coming from the bin, you know, nicely, but it was obvious she meant we should clean it.'

'Fuck it,' said David. 'Don't worry about it.'

'Well, it was a bit embarrassing.' Marly chewed her bottom lip. 'She said, "It's very auspicious I caught you because the new tenant Jason's moving in on Saturday." You know how she speaks. He's been commuting all the way from Hampshire if you please.' Marly grinned, being Mrs M. '"All the way from Hampshire if you please. He's an optical technician apparently."'

'She's the sort of person,' David reflected, stirring the

seething red mass on the stove, 'who'd talk about condiments. And utensils.'

'Mmm.' Marly started to unlace her muddy old trainers.

'What an arse!' cried David – it was a ritual – as she bent over.

'I know, I know. People'd give their eye teeth for this arse.' Hovering barefoot on her way to the sitting room she added, 'There was this little kid in a buggy like a dodgem car with a stick thing up the back his mother was pushing him round with. It was dead cute. He was pretending, you know, to steer the wheel. He had little goggles on and a gas mask thing for asthma.'

'Pollution,' David corrected, smiling at the image of a begoggled baby in a bumper car, gleaning what he could from her mishmash of words. Her sentences got worse – strange to think she'd once been Ophelia – as if her brain were disintegrating or moving too fast for her mouth. She made stuff up half the time to fit her own reality, swapping meanings, pouring words out all jumbled up, all mixed up like vomit. She set no store by the things she said, calling him all the names under the sun, not caring whether they hurt or pleased. And yet she set great store, a squirrel's store by his words, hoarding up something he'd said unthinkingly years ago and bringing it out like a ripe nut in every argument, her bright eyes twitching. 'That thing you said to me in Birmingham, two years ago.' She was a squirrel for hoarding that sort of thing. 'What thing? What are you on about?' And yet, he thought, softening, she'll be sitting right now on the settee with that wretched book of hers, staring at the Moses basket and the brightly coloured nursery – how she loved the brightly coloured nursery – reeling off the things you should eat when you're pregnant: sardines, broccoli, raspberry leaf tea. (He knew them off by heart. He even knew the weight a six-month foetus should be.) It was a crazy addiction she had, a craving to know, to participate vicariously in a process she might never experience. He congratulated himself on the phrase – to participate vicariously in a process she might never experience – not bad for a dim, narrow, weak-minded mathematician! Still, he thought, frowning, any phrase was better than stealing a begoggled baby in a bumper car!

'No, but anyway,' Marly continued as they settled into their food, 'it's like I'm a fugitive from my own lies, my own life. I sat here for ages waiting for her to go and then I thought, you know, I'm meant to be at work – she must have thought I was a right mess – so I went up the cemetery.' She didn't tell him about the boys with a ball like an old moon. At first she'd told him everything – it'd been like a burden being lifted from her shoulders – babbling away the stored-up years, every little secret, every last dream, until she was emptied, serene, ready to be filled again with his love. Now their communication was deeper, less tangible – an intimate code of intercepted utterances, delicate tappings, invisible springs and hieroglyph smiles that affirmed their knowingness, their habitual togetherness. Marly sometimes felt that the code half stifled them and it was then she babbled away as in the early days while he, puzzler that he was, took refuge in trying to decipher her heart.

'You're a poor little thing,' he said, smiling a little between forkfuls.

'I am a poor little thing. And the sooner you realise it the better.'

'I do realise it,' he said, sadly this time.

Marly stiffened. Poor little thingedness was all very well for getting sympathy but not pity. Self pity was alright but pity from others she didn't like. 'I caught a bit of Oprah,' she said, changing the subject. 'It was terrible....'

'Caught a bit,' scoffed David. 'You had a lovely old time of it, sprawled out here with your feet up.'

'No I didn't,' indignantly, 'I told you I was up the cemetery.'

Zillah Bethell

'I know, I know. I was just having a laugh with you.'

'Well, anyway,' Marly went on, irritated a little by his effervescence, 'there was this kid who'd been attacked. It was ninety degrees apparently and the puppy had a seizure. It was so bad they couldn't show the pictures – he was just skeleton and teeth.'

'Jesus,' David muttered appropriately, not yet having a clue what she was on about.

'They made a face for him out of his arms and legs – like me mam, d'you remember, when she had her neck grafted with fat from her bottom. She said her backside afterwards looked like a wrinkled elephant's. Oh dear.' Marly lapsed hysterically into a giggle.

David nodded, remembering. 'It's alright, my love.'

'They'll be transplanting faces soon apparently. They had this monkey – it was horrible – with a transplanted head. They said, "It's so exciting, his eyes are tracking us." They kept going on about how marvellous it was they'd saved this kid's life and everything with this miracle surgery but... I mean... you should've seen him. He looked terrible.'

David rolled his eyes in mock despair. Here we go, he thought.

'I mean it's hard enough for most people to live, to exist, let alone a kid with a face made up of arms and legs. What sort of life's he going to have?' He'll miss out on the adolescent vitamin for sure, she thought. 'I don't know, it should be wonderful, the fact that he's alive and that but... it might've been better... people have such terrible lives.'

'That's true,' said David tonelessly.

'It's like the bit of an end of a documentary I saw...'

'Yeah, yeah, bet you saw the whole...'

'No, seriously, when you were at your evening class. There was this Russian woman who had to sweep the streets from ten thirty at night till four in the morning and she only got paid three quid for it. We don't know we're born,' Marly added.

14

'That's true,' agreed David and then quickly, 'I love you,' because it was his job, he felt, to nip things in the bud, to bring her back before she was anywhere near close to the brink. 'I think you're marvellous.'

'Am I?' she cried, falling as always – childishly eager – into the trap. 'In what way am I marvellous?'

David put his finger to his chin as if pondering the question for the first time. 'Every way. Ironing shirts, washing socks…'

'Hor*rid!*'

He laughed and opened his arms wide. 'You're beautiful and soft and gentle and,' stupidly, 'you're a poor little thing.'

'I'm alright,' Marly pushed back at him, sealing up the vulnerability, pleased to hear she was such things yet feeling none of them.

He put the television on then, flicking through the channels with a cumbersome grace, his arms still close about her.

'You don't care do you?' she remonstrated, breaking free, feeling there was still some point or other to be made, that the depth of their discussion wasn't up for grabs, didn't warrant the usual crisp-packet-in-the-cinema routine which he employed for effect in moments of high seriousness. 'D'you want a crisp?' he'd whispered once, loud and rustling into the dark, tense, tenterhooked silence, much to Marly's amused embarrassment. 'D'you want a crisp?' She eyed him suspiciously now but he was innocent enough, his face sad, angry even.

'It's because I care. To distract you. Stop you moping about.' And it was true he'd turned it on to distract her, as well as himself, from her misery, her unrelenting misery that brought him down, sometimes, as low as she. I work hard all day, he thought, and come back to this.

'I'm not moping,' she muttered sulkily, sitting very straight on the sofa and opening her book at 'Lilian's Caesarean Section', tears welling up in her eyes. He'll never understand, she thought, it'll never work, and she read a sentence blurrily over and over: 'I felt I'd missed out on the real thing, having a Caesarean. I felt I'd missed out on the real thing, having a Caesarean. I felt I'd missed out on the real...'

David chuckled and nudged her. She focused even harder on the sentence though her ears, in spite of herself, were listening. 'I felt I'd missed...'

'In a tropical jungle like this one,' came an excited little whisper from the television, 'bright colours signify genuine nastiness.' Marly looked up and saw a man in shorts and a Panama hat. 'But this little humdinger of a treecreeper's got everything he wants right here under his very nose, a veritable cornucopia right under his nose. Figs! It's all he eats. He relishes them, can't get enough of them.'

'Relishes 'em,' spluttered David. 'I bet he's sick to death of them!'

Marly giggled and put down her book. 'You'd be off for a slap-up curry,' she teased, sarcastically enough to sound as if she hadn't quite given in yet. 'With ketchup,' she added.

'What, what!' David obliged, being the proprietor of Mariners where he – she never let him forget – had had ketchup with everything. Mariners, where they'd stayed two nights for one of his interviews, where Marly had laughed and smiled at the sea view, the little sachets of hot chocolate, the bourbons and custard creams; and the proprietor who'd looked like a toad, made his own clocks and gone about saying 'what what' all the time. '"Full English breakfast is it again sir? With ketchup? You're a brave man sir. What what!"'

'You scoffed all the custard creams,' she reminded him delightedly. 'Remember that china dog on the mantelpiece you said looked like it had worms!'

'Well, it was the position of its legs,' David explained for the umpteenth time, knowing how much it amused her. 'It was uncannily like our old dog Rosie when she slid her bottom....'

'Yes yes, thank you very much. I think we've heard quite enough about that. Mind you,' Marly's eyes glimmered, 'I had a worm remember, when I was little.... It kept sliding back up my...'

David leapt up and ran out of the room, pretending to be horrified at the story.

Marly giggled and he came back in. They sat together in happy silence, holding hands beneath the red sleeping bag and watching television. 'At least he's passionate about it,' Marly said after a while, meaning the man in shorts and a Panama hat. 'I bet you wouldn't mind a few students like that.'

'Well, I don't know,' David grimaced. 'It's not normal to be keen at their age. I think I prefer Ross Newman's belching. Honestly, that's all he does: leans back on his chair with his can of coke and belches!'

'He doesn't!'

David perched himself on the edge of the sofa with a dopey expression on his face. '"Do we need our books today sir?" Every bleeding lesson he says it. "Do we need our books today sir? Do we need our books on Friday sir?" I said: "Bring 'em anyway, it'll keep you fit!"'

Marly rested her head on his shoulder and listened to his anecdotes, knowing he was making an effort and grateful, too, for every last detail of Ross Newman's belching, of Anton the French teacher who always said 'Bonjour Class' and whose students ran amok and sent messages to each other on their mobile phones, because these were things that connected her back to a world she was drifting away from further and further each day, swinging out into orbit; and only David's arms, she sometimes felt, (he being the only one she trusted) could clutch her back.

They read their books after that, drifting off into other worlds yet side by side beneath the red sleeping bag, shoulder to shoulder, thigh to thigh, heartbeat almost to heartbeat, nodding off now and then like an old married couple or stopping just to peek at where the other was at.

This was Marly's refuge, her retreat from a world that lay beyond the confines of their cramped little rundown flat, where the rats played and the green mould grew. She sat reading books amidst the refuse of her life, books she'd read as a child over and over, dear and familiar like a pair of old shoes, the woman who lived in a shoe. Trying to regain a part of herself she'd lost, a part that had burnt out, died. Striving to resurrect herself, ghostly, in those ridiculous too-tight shoes. Whittling time away to bone washed up on ancient beaches, to daylight dimmed in the eye of an ant. There was no need for any other, no world to let in here. If I could shoot the world to bits, she sometimes thought, we might just make it.

She wrote that night in her gratitude diary:
1 Saw a ball like an old moon.
2 Slept ok.
3 Didn't check cheek.
4 D told me about R. Newman.
5 I am alive.

She always wrote 'I am alive' for number five, not because she was always grateful for being alive, but because she thought that if she didn't, something worse might happen.

# Three

She had one of her nightmares that night. It started off pleasantly enough – they always did – with her and David skimming stones from the pebbly bank of a swollen river, the softly slanting rain dribbling down their noses and between their toes. The river was brown and swirling bric-a-brac, dead wood and submarinating trolleys; and on the sandy bank opposite was a little forked set of bird-prints, like arrows. (When you saw only one set of prints, came a voice in her head, that was when I carried you.) 'Here's a good flat one,' said David. 'Try that.' And she flung the stone bouncing – once, twice, thrice – across to the sandy shore, like an India rubber or little superball. 'What must we be to the fish,' she decided, all knowing and omnipotent, 'in their watery mirror but glowing ghosts or wide-awake trees'; and she spread her arms wide in an arc to encompass the small green field by the pebbly bank and said to David with great serenity or was it solemnity: 'I shall grow vegetables here. It will be like a garden of Paradise. There will be birds and flowers and all beautiful things. All bright and beautiful things.'

'You're a bright and beautiful thing,' he replied, holding her, before turning into a small flat stone in her hands which she flung bouncing – once, twice, thrice – across to the sandy shore, like an India rubber or little superball.

And then she turned, herself, into a short fat farmer

from Idaho and said to herself (for she was both the short fat farmer as well as the painted lady hovering in front of his nose in search of cabbages): 'you'll grow no watermelons here no more. I used to grow 30lb Jack in the Beanstalk watermelons afore the river changed its malignant course.'

And she saw, with her own eyes, that the top of the precious field, where she was to grow all the bright and beautiful things, had been nibbled away by the hungry river, great clods and chunks of earth – still growing grass and golden buttercups – sitting halfway down the animal's throat; and the beach where they'd skimmed stones was really the great naked pebbly belly revealed as the beast swerved out again. 'How disgusting,' she said as the sweet-toothed Ivy sped down with the current on a little dead wood tree, her arms flailing. 'You, you,' she pointed and screamed. 'Left mammary. Your fault.' And her father's purple fingers curled up through the dead wood branches, like some maleficent river god making a grab at its pretty queen.

She screamed in her sleep and woke up sweating and clinging on to the last few shreds of the dream. How ridiculous to feel such agony in such a thing as a dream. How ridiculous the mind can be, she thought, and lay trembling and watching the headlights of cars as they passed like illuminating beacons across the curtains. 'I hope it is cancer,' she remembered herself saying so many years ago in a similar room, enraged little fists pumping the pillow of a toy bed by a toy chair, toy bookcase, toy Tobermory lamp. How she wished she could get up now, touch every last poster – Duran Duran, Blondie, Adam Ant, Spandau Ballet – and make it alright again. That magical sequence of cause and effect and that perfect little ego at the core of it. Believing, in those days, that touching posters, watching magpies and stepping on lines could alter an iota, a destiny; a life even. Stranger still to think that these things lingered in the adult mind, mushroomed, even though no longer believed in; the ego so battered by cause and effect that it clung on to the slightest, littlest, remotest hope that it still had control of cause and effect through the arbitrariness of magpies, posters and stepping on lines – though Ivy, of course, had died. No amount of stuffing cushions into covers could keep her soul in place. Bleak news, I'm afraid, the doctor had said. (They were always afraid.) She's got five years at most. What a lot of rot they talked! She'd gone on for ages after that – the everlasting Ivy, the sweet-toothed Ivy, the one-breasted Ivy. Stuffing marshmallows into her neck until they oozed out of her globulous eyelids. Biting into her marshmallow arms, even her marshmallow legs. Delusional, hallucinatory; sinking slowly in fits and starts – a death of agonising slowness bit by bit – into that banquet of bluebells. Better to go, Marly decided, touching posters in her head, in one fell swoop; and the cells proliferated like the fungi in the bathroom, the rats in the kitchen, giving each other a leg up. UB40. What am I gonna do? Sign on. See Terry. What am the fuck I gonna do?

She woke David up then, before her thoughts spun too far out; and told him about the dream, exaggerating details here and there to justify having woken him.

'Typical!' he muttered, smiling sleepily, the tip of his aquiline nose (how like her mother's) and the whites of his eyes just visible in the strangely illuminating darkness. 'That's all I am to you, a stone, to be flung across a river.'

'Don't be stupid,' she replied crossly, sitting up. 'It was horrible.'

He kissed the top of her head to show that he understood and said: 'I had a strange dream too. Rasputin was after me – I was running like a maniac round the launderette – and then I had this brilliant idea of hiding in his havers…'

'Let's just go,' she interrupted, suddenly clutching his arm. 'Anywhere. Away from here.'

'Anywhere,' he agreed with a mock shudder, 'to get away from that nutter. Honestly, he was shouting…'

'No, really. We could, you know. Somewhere by the sea. I'd be well, I think, by the sea. I could work again; you could find a job.'

'What, like Bonnie and Clyde,' he suggested with a touch of sarcasm. 'Start robbing banks?'

Marly sighed and felt herself detaching from the man at her side, the man who loved her, cared for her, did almost everything for her, except go along with her dreams; and her mind dropped (as it too often did) like an injured animal, into its cold, dark, lonely lair while the rest of her carried on with the daylight. 'It doesn't matter,' she said impassively. 'You've got no soul anyway.'

'And you've got no head,' he responded lightly, kissing the top of it again before adding in a softer tone: 'I love you, you know, Marly stole some barley Smart! I think you're magnificent.'

She lay without responding in the comforting warmth of his arms, listening to his words in the soft cocoon of his weaving, snug as a bug in a small green rug; and her mind crept bit by bit, almost reluctantly at first, out of its cold, dark, lonely place until all at once she was there back with him, her wounds wide open for him. 'I can't take any more. I can't... really can't... take any more,' she sobbed.

'I know, my love, I know.'

'It's like I'm on this road,' she babbled, 'and I can't turn back. I'm trapped, cornered at the end of it. That's what it feels like now, that I've come to the end of the road – I really have. I can't see any future,' her voice trailed off, 'any future at all....'

'Yes you can,' almost sternly. 'You're in a tunnel at the moment, that's all – it's a blip. It doesn't mean,' he added in what Marly called his wise old Gandalf voice, 'it isn't daylight outside.'

'Maybe not; but I can't see it. That's the business of the tunnel, not believing there's anything else, however many times you've been through it. People say get help, but you can't, you're a vegetable, you can't even pick up the phone – you've seen me. And even if,' she went on, drilling it in to him, 'I did believe I could get through it, even if I did believe that, I still know I'll be back here again and again and again like some sort of stuck record, some sort of sick joke. That in itself,' she added wearily, 'is enough to kill me off, the fact that I'll be here again, that it will go on like this forever.'

It kills me too, David said to himself, clinging on to her as if he might hold her up with his own arms, seeing you like this, dying away a little more each day, no matter what I do. But aloud he said: 'You don't know that,' lightly, gently, because he knew she knew or at least thought she did; but he wanted to hold out a little piece of hope for her to latch on to if she would; and surprisingly, tentatively at first, hands out and palms towards the ceiling in an almost prayer-like gesture, she did.

'We-ell. I suppose I might be alright, one day. It's not impossible.'

'Course you will,' he leapt in, sensing his advantage. 'You'll be fine, one day, see if I'm not right.'

'I'll always get depressed though.'

'Ye-es, you'll always have that tendency, but you'll deal with it better, that's the thing. It won't happen so often and you'll have better coping mechanisms.'

'Maybe I'll have children,' she cried then, almost wildly, hands clutching the sheet. 'Live by the sea?'

He kissed her warmly. 'Course we will. Think of some names,' he added, knowing how much she liked thinking of names.

'John,' without hesitating. 'John's a good, strong, masculine name.'

'I'm rather keen on Neville myself. Neville's got a good sort of ring to it.'

'Neville!' she spluttered.

'And Petunia. Petunia's a good name…' but he had lost her again to the stillness – that strange stillness that came over her when she was leaving him – and the faraway look in her eyes. 'Petunia,' he repeated, nudging her.

She gave a bitter little laugh. 'Who am I trying to kid? I can't even look in the mirror.' And she added, as if suddenly remembering, though he knew she'd simply been resisting the temptation to ask: 'How's my cheek?' and thrust her face, tongue stuck out to see if it hurt, towards him.

'It's fine,' he assured her. 'Perfectly fine.'

'You can't see in this dark,' she reproached him; and he thought for one horrible moment she was going to take him round to the landing light where he stood, often for minutes on end, squinting, staring, straining his eyes to see some imaginary or minuscule growth or blemish that had suddenly come up on the side of her cheek. (Was it like that yesterday? Is it worse than that thing I had in Birmingham? Will it go?) 'I've got magic eyes remember,' he smiled.

'Will it go?' she insisted.

'Course it'll go. It's saying *'Au revoir la monde'* this very moment!' He waved his hand in a comical gesture above the sheet.

'*La monde.*' she half laughed. 'You sure?'

'Hundred per cent.'

'Positive?'

'Posidrive. Your Uncle Dave's got magic eyes remember.'

'I remember,' she sighed; and he, trying to steer the impatience out of his voice (for fear, at this time of night, of the endless and inevitable recriminations and accusations on her part, cajolings and reassurances on his if he didn't), said quite firmly, 'Honestly, it's fine,' but some nuance must have escaped or betrayed him, at least in her imagination, for she turned quite suddenly and violently away from him towards the wall, childishly dragging the blanket along with her.

He lay there, partially uncovered, gazing a little abstractedly at the stars Marly had pasted to the ceiling and arguing the toss whether to turn round and comfort her. It flickered through his head that he had GCSE coursework to mark in the morning, and he thought for the first time how oddly the stars were arranged: great clusters then nothing, great clusters then nothing and he began systematically to straighten them out in his mind's eye, each and every one, until they lay more evenly spread. She was making little mewing noises now, strange huffs and snorts that meant (at least he always thought they meant) he should turn round and comfort her; but he lay quite still, cold and gazing at the stars. How stupid that little one looks, he thought angrily, alone and peeping over the wall like that. No spatial awareness, she's got no spatial awareness at all; and he thought, at that moment, how close he came to hating her sometimes with her proud little head turned away and her little legs thrashing to keep herself warm. (Cold hands, warm heart, he'd said to her once, but it wasn't true. She was vicious and pitiless as ice inside too, a splintered, fractured chip off an old, hard, glinting and very dangerous glacier.) But he knew, at the same time, that this feeling close to hatred was simply the obverse of his love for her, the same coin, the same feeling. It never went, it never went, stubborn as mud that love never left him, that feeling. It would go on, he thought now, to eternity, until his bones were dry; and it boomed suddenly in his head, reverberating like the acoustics in an empty room, that he loved her, that she was suffering and, that being all that mattered, he turned, enfolded her in his arms and said fiercely in a challenge to the dark and the doubts that surrounded them: 'I love you Marly. I love you terribly. I always have and I always will.'

And she, hearing the echoes in his mind, spun round almost as violently as she'd turned away from him and nestled her head to his chest, her voice coming up strangely muffled, as muffled as his had been echoing: 'How much?'

He pondered a while, drawing inspiration from the ceiling. 'See the distance from the earth to every single star in the galaxy?'

'Yeah?'

'Multiply that by infinity and you've got it!'

'That's not much!'

'Why I oughta just…'

'Will it be alright?' she interrupted him eagerly.

He cradled her gently in his arms, seeing her now soft, shy and fleeting as a robin or a drop of rain. 'It'll be perfect,' he smiled.

'Tell me how it'll be,' she pleaded, 'in our cottage by the sea.'

He stroked her soft-as-featherdown hair and, seeing his way clear again to helping her, said: 'It'll be like this….'

# Four

'You've got your own little shop,' he began in his *Jackanory* storytelling voice, 'on the seafront.'

'I've never had a shop before,' she interrupted him a little anxiously.

'Well, you have now. Picture it. You can hear the seagulls croaking away there you can and you've got a little shop on the harbour front with a green door and those little sort of Victorian windows coming round; and all the kiddies come up and press their chocolate-smudged lips to the window, looking in, peering in through the frosted panes.'

Marly giggled. 'Thinking of yourself now, ain't you: chocolate-smudged lips!'

'I am thinking of myself, yeah. Thank you very much, yes! Anyway, there they are and they're smeary and they say: "Mummy, mummy, what's that shop over there; it's ever so pretty." Like that, see.'

'I see.'

'And then the parents come over and they're bedazzled – they're bedazzled by the little shop, they are. They look in the window and their breath is taken away.' David made a noise like a cross between a snort and a sigh – 'like the wind taking their breath away' – and Marly smiled in the darkness. 'They go in, you see, and all your shelves are up, you know, with all your... wondrous things.'

'What wondrous things are they then?'

'Oh, pebbles and shells you've collected and decorated in your...' he looked up at the stars, 'uniquely artistic way. It's a lovely painted room,' he added quickly, 'nice big room with a wooden floor.'

'Oh, I likes a wooden floor,' Marly playfully entered in.

'As you walk across the floor it creaks in that nice way, that sort of reassuring way of creaking.'

'I know.'

'They come in, they do, and they look at the array of your wondrous things and they say: 'Ooh, this is just right for Uncle George this... that'll do nicely for Aunty Beryl... your mother would like this, John!' And they scoop things up and rush to the counter and pretty soon word's getting around, you see, spreading like wildfire... and all the people from all over the country, from John O'Groats to Newcastle to Land's End to the Isle of Wight... they'll all be coming over they will, to see your little shop. They have to bus 'em in they do, there's so many,' he added and she laughed delightedly. 'There's like a special bus service to get 'em in, and they all have to queue up outside. You'll be outside saying: "Single file please, single file please. There there, don't push now... plenty for everyone!" See that? And all the shops down the street, the little people who run them, they'll be sticking their heads out the window saying: "What's going on here?" They'll say: "That's a very big queue for a little shop, that!"'

'There's loads of 'em,' he went on, blowing his nose on a little piece of lavatory paper, 'hundreds of 'em, different people from all over the world.'

'All over the world now is it?'

'Course it is... from Buenos Aires... Philadelphia... and, you know, you got magnates, oil magnates from Dallas coming in saying, "Gee, what a cute little thing." And you've got a little nun in there, a little Irish nun saying, "Oh Mary, me lord Jesus, Bejesus! Oh, look at them, they're so beautiful. My word, I'm torn, torn I am!"' And then there's another little Irish bloke,' he went on, raising his voice above

Marly's laughter but deepening the accent, 'who says: "Don't you worry you little in the veil fella..."'

'In the veil fella!'

'"Don't you worry you little in the veil fella. We'll have a bit of a pact, you know, a bit of a pact if that's not the wrong sort of word to use with a nun. I won't say anything about er Sister Mary who's in the family way as we all know, we all know that. Now, come on, don't deny it." David tapped the side of his nose. '"I've got a little bit of a flutter on Run like the Wind in the Kempton Park at 3.45 this afternoon... fol diddly fay..."'

'Fol diddly fay!!'

'Anyway, there's the Prince of Persia or someone behind,' David went on, getting a husky Arab voice ready, 'and he says: "Ah, that is my horse. I own that horse. It is mine. It will win." See that? They're all in the queue waiting, all waiting to get their trinkets off you see. There's even men from the BBC,' he added, with a flash of inspiration.

'The BBC?' Marly exclaimed.

'They come down they do, the men from the BBC, come in their big van. They pull up on the front, they do. There's Alan Titchmarsh or someone coming out, you know, he's presenting it, he's putting his tie on; and they come and they shake your hand and they say: "Look, we'd like to make a documentary about you, we've never heard of such a phenomenon. Everyone'll be very interested in this, this is gonna be a top programme this, you know, we're gonna have viewers from all over the world tuning in just to see how you get on with selling your little things here." He paused, looking at Marly, then added in a softer tone, 'So he has a little interview with you see.'

'Does he?'

'Oh yes, he has a little interview with you...'

Marly lay still, waiting for a while, before asking almost impatiently, 'What's he say then?'

'He says,' David began, holding up a pretend microphone,

'"Well, Marly, how long have you been working in this er little shop then?"' He paused before pushing the microphone towards her. 'What will you say?'

'Oh, just a year now,' Marly muttered reluctantly.

'"Just a year is it? Just a year? And in that year I suppose you've seen business boom?"'

'Oh, I ain't done so bad, no.'

'"Ain't done so bad? Well, the queues in the street... I mean, we had trouble as soon as we hit the M25. We've just been in traffic since the M25, you know, two hundred miles away. It's just, I'd hardly say it was, you know, not doin' so bad. I'd say it was doing very well."'

'Yeah, I s'pose. Ain't done so bad.'

'"Well, you're doing marvellous, marvellous ain't you?"'

'Yeah,' reluctantly.

'"Yeah?"'

'Yeah, not so bad.'

'"You must be raking it in."'

'We-ell.'

'"You must be..."'

'Keeps the wolf from the door.'

'"Keeps the wolf from the door? I should say! Keeps the wolf from the door with all that lolly."'

'Yeah...' then suddenly: 'It's better than when I was living in Dartford.'

'"Oh right. I see."' David eyed her warily.

'Got a bit more money than I had then.'

'"Got a bit more money, yes. Very nice. Yes and..."'

'Had a terrible time of it there I did.'

'"You had a terrible time? Why? What happened? What happened then?"' David, alias Alan Titchmarsh, asked a little wearily.

'Well, I was very unhappy. I was very ill. I've been very ill I have.'

'"But you're not now though are you,"' very firmly. '"You're now..."'

'No.'

'"No, you are fully recovered, fully recovered you are now,"' hurriedly, '"and rolling in it as I can see. Well, I'll shake your hand there Marly. This is Alan Titchmarsh reporting from..."'

'Thank you for coming down.'

'"My pleasure Marly..."'

'Yeah,' triumphantly.

'"...to see such a phenomenon... and, I tell you what, can I have some of those little trinkets over there please?"'

'Oh yes.'

'"Just the little blue ones. Lovely thanks."'

Marly put her palm out. 'These are made out of... of...' with inspiration, 'scallop shells.'

David took the imaginary object. '"Scallop shells? That's very inventive, I must say. Very inventive. Genius. Yes."'

Marly added, almost animatedly, 'Would you like a bit of pasty I'm cooking up in the back kitchen?'

'"Well, I'd like a bit of pasty thank you very much, yes. Have you got brown sauce?"'

'Yes I...' Marly collapsed into a giggle.

'"Are you sure it's alright to leave your boyfriend dealing with all these customers here? He seems very busy... look at his little arms going up and down like..."'

'He'll manage.'

'"...flashing blades, they are."'

'He'll manage,' Marly laughed again.

David paused a moment and kissed the top of her head. 'So he makes a little programme see?'

'Does he?' she asked, her eyes very round.

'A little programme about you.'

'Oh, that's marvellous that is.'

'And...'

She rushed in. 'I bet everyone sees it. I bet the Queen sees it!'

'Oh, the Queen sees it. She says: "Philip, Philip, come in

here. Look at this." And she gets down the shop see. And you'll have sales, you know, you'll have a proper little shop.'

'I bet, I bet. Will I go to lots of parties and that?'

'You will probably.'

'Will people want to see me at the parties and that?'

'Well, like I said, you know, you'll have your princes coming down… they'll probably take you to royal balls and galas. They'll say: 'It's only for very special people this.' And you'll stand in the great ballrooms next to the enormous paintings which are fifty foot tall and thirty foot wide… and the great draperies, the great drapes hanging down the walls, great silken drapes worth a million pounds each one they are, see. And the great chandeliers, you know, that sparkle like all the stars shoved into one spot. See that?'

'Yeah,' Marly replied, her eyes glistening in the dark.

'You'll dance with princes and dukes and earls. And even the Queen will break tradition just to have a quick scoot around the floor with you!' He smiled tenderly. 'You likes that don't you?'

'Oh, it's nice.'

'That's right. And, you know, you'll have your own little cat and dog.'

'Will I?'

'Oh yeah, you'll have little Snowdrop.'

'Aaah!'

'Who'll get fed bits of… orange from the man from Delmonte, cos he's in the queue with his little hat on. And his white suit!'

'Nice that.'

'And er…Tipperary, the little cat, who sits in the window of the shop on his purple and gold cushion.'

'That's lovely that.'

'Keeping an eye out on the old fishmonger down on the front there, flapping his fish about.'

'What's the front like then?' Marly asked curiously, propping herself up on her elbow.

David thought for a moment with his eyes closed. 'Well, you're on the harbour where you can see all the little white sails cos all these businessmen, they come in their boats, you know, and hop off to get your trinkets. There are lots of little shops on the front there, too, but none of them are doing half as blinking good as yours! See that?'

'I likes that.'

'That's right. I know you like it.'

'Good, that is.'

'Well, it's the truth. It's the truth see. And they get a bit jealous… and one or two of them, they have to kind of shut up shop and move somewhere else.'

'They do?'

'Cos they can't cope with all the customers queuing up, you know, they just sort of stand past the windows, they don't go in *their* shops.'

'No.'

'Just queuing up past the windows, they have to push past them in the mornings, they do.'

'Oh dear,' gleefully, 'that's terrible.'

'That's right. But, you know, what you do is, on the quieter days, you have a bit of lunch or whatever and you shut up shop and take a walk down to the little front and watch the waves sort of lapping in gently.'

'Oh, that's nice that.'

'And you look around at all the people there. There's a woman reading her Jackie Collins novel, engrossed, great big hat on her head, great big sunglasses, you know, you can't see her face. She might not have a face; it's just buried in her Jackie Collins novel. And, er, there's a couple in the water…'

'Oh yeah?'

'Young couple, you know, getting very frisky with each other… very frisky. Practically "en flagrante"..!'

'In your dreams!'

He laughed delightedly.

'Yeah, yeah, in your dreams you little munchkin!'

'Eh? Honest it's true! It's true, it happens. I can see it now, it's bound to happen! They'll be splashing about there, you know, you'll kind of cough, avert your eyes a bit.'

'Mmm.'

'And there's a little kid scooting about on his skates all over the place. He's gotta be careful he doesn't get sand in 'em mind.'

'That's fun that.'

'That's right. And he's talking to Jack, the old sailor. He's sat on a great big barrel is Jack, wrapping his ropes around, sorting his ropes out.'

'Oh yeah, they do that don't they, fishermen.'

'They do. Exactly. That's the sort of thing they do when they're not fishing,' David grinned. 'And, er, he's got a pipe in his mouth, you know, not the little boy now, that's the…'

'Fair enough.'

'…fisherman… and the little boy's saying, "Tell us about the sea, mister. Tell us about the sea."'

'Tell us about the sea!' Marly laughed in mock disgust. 'He's not gonna say that is he?'

'Course he is. He doesn't know much. He's never been to sea has he.'

'He'd say: "Tell us about the *critters* in the sea."'

'We-ell, I suppose he would…'

'"Tell us about the octopussy," he'd say.'

'Yes, I suppose… no no, he'd tell him about the sea.'

'Alright, carry on then, carry on.'

David made a noise somewhere between a snort and a cough. 'He'd start puffing his pipe like that.'

'Fair enough.'

'"I spent thirty years on thart sea there. Thirty years o' my life on thart sea; and I tell yer what, I tell yer what, it's a tough…"'

'Is he Irish as well is he?'

'No, no, no, he's Cornish innit! My accent's alright, it's your hearing that's funny.'

'Yes, yes. Very good, very good!'

'Puffing away on his pipe like a good'un he says: "I tell yer boy, it's a tough life on the sea." The boy says: "Tell us about the sea monsters then mister...."'

'Go on then, carry on.'

'"Oh, I tell yer, there's some narsty sea monsters I've seen, the worst one bein' the krarken!"'

'The kraken?'

'The kraken, yes. He says: "The krarken... I was on the South China seas in my boat *The Plimsole* when..."'

'*The Plimsole*?!'

'"Thirty year ago. And I tell yer boy, I TELL YER, it was a right frightenin' experience. There I was standing, I was Captain of *The Plimsole*, surveyin' the surroundings, when all of a sudden a great slippery arm came up the side of the boat. And on the other side of the boat another great slippery arm came up. Then another three slippery arms came up each side of the boat: there were eight slippery arms! He was a giant octopus, that krarken, a great big giant octopus!"'

Marly giggled.

'"He was I tell yer,"' excitedly. '"He started rocking the boat and all the men were panickin' but I didn't, I didn't, see...."'

'Course not!'

'"I kept calm, I knew what to do. We were transporting pepper see, we were transporting barrels of pepper that day to the South China seas...."'

'What they transporting pepper there for?'

'They haven't got it there that's why,' David replied in his normal voice. 'Dear oh dear, you don't trust me at all do you?'

'No, carry on.'

'Anyway, and he says: "I tell yer boy, I knew what to do. I knew the krarken had a very large nose so what I did was I said Come on Harry, get this barrel overboard. And we opened the top and we threw it overboard and all of a sudden his arms kind of started quiverin', they started a quiverin' on the side of the boat they did cos, you know, he's affected badly, the krarken, by pepper… and he makes a sort of puffy noise and all of a sudden his arms flailed about and he went Awhoooshoo…!'"

'Didn't that turn the boat over?'

"'I tell yer what it did boy, I tell yer what it did…'"

'What did it do?'

"'One minute we were in the South China seas…'"

'Yeah?'

David paused for dramatic effect. "'Thirty seconds later we were in the South Indian seas, I tell yer! He sent us flying through the air he did!'"

'Bet he did!'

"'Honestly, I tell yer boy that's the truth.'" And then in the little boy's voice: "'That's a load of old rubbish mister!'"

'I bet he did,' Marly laughed. 'I bet he said that's a load of old crap you fucking…'

"'That's a load of old rubbish mister. There's no such thing as a kraken." "…I'll kraken you round the head in a minute young boyo…. Run along my lad, run along…'"

'I bet he says you fucking nobhead doesn't he.'

'Well,' David laughed, 'he doesn't say you fucking nobhead no. He's not quite at that age yet!'

They dissolved into helpless laughter for a while and David took a sip of water from the lipstick-clouded glass by the side of the bed. Marly smiled dreamily and nestled her head in the crook of his arm. 'You tellin' the truth now?' she asked, childishly hopeful.

'That's the truth yeah, that's how it's gonna be. It's guaranteed see.' He squeezed her arm. 'And I'll get myself a little job mending shoes just down the road. You can come in of a lunchtime, I'll be sorting the soles out on a pair of alligator skin tips!'

'Fair enough.'

'So, you know, at the end of the day you shut up shop; you say: "Go away everybody. The shop is shut, it will not be open now..."'

'Do I live at the top of the shop?' Marly asked suddenly.

'Oh yeah, it's a lovely little flat overlooking the sea. You've painted it up and you've got all your bits there...'

'Is it big, the flat at the top?'

'It's a cute little flat, a cosy little flat, not cramped, not the sort of thing you'd give yourself a neck-ache standing about because the roof's so small. You can stretch about in it, it's very nice; and, you know, Snowdrop and Tipperary will be up there – they've got little baskets there.... And I come along from the shoe shop, me hands smelling of leather, I come up and you cook a nice little pasta meal for us, nice little pasta meal,' he repeated, nudging her.

'I see. I cook it up do I?'

'Oh yes. Course you do! I've been slaving away in the shoe shop. I've been trying to nail some soles on, mush!'

'I'll nail a sole on you in a minute, darling!'

'That's not very nice is it? I mean I'll do the washing up.' His voice became gentler. 'Anyway, at night we can go for a walk down to the beach can't we. We can walk down the little cobbled street down onto the beach, Tipperary and Snowdrop following us. We can take our shoes off and run down to the sand, get the sand between our toes and have a little paddle in the water.'

'Oh, it's nice.'

'You can feel the waves sort of lapping up; we watch the sun going down; listen to the seagulls squawking. We can go and stand there and hear the silence of the sea sort of coming at us.' He took hold of her hand and they both lay very still. 'I'll hold your little hand, Tipperary will be down by my side, Snowdrop will be down by yours, paddling their feet. See that? And we'll sit on the shore we will, watching the sun dipping itself into the water until it's gone.'

She murmured something, her eyes staring.

He went on slowly, intently. 'You can see the boats in the distance, you can… the ships going off to far flung lands, going off to America, going off to Africa, to China… Australia…. We'll wave at them and they'll wave back.'

'We wouldn't see them if it was dark,' she pointed out in spite of herself.

'We-ell, I mean they can. They've got fantastic equipment these days, these ships. They can see us and we can see them… sailing off….' He waited for a moment.

'And then late at night we can walk back home, back to your little flat. Snowdrop and Tipperary are rather tired now: they've had a busy day, you know, cos Tipperary's been trying to get his fish, Snowdrop feels rather stuffed up with orange segments….' They laughed together and the mood lightened. 'So we walk back through the quiet streets and the only noise you can hear is like a piano being played and a sea shanty being sung down at the er… Lobster Basket on the corner. You can hear this sea shanty being sung about "The Krarken and how I fought with him!"'

'Oh yeah? How does that go then?'

David sang in a Cornish accent, ridiculous above the sheets.

'I knew a kra-ken
 And he tried to get me back-en
 I'll get him back-en
One of these da-ays.'

'That's a fucking good song innit? I've never heard such rubbish in me life. Call that a sea shanty?'

'It's a shea shanty of a short,' he chanted.

'It's a shea shanty of a short.
 It's a shea shanty of a short!'

They collapsed into giggles and he went on as if winding up the story. 'Then we go back to your door, you see, and in runs Tipperary and in runs Snowdrop; then you turn round and give me a kiss on the chops.'

'Ah, nice that!'

'It is nice that. You likes giving me kisses!'

'Yeah, yeah, I do and I don't.'

'Eh? I thought you'd enjoy that bit.'

'I did enjoy that bit.'

'Anyway, you go upstairs, put Tippers to bed, give him a kiss and say goodnight little Tippers!'

'Tippers!'

'Goodnight little Snowers... give him a pat on the head, then you put your jim-jams on but before you hop into bed you stare out the window, see.'

'Oh?'

'Stare out the window up at the sky, the perfectly clear sky, looking up at the stars twinkling.'

'Aaah.'

'Looking for Ursa Major, Ursa Minor, Ursa Middle...'

'What ones are they then?'

'Eh? They're constellations ain't they, I don't rightly know do I? I don't know much about it. Anyway, you'll be looking up at them, watching their reflections twinkling on the sea.'

'Lovely that,' Marly yawned.

'Then you hop into bed and have nice dreams about fish... and... paintboxes... and...'

'The kraken?' she murmured sleepily, turning onto her side.

'No, not the kraken no,' David replied, moulding his body round hers and tucking the blanket up high about her long cold neck. 'He's a bit frightening.' And he lay there listening to her drifting peacefully off though his own head, too busy for sleep, sang songs and watched the headlights of cars as they passed like searchlights across the curtains; and waited for the dawn.

# Part two

# Between Scylla and Charybdis

# Five

Terry lived in a very white house with a very red car parked outside. Too red, Marly always thought, for a spiritual man. The inside was no better: lots of bright clean spaces and thickly, discreetly carpeted floors for souls, no doubt, to lay themselves down and almost, but not quite, bare all. It might have been a cross between a mosque and a tea shop with its strange blend of smells, wails and murmurings from behind closed doors, its spiritual mumbo-jumbo on the walls (Go-with-the-sunshine Dr H cures Mr Kwon's lumbago with crystals and acupuncture, love and light) redeemed in part by the certificate signed (by some meteorological society), sealed and under glass, of the 'Terry & June' star. It twinkled above the rest like a saint bathed in reflected glory and Marly often imagined two stars in twin beds, one of them tall, grey and thin with wide, vitiligoed arms, the other short, fat, rotund with a pink rinse and pearls. Unearthly pearls the colour of amethyst, unearthly pink rinse the colour of candyfloss or coral before it bleaches, before the algae flee it. Or maybe she just ate too many raspberries, being a nutritionist; it was known, after all, that too much beta-carotene turned you orange – like something out of the chocolate factory, Augustus Gloop was it, or Verruca Salt? What you ate had a profound effect, especially in fairy tales: drink me – spinach – fairy-moonface cakes. Eat your greens, it said – above *Hello!* magazines and appointment cards –

43

and you'll grow forearms like Popeye. Amazing what you believed in, thought Marly, stepping briskly up West Hill, her feet tapping out the rhythm of sea green mushy pea green jelly bean green greens, when you lost your faith in everything else. (Ivy chewing on pineapple skins, wrinkling like a crocodile; purple fingers mashing 'em up, smiling a crocodile smile.)

She swept in through the stained-glass porch, past the receptionist who stank of scent and always said: 'May our wishes come true this month, this week, this afternoon'; and went to sit on the one remaining chair in the hallway, the other being occupied, astonishingly, by a delicate little dark-haired girl reading *Black Beauty*. Marly felt like saying, as she perched, clumsy, old and ridiculous, beside her, that the remainder bookshop in town sold hundreds of horse books – the *Black Stallion* series for a start. She knew because David brought one back for her each week wrapped up in a brown paper bag.... Only a quid, they were brilliant... about a boy who got stranded on an island with a horse; he fed him carrageen (it's a seaweed) and learnt to ride bareback, his arms straight out like an aeroplane, into the waves.... But instead she sat there silent and staring at sunshine messages through superglued glasses, trying not to sneeze at all the scent in the air and listening to Terry's voice coming from one of the darkly, discreetly, closely kept doors. What a danger his soul must be, she thought, privy to a hundred-and-one little secrets. What did he do all day with those fears, anxieties, sores and complaints? Did he feed off them in the thick, foetid air, a vitiligoed mushroom in a dark space; or did he leave them there, a shadowy mantle to be put on, put down and passed along, like some modern day Elijah or John the Baptist, his burden the psyche, sciatica, haemorrhoids, the curse.... She blinked at the sunshine through blue-tacked glasses, a migratory bird, twitchy, wanting to be off; overly conscious of the girl at her side and wondering why the longer the silence, the harder it was to break. The girl coughed and turned a page; and Marly shuffled uneasily around in her seat, trying to catch her eye so that it wouldn't seem so abrupt when she asked, a little stupidly: is that *Black Beauty*?

'Is that *Black Beauty*?' at last, out loud.

'Yes.' The girl seemed quite unsurprised to be asked, totally composed and at ease with Marly's proximity.

'Oh, that's a good book.' How easy it was. 'I love that book.'

'I've only just started reading it,' the girl explained, indicating the page she was on.

'It's a good book,' Marly repeated. 'The *Black Stallion* books are good too. Have you read any of them?'

'No.' The girl's eyelashes splashed against her cheek. The tip of her nose, Marly noticed, was freckled.

'They're very good as well.... Have you got a horse?'

'No... but I have riding lessons.' Her eyes lit up. 'I ride a horse called Tarka.'

'Oh,' smiled Marly. 'What's he like?'

'He's a chestnut with a sock,' the girl announced proudly. 'He can jump as high as three foot six!'

'That's brilliant,' Marly enthused; and was about to get into a good old discussion of dapple greys, blue roans, cavaletti and palominos when the door opened and Terry came out saying 'You'll feel like a new woman,' to a little, old, sad-looking woman in a grey suit who disappeared through the stained-glass porch. He beckoned Marly in.

Smiling an apology at the girl, she went into the bay-windowed room to her seat in front of the old piano, wondering, as she always did, if he ever gave anyone a tune, for healing purposes of course. (*Give us a tune, said the old Dad. Can you play Chopsticks, Érotique, the Waltz of the Blue Danube? My piano teacher used to get very close and talk about murders and bargains.*) She took off her glasses from vanity or habit, folding them up in her lap, and everything became very vague like an impressionist painting. She knew there was a book of dreams on the table in front of her, described and interpreted Victorian style and a variety of cards from well-wishers and grateful patients; somewhere to her left, a suitcase filled with pills and poisons in differing potencies with strange names like Belladonna, Pulsatilla, Sepia and Natrum Mur; and best of all, on the wall opposite, a picture of a woman with a row of children behind her, all in the shape of a cross – the woman being the stem of the cross, the children its arms. Marly liked the picture very much. The woman had green eyes; and it reminded her of something out of a dream or a memory.

'How have you been?' Terry asked, settling himself into his black leather chair and smiling kindly.

Marly hesitated, staring at his bad gangster face with a myopic eye and wondering what to say. Sometimes she told him things quite unconnected with her illness, though never the whole story, never the full picture, despite his air of having heard it all before. She had a feeling he was more interested in affairs of the heart than in bowels and stools, headaches and depressions, his own having been quite broken as a young man near Wormwood Scrubs. He had an unflurried ease about him, as though he'd been surprised long ago, many times, and had now grown calm on a surfeit of wonderdom. And yet, she always thought, he also gave the impression of regarding the world with a perpetually raised eyebrow, like a newborn, as if to say that although he'd been here countless times and knew his way around the block, he was willing, even eager, to try it again by another route. 'I'm learning too,' he sometimes said, much to Marly's dismay.

'Alright,' she replied a little reluctantly. 'I'm thinking of moving.'

'Oh?' He sounded surprised. 'When?'

'After Christmas. Somewhere by the sea.' And she added inanely into the lengthening silence, as if it might make a difference: 'I love the sea. I was born by the sea.'

'Have you discussed it with David?'

'Oh yes. He knows I love the sea. He's always known I wanted to move.'

'Only, if you don't discuss it properly,' Terry went on mildly, 'it could cause devastation.'

Marly smiled at the word. 'Oh, he doesn't like the idea of course, but he'll go along with it for my sake. He's very supportive. He just wants me to be well.' The implication being, of course, that she would be well far away from the noise and traffic, fumes and pollution. I even had a dream, she wanted to say, where I was skiing down the slopes at Val d'Isère, in a bikini made out of sugar and exhaust, my hair different every time – though she'd never been skiing in her life before.

'Well, just so long as you talk it through together.'

'Oh yes.' Marly dismissed it as a given.

'I nearly went to New Zealand,' he confided suddenly, the way he did sometimes, 'but I got married and moved to Orpington….' He shrugged his shoulders. 'Sometimes I think I'd like to retire to the country but my wife says it's a bad idea, we have our friends here, our work. What's the point? Seems a shame, after building something up for twenty years, to let it all go and start again somewhere else.

'Yes,' Marly nodded, a little uninterested, thinking he was an idiot to stay twenty years in a place like this and thinking, too, that June, his wife, was evidently a meddler, too busy with her candyfloss and wok.

'How about having a holiday by the sea?' he suggested then. 'It's not so drastic.'

'Well, yes, I could do that,' Marly answered politely. 'I'll have to see….'

'Think of it as being, say, a minister in a place like Tower Hamlets for ten years, then suddenly getting a job as Archbishop of Canterbury. Adapt to a place, make the best of it... anything can happen.' He opened his arms wide as if to encompass that anything.

'Oh yes I see, that's a nice way of looking at it,' Marly smiled, though she sensed his disapproval and was piqued. Wasn't she meant to wrench destiny her way for a change? Hadn't she lived long enough in squalor and green mould? Wasn't she meant to follow her dreams? Simple ones at that: to live in a house by the sea, grow turnips and rhubarb, radishes and sweet peas; walk through sunflowers and sea mists, green lanes and bluebell woods; swim in the rain before breakfast, maybe keep a pet cow... I'd call her Moon, she told herself now, my very own pet moon; then she stopped as an image of her own small, battered, insignificant self came back to her and she felt herself going down, ridiculously, like a lead balloon or a bad joke. 'I just want to be well,' she all but pleaded with him, 'so I can do these things.'

He nodded gently and leant forward with his hands on his knees. 'How have you been?' he asked again. 'You seem a bit better to me.'

Her mind turned against him. How could he pre-empt her like that? How could she say now that her life was bad, that she had no life, that the pills he gave her didn't work, made her worse, made her feel like she had no future, made her want to tear herself up. And she sat there grinning at him, a gentle thing so full of rage, not telling him, never telling him about the sheet lightning that shot out of a clear blue sky in their cramped little rundown flat where the mice played hide and seek and the green mould grew to gigantic proportions, except in euphemisms of 'I hurled a cup', 'I got a bit angry', 'I even stabbed the breadboard'. (*My spider-killer, she called him. An ironic name as it turned out: he kept her under the floorboards wrapped up in a web of his own. Can you play Alice where art thou? Ave Maria, a Clementi sonatina?*)

'Not so bad,' she sighed at last, 'though sometimes I feel like it's a desert behind and a desert in front,' and she saw the corners of his mouth lift a little as he wrote something down and thought that it probably did sound funny, in an objective way, to a man who'd lost his heart near Wormwood Scrubs.

He put his pen down. 'You've been going like this,' he explained, waving his arms about like a windmill or a drunken bird, 'and we need to get you like this.' They were straight out then like an aeroplane.

Riding bareback into the waves, she thought, riding bareback into the waves. Seahorses were real in my day, seahorses were real... (*They do a good snail soup at the Champs Elysées. Half price on Fridays.*) and her head drooped a little as she answered his questions on diarrhoea and flatulence, blood, pus and guts. Any blood? No, nothing: it raced around her but never out of her. Any pus? Yes, lots of it: spinning out of her like cow's milk. Any guts? No, none; they'd left her along with the plane ticket out of here bareback into the waves. She sat with her elbows resting on the edge of the old piano, stubborn and shy (as the little boy she'd seen in the supermarket shouting fuck fuck fuck at the broccoli, his head jerking from side to side,) feeling humiliated, embarrassed, pried into, pried open.

'You said last time,' Terry went on, shuffling his notes like a fly shuffling its legs, 'that you were suffering from irrational thoughts. Any more of that?'

'Did I?' cried Marly, surprised. So that was how he transcribed her thoughts. Irrational were they? Irrational my foot! Well, of course, she was a woman wasn't she, they were bound to be; men, on the other hand, were deeply logical – David had taught her that – with their statistics, their percentages, their little Venn diagrams. Women were weathercocks, chameleons, what about daggers at dawn – how rational was that – for the hand of a fair lady? Men! Huh! The word was a joke. She spat on it, rolled it into a ball, then flicked it somewhere for someone to tread on.

'Not so many. I still look at my cheek a lot – I feel most of the time like a piece of trash – and the kettle has to be switched off.'

His mouth twitched again but his forehead frowned. He consulted a book for a moment in silence then jotted one or two things down while Marly stared blankly out of the bay window, feeling a bit like a goldfish. Then he got up, went over to the suitcase and tapped a few pills from a vial into a small brown envelope; she didn't bother asking what they were any more, she just sat there accepting, taking her medicine, hoping, despite all, against hope that they would help. 'These'll make you feel bright and shiny,' he told her, licking up the envelope.

She gave him the money David gave her to give him.

'Now remember,' he admonished her, helping her on with her raincoat, 'don't make any rash decisions. Take a holiday!' His arms waved airily like twigs in a dry wind. 'Enjoy yourself! That plant of yours,' he added, 'is flowering again, after a barren patch it's got some blooms.'

Pushing her arm through the elasticated sleeve, she eyed him suspiciously, not trusting him an inch, thinking he was saying it to make her think she would be flowering again, blooming again after a barren spell. (*To a Wild Rose, Romance sans Paroles. Flowers for a flower, he said; and his heart went like a piccolo.*)

'I am glad,' she said with nervous animation, fingering the brown envelope in her pocket; and she made her way to the stained-glass porch, reminding the little girl (who was still reading *Black Beauty*) as she went, about the *Black Stallion* series, with a faintly ridiculous waggle of the head.

# Six

It was cold outside; and a yellow wind blew hard from the factory, or was it Littlebrook D, Marly didn't know exactly. All she knew was that the sharp east wind brought the smell of burnt toast along with it and now, ridiculously, the echoing sounds of 'Yankee Doodle Dandy' from an ice-cream van. It stopped a little short of macaroni. It always did. You never heard the whole thing; only snatches of 'Greensleeves', 'Doodle Dandy' and sometimes 'Danny Boy' – what a tiny repertoire they had, to be sure – as if the van had come to a halt in the fog and yellow wind and the song had melted away into the ice creams. She thought about the girl with the little freckled nose and wondered if she played the recorder. That was probably an irrational thought. 'Enjoy yourself' she muttered, kicking a few leaves off the pavement and wanting to shout 'Bloom' at them. It was alright for *him* with his blueberry muffins, his peppermint tea, his bright red car and his very own pet star. Didn't he realise she was on the verge of suicide? Didn't he realise she could kill herself in a trice? It was no laughing matter, his mouth twitching away like that. Did he think she hadn't seen him? She pulled her hood close and shuffled on down Miskin Road, past her landlady's house – what a monstrous spectacle of extension and accumulation and they couldn't even provide a decent Hoover – and peering up now and again through the half-hearted trees at the pale

blue tower where David worked. She imagined him leaning
out of his pale blue tower and waving at her; but of course
he wasn't. He was probably hidden away in the prep room
off the maths department, surrounded by corrosives,
combustibles, beef suet and magnesium. He sat there and
phoned her sometimes when he was going to be late,
making a little joke about something being inflammable
then breaking off with a shout, then silence as if he'd gone
up in flames. Absurd how he laughed at his own silly jokes.
She was surrounded, it seemed, by laughing men. Bright
and shiny indeed... she would ask him then if he could find
the pickled baby, the pickled baby in a jar, there was always
one in a prep room, at least there was in her day, locked
away and under key in case it escaped and brought out now
and then like a beautiful freak for kids to have a laugh at.
'What the fuck is that?' 'That's your twin brother that is,
Jabba!' 'Is it alive, Miss?' Mock horror, mock disgust,
playing it up for laughs and you, somersaulting now for the
crowds. Pickled egg, pickled prune, pickled ship in a bottle,
marooned on an untidy bench amidst tripods and Bunsen
burners, a row of sharks with bits in their teeth, playing jacks
and saying 'ace'. You were ace with your tiny hands and your
overgrown head; there was obviously something quite
wrong with your head. I wonder what you wanted to be: a
dancer, a fireman, a film star; a business tycoon. You might
have grown to be a kid who shouted fuck fuck fuck at the
broccoli; you might have ended up just skeleton and teeth –
or even, worse luck, behind a hedge with a shoe missing,
your clothes ripped to shreds. Your soul must be very old,
preserved in that little bottle, like Ivy ever bottling between
a rock and a hard place, between jams, pickles and
gooseberry fools. You must be older than Tiresias.

'Bloom!' she wanted to shout again at the leaves
spreading before her like a patchwork quilt right the way
down the street; what had happened to the leaf sweeper?
Did he prong them with his fork then curl up in bed or was

he extinct like the chimney sweep; and were they left to
decay, those leaves, or fall down manholes – and she
vaguely wondered if the queue would be very long in the
job centre. It usually was, stretching away like the leaves to
the big glass door where the guard sat, between naps,
looking at his fingernails and counting his rings. He even
had one on his thumb, a little to Marly's disgust. What good
was a security guard with a ring on his thumb and a little
Saint Christopher round his neck – unless there were rivers
to cross in the Department of Social Security. Bernie
Mungo, unofficial pilgrim of the DSS. Bernie Mungo,
counting his rings like lucky stars amidst petty gods,
Samaritans, tax-collectors and Pharisees. There'd been a
disturbance once in the review section and someone had
shouted out 'Get Bernie Mungo!' though he was right there
in front of them by the big glass door, looking at his
fingernails and waiting to intervene. Sometimes he stroked
his moustache or got up and walked around, looking at the
jobs as if he didn't have one. She'd heard him say, in a low
soft murmuring voice, that he was saving to go to Jamaica;
and she wondered if, when he counted his rings, he was
reckoning on the rivers he had to cross before he got to
those deep, glowing coral reefs, those frangipani trees; the
talcum sand that burnt your toes and the warm and oily
mangoes. What a name for a girl Frangipani would be.
Frangipani Mungo: tall, dignified, shading her eyes across
the wide, blue Sargasso sea. Did he think of her, on those
cold grey days, when the petty little gods were shouting
'Get Bernie Mungo' at him?

The man who'd caused a disturbance in the review
section was a trained joiner, so he said. He'd been laid off
after twenty-five years he said – 'You wouldn't treat a dog
like that' – and was suffering from psoriasis. They were
offering him a job as salesperson in the burger bar on the
High Street and he was saying that it was silly pay, that he
was a trained joiner, that he'd got his apprenticeship at

fourteen, that he was under the sunlamp most days and he wasn't going to put on a hat and sell chips.

The woman, whose hair bunched up at the back like a little mushroom, replied: 'You will most emphatically be doing more than selling chips. Briefly, (as well as 'most emphatically' she kept saying 'briefly' the way people do to get you off guard before launching into an account of their grandmother's boils) briefly, 'salesperson' covers a multitude of tasks: clearing tables, emptying bins, keeping the oven in good order, operating the milk-shaker, the cash register and customer relations. Flexible hours to suit applicant. Experience preferred but not essential as training will be given. Good career prospects for enthusiastic applicant. Applicant must have a neat and tidy appearance as job involves liaising with the public. Uniform provided.'

'Oh good,' said the man a little sarcastically. 'Thanks very much. This is forcing me to go out thieving, this is.'

The woman ignored him. 'Taxi service provided after hours for female members of staff.'

'Oh well, there we are then,' said the man, getting up, and his fingers were shaking holding the application form. 'I should be retiring now, I should be going round America in a camper van,' he half laughed; and Marly had recognised that hopeless humour wherein a dream is revealed, or something true or very dear, behind the joke. 'You, all of it, the whole thing's just forcing me to go out thieving.'

'We are most emphatically not forcing you to go out stealing,' huffed the woman. 'We are, briefly, offering you a position as salesperson in the fast food establishment on the High Street.' And she began reading off the card again, very precisely, very officiously; the man began shaking even more violently. He was shaking so much he was almost quivering the way very old people do, who are soon to return to inanimate matter which quivers, apparently, almost invisibly. (That's when they called for Bernie Mungo.)

'What else am I supposed to do?' he ranted. 'I haven't

got no other option but to go out there thieving... twenty-
five years! They won't get nothing out of me now. You can't
survive on silly pay; I've got responsibilities in Basingstoke.
You wouldn't treat a rat the way I've been treated....'

Everyone was holding their breath by this time and
that's when Bernie Mungo stepped in, quietly ushering him
out with an arm about his bony shoulders – he seemed
quite grateful to be taken away. The woman slumped back
with a look of relief, though when Bernie Mungo came in
again she leapt up and collared him with her peacock-blue
nails. 'Couldn't you see,' she screeched, jabbing at his Saint
Christopher, 'couldn't you see he was leaning over me in an
aggressive tendency?'

It was tempting, Marly thought, awaiting her turn to sign
on, to lean over everybody here in an aggressive tendency.
Either that or you became very grateful for anything anyone
did for you; or a mixture of the two like the man with
responsibilities in Basingstoke. Something about the place
was catching, like a dose of the flu. At first you sailed
through the motions, inviolable, intact, supremely aware that
you weren't meant to be here, that you were just passing
through and then, bit by bit, as week turned to month and
month turned to year, you suddenly found out you'd caught
the cold for good. You were the shifty one at the back of the
queue in socks and sandals, eligible for any old job under the
sun you'd been unemployed so long; adept at lying, at
making up excuses on the spot, at hedging, evading, at
putting on the grateful face, the 'Oh really I didn't know that,
I'm so sorry' face, the simple face, the interested face – so
many faces even Worzel Gummidge would have a job
screwing them on. And, worst of all, you never quite
understood how you got to be that shifty-looking one at the
back of the queue, never saw the slow degradation (except
in the eyes of passers-by which you avoided), never felt the
silent virus creeping up on you in your unwashed hair, your
unmade-up face, your unclean clothes, your unpolished

shoes, until it was far too late. (It was like knowing someone was dying yet never fully realising it until they were dead.) And though you still went through the motions and put on different faces, you weren't quite sure who the faces belonged to; the spark of defiance you'd kept inside had been snuffed out somewhere along the line – they'd snuffled it out of you like pigs after a truffle, gobbling through your heart and lungs to get at that little truffle (and they stank as bad as you); or in the end you gave it up willingly enough, sick and tired of the struggle, and laughingly watched them share it out and maul it about like children with birthday cake – horrid little trotters...

Marly wasn't quite sure who 'they' were exactly but she thought of 'they' as an amorphous somebody who kept you in the dark and told you half truths about the films you watched, the books you read, the food you ate and the lives you led; who fed you gobbledygook about war crimes and UFOs, GMOs and nuclear waste; who made decisions above your head, leaving you bewildered and constrained – waiting for a hip operation or mummified in red tape; who fudged and dodged behind a sugar mountain of lies, so many lies you couldn't even recognise the truth when you stumbled upon it, so many lies even Pinocchio would have died from his nose out of sheer embarrassment. (How well she understood 'they'!) It was a world of make-believe, they should have said, with everyone so scared they didn't fit into it: not good enough, not clever enough, not pretty enough, not rich enough. Even the good, the clever, the pretty and the rich ones were scared in case somebody gooder, cleverer, prettier or richer came along to topple them off their golden throne. And so we all clung on to a time when we had been good enough, clever enough, pretty enough and rich enough, even if it was one night twenty years ago when we'd had some champagne! That night I was sensational, the world at my fingertips, the world my piano. I could trill and thrill upon it with my arpeggios, my chromatics, my scherzos, my vivaces, my little diminuendos, my great roaring crescendos... like a lorry going up and down the length and breadth of Britain, through Glasgow, Felixstowe, Heathrow, Walthamstow... all England, my arpeggio! The world, my oyster shell! That night when I wore my sea-pink dress and you told me I looked sensational....

It was her turn. She stepped up to the desk and handed over her UB40 card. (Marlene? After Marlene Dietrich? No actually, but she might as well have been for all the signatures she had to write. Once a fortnight for thirty-seven months. How many signatures – David would work it out for her – was that?)

'Have you done any work since you last signed?' The girl had long plaited hair and eyes like small brown beads. Nicked no doubt, Marly thought ridiculously, off her grandmother's best necklace.

'No.'

'Well,' said the girl as Marly wrote M. Smart underneath the rest of the sprawling, spasmodic, ever so many M. Smarts, 'let's see what we've got.' She tilted the computer for Marly to see. 'Care Assistant at the Limes.'

'Oh.' Marly's heart sank. The Limes was a psychiatric institution a few doors down from where they lived; she passed it every day on her way to the lake. A long, low, sloping building set away from the road behind some trees and a little electricity transformer covered in graffiti and signs saying Danger of Death (which David found amusing in his rather pedantic way, there being no danger in death itself, so he said). One time a woman had appeared like a phantom from behind the trees and asked Marly if she'd seen a man wandering about in a pair of furry slippers; then she'd said suddenly: 'Where's the parade?' Marly had replied that she didn't think there was a parade that day and the woman had gone back in, sighing and wringing her hands. Marly had an idea Rasputin came from the Limes;

she also had an idea she might end up there the way she was going. 'What does it involve exactly?' she asked cautiously. 'I suppose they want experience,' she added hopefully.

'No, training will be given. To help with elderly residents, serving breakfasts, lunches etc. To help residents bath, wash, toilet, dress etc. Uniform supplied. £4.55 per hour. Duration: part-time permanent.'

'Ah.' Marly tried to feign enthusiasm. 'I could give it a go.'

'There's another one here delivering fish to local area. Applicant must be willing to handle cold wet fish.' The girl made a face. 'May have to lift up to 25 kilograms.'

'What, is that a shark or something?' Marly grinned after a few moments hesitation while she'd been thinking up the joke and wondering whether to say it; and she thought of the glistening eyes seeing through a supermarket glass darkly; and Ivy's eye like an agate ready to be pocketed (they'd got her rings for sure in the crematorium). 'They're not really dead,' David had joked with his fish and chips, 'if you can't see their eyes.'

'Oh yes,' the girl smiled back. 'Exotic foods are very trendy these days aren't they. Me and my boyfriend went out the other night to the Papermakers' Arms. D'you know it?'

Marly shook her head.

'Just down the road by the garage. They've got a new menu full of things like wild boar and venison. We had ostrich burgers! They're a bit like chicken only greasier.'

Long necks in tutus, thought Marly, and they always looked so ungainly – though nothing deserved to end up in a bap.

'Must have knowledge of local area,' the girl added. 'The last one had to keep stopping to look at the map apparently.'

'Oh dear,' Marly smiled with relief. 'I haven't got that I'm afraid.'

'Well, no,' the girl agreed, 'if you didn't know the Papermakers' Arms.' She made it sound like that was the be all and end all and she clicked the mouse quite firmly to see what else was available while Marly looked earnestly at a *Back to Work* leaflet, though she couldn't see much of it without her glasses on. 'That's all we've got today,' the girl said at last, clicking off and sitting back.

'Ah well,' said Marly, getting up and making a bit of a thing of putting the Limes application form very carefully into her rucksack, as if it were something quite precious, 'goodbye.' The girl smiled in return by pressing her lips together and for a moment her eyes gleamed as though someone had breathed on them then polished them up.

Bernie Mungo was standing outside smoking a cigarette; he looked very thin in his navy blue uniform and Marly wondered if he was cutting back on food so he could get to Jamaica all the sooner. She gave him a faint smile, which he didn't appear to notice, and cut across by the Daisy launderette where a little girl sat with her nose pressed up against the window. What a name for a little girl Daisy would be, she thought, like something out of the twenties. Daisy, Poppy, Rose and Lilibet doing the tango and the two-step, with their bright, bobbed hair and their sleek red tunics; though Poppy at the age of forty would have a faintly ridiculous ring to it and then, of course, there were the soldiers.... Marly stopped abruptly by the memorial for the dead and readjusted the straps of her rucksack. People were pouring into the library from all directions with piles of books, videos and music tapes; and the gardener's truck was stuck slap bang in the middle of the front gates – one man suffering under a load of Disney videos and a massive tome entitled *Collectors Guide to Inkwells* veered round it with a menacing expression on his face and Marly turned and hid a grin as she inched past it herself in the opposite direction. It was full of flowers, she noticed, like feverish faces in hospital beds – red, green and bluish-tinged to match the seasons and celebrations or after-effects of celebrations (colour co-ordinations even Ariel couldn't mix, trapped as he was inside his pine). Though the brain itself, Marly decided, trudging into the park, had its own seasons: its own awakenings and dormancies, witherings and evergreens; its own acorns and tulips, brambles and perennials. To her it was always an agonising spring (someone had said April was the cruellest month and it was true) where dragonflies darted around you like fish and the April rain lost everything to death and decay in a banquet of shy peeping bluebells while she, Marly, stood ready and waiting to ripen out of something quite green, though she was already quite ancient. As ancient as the soldiers for whom it must always be poppies and forget-me-nots, like the poem she'd read once: S*teffi.Vergissmeinnicht.* Steffi. Forget-me-not.

She came across the gardener quite suddenly round the corner, weeding with one hand and holding her hair back with the other. It was extraordinary to see someone doing such a thing and Marly almost stopped dead in her tracks. She wanted to shout out, in David's voice, 'Tie it up Missis, for Christ's sake tie it up'; but instead she sat down on a bench a little way away, partly because she wanted to watch the extraordinary gardener and partly because it was a rule of hers to spend at least two hours outside out of every twenty-four – otherwise she got stuck in their little rundown flat like a small round vegetable in a cardboard box, peeping out at the ceiling or Oprah Winfrey shows and waiting for David to come home. She fished her glasses out the better to see the girl and spread the Limes application form out on her knee lest anyone should think of approaching her. It didn't do, she'd discovered over the years, to sit on a bench all alone and stare into space, unless you were Leslie Finch waiting for a kid. You needed a dog, a cigarette, reading material or a sandwich to disguise your solitariness and keep the buggers at bay (though once she'd made the mistake of smoking and eating at the same time and she'd been rumbled) else they came right up with their Labrador dogs and said things like 'Cheer up love, it might never happen'. Did they want her to shout at them? Did they want her to beat the living daylights out of them? 'My mother's just died an agonising death, I can't eat, can't sleep, can't get up, can't go down, can't live, can't love, can't look in the mirror, can't do this, that or the other and you're telling me... I'm reduced to the state you see before you now: unkempt, old boots, David's pants, thin legs, fidgeting, hiding away from your inquisitorial eyes and you're telling me.... I'm one stage away from beer cans and insanity, on the scrapheap, the dungheap, clapped out, down and out, finished, kaput, one foot pushing the daisies up, the other pirouetting about my neck and you're telling me it hasn't happened yet, you silly old bastard, you silly old fart. Once I played Ophelia in a small town theatre. Look at me now. Once I read poetry. Now I just want to beat the living daylights out of you with your 'cheer up love' and your Labrador dog.... (Those are the things she might have said; but she always mustered a smile in reply and patted the dog on the head.)

The gardener's hair was electrifying, strangely volatile, it seemed to Marly, as she shifted uncomfortably about on the bench which was slightly wet and tried to dry it out with the bottom of her anorak. It looked as if it might fly off at any moment with the pigeons that raced around the top of the Tudor church or lined up on the tower disguised as battlements. Even the nimbus of a saint it could have been, the way it sprang away from her round ruddy cheeks, though it wasn't golden the way a saint's would have been but the colour of the mice that slipped into the kitchen for crisps and crusts of bread. The colour of Marly's to be exact – mouse brown – though she'd often tried to brighten it up with lemon juice, chamomile flowers and (one terrible time) household bleach. David sometimes flattered her by saying it had flecks and shades of autumn in it. Flecks and shades of autumn indeed! Marly snorted in delight. Almost a name for a horse: Shades of Autumn, Autumn Velvet and a filly foal Autumn Butterfly by some great Arab stallion who shared tents in the desert with sheikhs and silver stars. What a lineage! What a descent! Nicking their dam's taffeta dress as they went and their sire's love of empty spaces. David's hair, she reflected now, taking her eyes from the gardener to the lollipop sticks, ants and cigarette butts about her feet, had flecks and shades of winter in it. Ridiculous really, at his age.... She kicked at an ice-lolly stick, trying to turn it over, wanting to see if they still had jokes on the back but it was stuck firmly to the ground and a couple of ants appeared to be sucking the last few dregs of sucrose and caramel off it. What did the big ant say to the little ant? You're too young to suck off so fuck off.... Even the ants, she thought angrily, had some fucking purpose; and feeling a sudden surge of restlessness, though she'd been sitting there less than a minute, she got up, threw the Limes application form into a bin and started off at a rapid pace around the flower garden.

Halloween faces popped out at her at intervals – witches, trick-or-treats, pumpkin masks and toffee apples – though they may have been dahlias and hyacinths for all she knew, even a premature Catherine wheel. The gardener, she noted, had just been joined by a young man in blue overalls; and they were pointing and gesticulating at a newly dug piece of earth where a couple of magpies (two, thank god, for joy) were hopping around, like Pegleg Pete, after worms, snails and *objets d'art*. Why does the early bird catch the worm? Because the night-time's damp and the worms come to the surface – she'd read it on the back of a cereal packet the other morning while David was brushing his teeth. The gardener was stamping now as though willing up a rainstorm and her hair was going like a whirling dervish; Marly got a little closer and slowed down a bit.

'We're not planting edelweiss or rare orchids. What did they teach you up there? We need hardy little shrubs that'll withstand the cold, bikes, tatty little children chucking their shoes up for conkers – see that pile of branches over there, that's kids going for conkers that is – not to mention black crows. Did you get my samosa?'

The young man, who seemed to be wilting under her gaze, brought a little parcel out of his dirty overalls and held it out to her as though he were begging for gold.

'You're a good lad,' she beamed. 'Go and get the beds then. And forget Liverpool.'

Marly stood stock-still, marvelling at the conversation, feeding off the bits of information like a vulture and storing scraps away for her mind to pick clean later. So lonely had she become that other people's conversations fascinated her; and she looked at strangers for company and occupation while David toiled away all day in his pale blue tower. Edelweiss! Orchids! Liverpool! Her head swam and she almost clutched the stem of a toffee apple for support. How huge the world was and alive. Overwhelmingly alive. Why could she not explore it? She stared hard at the gardener: it certainly wasn't a saint's face. It was a sort of primitive-looking face if a face could be such a thing, hewn out of granite by a craftsman with bad eyes and a blunt instrument, though he'd pinched a bit of blue sky for her eyes and crushed a rosebud for her mouth which was now, at this very moment, stuffing down the samosa. No, not a saint's face, but a jovial monk's perhaps, like Friar Tuck. David's face was a saint's face and Ivy's too for that matter (bordering, in her case, on martyrdom): aquiline, defined, chiselled out of porcelain or cut-glass crystal with eyes – goodness me – they must have searched far and wide for those eyes.... Whereas mine, she thought, sighing and stooping to sniff a trick-or-treat, was cobbled together like Frankenstein's by a craftsman on speed! (What d'you think you're looking at? Can't quite make out. D'you want a photo or summat? No ta, it'd break the camera.) Mind you, she added, changing abruptly to the 'you' form which she did sometimes when talking to herself, you were lucky enough to be given the feet of a water nymph; and she smiled to herself with bitter irony and clumped out of the flower garden in her shabby old boots, her neck poking forward like a witch's hat or a dunce's cap.

It was getting colder; and the park was almost deserted except for a few people walking quickly into town and a young boy with his hands in his pockets, obviously skiving off school. Marly pretended not to notice him and made her way, as she always did, along the little path beside the Darenth stream. Luckily it was brown today and full of debris so she couldn't see her reflection broken up and tumbling among the clouds and the trees; it must have passed invisibly beneath the stones and grey fish, silent as a secret. Her head ached with the wind and the fumes drifting like smoke above the trees from the burning tyres on the old Canterbury road; and as she made her way along the same old route she trod around the same old thoughts in her head, never budging an inch to the right or the left. Did he love her enough for her to love him back? Did he love her enough for her to take the risk? It didn't do to go left when she always went right and it didn't do not to stop at the old oak tree where no yellow ribbons ever decorated the boughs, only yellowing leaves which were flying now, like butterflies, to the ground. She wanted to catch one and make a wish and for a few moments she leapt about like a small child, her face breaking into a smile, here and there, up and down, hands out and eyes to the sky after the catapulting leaves; but a capricious wind blew them near then out of reach, like all wishing things, (what a lot of bellows the gods must have) or she guessed wrong and lunged in the opposite direction. Please may I be well, she whispered prematurely each time, her fingertips brushing the edges of discoloured and decaying things spinning down and down; and then, as the rain fell, she gave up and sheltered beneath the heavy old boughs. It must have seen all sorts, she thought, staring at the scaly bark ravaged and filleted by lightning and penknives, axes and naturalists. It must have seen the equivalent of hundreds of Oprah Winfrey shows: freaks and spiritual gurus, tramps and madmen, lovers and serial killers. Bohemia must have wrung her hands beneath these very boughs, bewailing and repenting her vows; even Waltzing Matilda may have squatted here just the other day in the hope of something better than ducks and broken bread. It sat there impassively and never moved a muscle, watching the world pass before its eyes like a giant TV screen. It must have witnessed the sublime and the ridiculous: bombs and hula hoops, hotpants and shooting stars, petty squabbles and Sunday fêtes (in the commercial breaks). Once it was an acorn and now it was very old, older than her grandmother – who was really quite ancient – older, even, than Tiresias. Its soul, if it had one, must be older than the hills. Did it feel the burden of having remained while everything else decayed, matriarch of the Dartford park? Did it creak down the middle and fart at parties? Had its heart been coppiced too many times to keep going strong; and did it rattle and shake in the breeze just for the sake of it, dead as a dead wood coffin inside too? What if he stopped loving her at fifty-two when she'd invested her life, her soul, her heart in him?

The thought didn't bear the thinking; and she circled round it as she circled round the park, letting the rain fall softly onto her face and hands, misting up her glasses and blurring her vision a little. The fair would be coming soon, as it did every year for Halloween and Bonfire Night, like some ancient pagan rite that signified the end of summer and the start of the crispy, crunchy, pinch-your-cheek months – the Ferris wheel a burnished god propitiated, in time-honoured tradition, with red-hot beating hearts and, depending on your 'cool' credentials, muffled or blood-curdling screams. The town, at this time, acquired a faintly carnival air: the market stalls crackled with life – slasher movies were up for grabs; supermarkets abounded with scary masks and black trees, bats and broomsticks; even the little bakery at the top of East Hill binned its currant buns and elephant toes and brought out new lines in 'petrifying pumpkin' muffins and sugar-coated 'ghastly ghosts'. People hustled and chafed, bustled and brrr'd, vivid as autumn leaves or a sun that seems to blaze most intently the moment before it goes under a raincloud. They craned their necks for the floats that crept at a snail's pace round the ring road (even the boy racers in their souped-up jalopies and stolen Orions took a back seat that night, the night the clocks went back) and strained their ears for the drums and tambourines that sounded like far-off distant thunder. 'IT'S SHOWTIME!' the mayor shouted into his crackling mike from his platform by the memorial for the dead, sucking on innumerable lozenges in case his voice went or, more often than not, having just got out of his sickbed. 'LADIES AND GENTLEMEN, IT'S SHOWTIME' – miles before the first float appeared, like a tardy bride, decked out in flowers and colours and bright motifs, with her endless train of courtiers and clowns, jesters and majorettes swinging their batons out of step and shivering in their miniskirts; t'ai chi experts who feigned and bowed to the cheers of an illuminated crowd; boys in their paper-made flying machines, faintly ridiculous, just sprouting beards; grannies in aid of Alzheimer's disease (unless they were waiting for the parade somewhere else); dragons who breathed a fairylight fire with slayers that came in their wake complete with fake, wobbly swords (manfully manned, of course, by a spinstered headmistress); and last but not least the little princesses, vacant, yawning, late for bed, who waved their little hands above the wrist like puppets on a sad production line or bona fide royalty doing the rounds....

And they all swept into the park, past the gardeners perennially deflowering the beds (they'll come up again and again if you let them), the hot-dog van and the candyfloss stall (spinning its skeins of silken breath); babies bawling, kids skedaddling, teenagers dropping like flies (due to cider and aspirin); goldfish hanging like baubles from hooks (in their little plastic bags, too easily spilt) and the tent full of cards, spells, crystal balls and crones you wouldn't ever want to meet in the dead of liquorice night. Glued-down toys and weighted hoops, metal hands that clutch thin air (not even the ear of a teddy bear) and an avalanche of glittering coins which never ever falls (like the wild boy surfing the waltzers, nonchalant and arrogant as the breeze) to the burnished god who stands centre stage, like a Colossus, astride the football pitch, juggling his people for the moon – only too-willing victims of sacrifice... up and down, round and round, he loves me, he loves me not.... Where Marly had stood (was it two years ago when it felt like ten?) almost touching the roof of air and counting stars as if they were smarties and smarties as if they were stars (what a lot of parties the gods must have), the daisy ring too big for her twiglet fingers but it might as well go as a noose around her twiglet neck... up and down, round and round, no at the bottom, yes at the top... Marly's ring, Boethius' ring. Where Leslie Finch had taken a kid (Surely not! A preposterous thought) to go find Mr Squirrel in his den and give him a hazelnut or two.... Dead drunk she must have been, on neon and moonshine, to say 'I do' up there at the top for all to hear, especially David, who grinned in delight and rubbed his hands as if he'd found his treasure at last, though the money jangled right the way out of his pockets as they hurtled back to earth.... (How could they go so high and so low?) And to write that night in her gratitude diary 'I am alive' for number five. 'Truly alive!'

And an extra one for number six: 'IT'S SHOWTIME, LADIES AND GENTLEMEN, IT'S SHOWTIME!'

# Seven

She pounced on David as he came through the door, not even giving him time to take his coat off.

'Terry says,' she launched in, bustling about the kitchen, 'if I got more love I wouldn't be thinking of moving.'

'Did he?' replied David, scanning the surfaces and sticking his nose in the air, doing his Sherlock Holmes thing with the dinner. Any minute now, Marly thought a little irritatedly, he'll be taking a peek in the fridge.

'Sausages,' he ventured at last, taking a peek in the fridge.

'No.' She got the grater out and started grating some cabbage quite fiercely into a small bowl. David went past her into the bathroom and she heard him urinating through the thin walls. Familiarity, she thought as she always did, really does breed contempt.

'He's given me stuff to make me feel all bright and shiny,' she called through. 'Apparently.'

'What?' – over the flush – 'Say it again.'

'BRIGHT AND SHINY,' she almost yelled it. 'You're deaf, you are… honestly, you need to see him more than I do.'

'What!' again, this time for effect. He came out with a grin.

'Very good, very good. He's given me stuff to make me feel bright and shiny – stupid bastard. Honestly, he hasn't got a clue, sitting there with his books… I bet I could understand them better than he does. He hasn't got a clue,

68

that's the problem, he hasn't got a bloody clue.' She scooped the cabbage from the back of the grater and almost flung it into the bowl, her fingers splayed. '*And* he said my plant's flowering again like it's some sort of sign or something. He said it deliberately, I'm sure of it.'

'We-ell,' David began doubtfully then immediately regretted it.

'Well what?' she burst out. 'Course he did. He knows what I'm like in that way, that's the thing. He knows how my mind works... at least he thinks he does. He hasn't got a clue really – I'm too good at acting. And then again,' she paused, amputated stump of cabbage mid-air, 'I mean, the thing is, sometimes I am alright when I see him; it's just the rest of the time he doesn't see me – not like you do.'

'No.' David's tone seemed to suggest (at least to Marly's ears) that he was only too well aware of that rather dubious honour.

'If I got more love,' she repeated, 'I wouldn't want to move probably – that's what Tezza says.' (It didn't seem so bad, putting it on to Terry, having him ask for love on her behalf.)

'He didn't ask you about your sex life then?' David half laughed. 'Dirty sod!'

'No.' She felt a surge of anger at his sidestepping and, after a few moments pent-up silence, she flung the grater down. 'Look at it, it's rubbish, it can't even grate properly – I nearly cut my finger off. It's rusty, that's the trouble, it's rusty because somebody, SOMEBODY keeps leaving it out on the draining board and not drying it up properly.'

David felt his stomach tighten – it was going to be a bad night. She was stressed, her movements awkward as if she'd been fashioned out of wood, her shoulders up round her ears – all signs that she was fast approaching what he privately termed the 'electric fence' stage. (Programmes included, his mind silently articulated: men as a four letter word; leaping and bolting at the least little thing; taking everything he said amiss; red-raw nerve action; and throwing things with the force and accuracy of a Valkyrie. Modus operandi: keep your trap shut or else and take over the sorting of all practical matters.) He took the grater off her carefully, gently nudging her out of the way.

'Here, I'll sort it out. You go put your feet up, watch Oprah Winfrey or something.'

She leapt onto the little step that separated the kitchen from the tiny hallway, her arms folded like a little old schoolmarm, her eyes glinting wildly behind the lenses of her tortoiseshell specs. She put them on, he sometimes felt, just so her eyes could glint a little wildly behind them. 'Oprah *Win*frey's not on at this *time*,' she said as if he were an idiot, elongating words and emphasising syllables the way she did when she was unravelling at a rate of knots.

'Have we got mayonnaise?' he asked to distract her.

The folded arms shrugged. '*I* don't know. How should *I* know. I don't know anything any more.' (Oh lordy, he thought. Red alert, red alert. EF proceeding to dumbshow in a matter of a microsecond. Modus operandi: snap her out of it sharpish.) 'Well, you should,' he said too firmly – Oh David you fool, you fool – far far too firmly.

The wooden frame that was now Marly bent from the waist to the fridge and the voice that came out of her was sharp and dangerous as a knife against stone. 'Well, let's see shall we?' Three jars came out in quick succession, each with a bang more furious than the last. 'Curry dip, chilli dip, red-hot pepper dip – more dips here than the Eastern Eye... and yet – how bizarre – they're practically empty. Most people, you would think, would rinse them out and put them in the recycling bag or the bin but Davey boy, little Davey boy (how her voice set his teeth on edge) puts them back in the fridge, for safekeeping I suppose.... No mayonnaise though, I'm afraid, alas no mayonnaise.' The fridge door slammed shut.

'It'll be foul,' he muttered with genuine displeasure, 'without mayonnaise.'

Her eyes gleamed malevolently and she straightened up at her post like a sadistic little sergeant. 'It'll be *fine*, absolutely fine. You should be grateful you've got anything. People'd give their eye teeth for raw apple and cabbage. (It came, he thought, probably, that sadistic little bent, from childhood memories of being forced to swallow fat – for good manners – lump by glistening lump.)

'I might go up the shop,' he proposed, putting down the grater, 'even so.'

'No you will not.' She practically barred his way, her arms and legs stretched out in an X, as if she were doing aerobics or bracing the walls for a Samson-like wrath. 'It'll do you good – Jesus Christ – to manage without mayonnaise for a change.... If that's the only problem you've got – dear God... it'll do you good,' she repeated, stepping forward to poke what she called his ice-cream, chicken-pie, chocolate-cake waist – though God knows why because he never got any; and then, as if she'd gone a little too far (though she was capable of a great deal worse than *that*), she turned and went through to the sitting room where the sound of her banging and cursing came through in snatches just loud enough (deliberately and infuriatingly loud enough) for him to catch: 'Oh what a tragedy! No mayonnaise... BANG... poor little Davey boy can't live BANG BANG without it!'

Marly looked at their reflections, far off on the TV screen: her own, tall and unyielding, the plate teetering on the edge of her knees; David's smaller, shrunken against the sofa, as if he had no torso, the plate in the middle of his lap, already half empty of course – the way he shovelled it into his mouth, like a forklift truck – eating around the sausages, saving the best till last like a little boy taking his medicine first. She sighed excessively and eyed his plate disapprovingly several times, in between small bites.

'What?'

She sighed again and shook her head and stared at his

plate again. 'I don't know, I really don't know... guzzle, guzzle, guzzle!'

'You've got to,' he joked, 'before the other animals get to it!'

She stared at the shrunken gnome on TV and the tall ice queen by his side, wondering what they were going to do. It was like that sometimes – she glimpsed the possibilities, probable outcomes, consequences of the things she said and the things she did but it never seemed to make any difference – the hag always rose, bubbling with lava and the ice queen froze mid-air. Her eye fell distractedly on the world map pinned to the wall like some sort of Holy Grail and she wondered if she'd ever get to Novorosysk, Corsica, Shangri-la.... The meal really was quite foul – a joyless, perfunctory little meal, the way it had been made; and she felt a weary sense of futility wash over her, something close to despair. No hope, no good, ever before and ever after... just endless repetitions of this feeling inside her. She grimaced and took a sip of water. 'We are not Neanderthals, we are not living in the Stone Age. We are civilised, with table manners. There are no animals here to take our food,' she went on with a bitter little sense of her own irony. 'Look at the way you hold your knife – all la-di-dah like a pen, yet you shovel it in like there's no tomorrow (though there is a tomorrow and tomorrow and tomorrow her mind said, and the ice-queen's voice came cold and distant as ice floes, starlit nights, thin chill silvery steppes and golden-mountain oceans). 'Did your father teach you that?'

David took the remaining sausage in his hands, swallowed it in two fierce gulps then licked his fingers one by one, with a slightly theatrical, pugnacious look on his face.

'Course not! He eats with his hands, he does.'

She decided to ignore him. 'Most people have scintillating conversation over the dinner table. They talk about ideas, things they've done during the day, their plans and hopes for the future – but I don't suppose,' she paused for a sarcastic little laugh, 'we'll get any of that here.'

'Alright then.' David leaned forward (and the gnome's face ballooned on the TV screen). 'How was your day?'

'It's not for you,' she burst out, 'to be asking me about my day, it's for you to be telling me about yours. It's always the same – me taking the initiative, me taking charge.... Without *me*,' she concluded with an angry little bite which made her even angrier because she thought she might've chipped a tooth on a metal prong, 'everything would fall apart.'

'There's nothing to tell,' he said quietly. 'It's all so mundane and trivial – too trivial to mention, to remember even.'

'You never do,' she cried. 'You spend half an hour on the phone with your mother and there's never anything to tell – you can't remember. You spend eight hours a day at work and there's never anything to tell – you can't remember. You spend six hours down the pub drinking yourself silly and there's nothing to tell – you don't remember. Is there anything at all you do remember?' she asked in a whine, munching solidly all the while as a foil to her rising voice and the hag that was rising within her – oh yes, she was rising alright – rising like new bread from blackened dough; rising from the wrong side of a festering bed; rising in the east like an old old old cantankerous old sun, rippling on the surface like a pond, bubbling with old sores, old hurts, bitter regrets, burning the naked eye.

And she rose, herself, and went over to the curtains, flicking them open to look at the little grey street where the little grey people (she being the littlest and greyest) went up and down, up and down ever after Amen, stumbling over roots that cracked the pavement open and brushing their way past dust-coloured leaves (How could they grow so close to the road?), peering into holiday brochures and calling their crumbledown houses 'Valhalla', 'Heart's Rest', 'Bedouin Cottage', crushed, squashed, entombed together. She licked the edge of her teeth in silent agony. She was crushed, squashed, entombed in a town, in a flat, in a body, in a mind, in a man she half loved, half despised who sat on the sofa still and opaque, as if he had no soul, who dwindled and loomed, dwindled and loomed, a shrunken or voluminous gnome; and more than that, worse than that, deep down, much deeper down a glimpse too, that if she ever got to the edge of the town, past the tulips and pretty cottages, bright fences and small dogs, if she ever got to the glowing coral reefs and bluebell woods, the frangipani trees and the Shangri-las – or anywhere else for that matter – she'd still be imprisoned in a body that had stopped at the doll's house and a mind that groped and spun in vain, like a rat in a cage.

'What's wrong?' David's fingers brushed her shoulder, lighter than feathers, softer than snowflakes. 'What's wrong, my love, what's wrong?' For a moment, just for a moment, she knew the possibilities, probable outcomes, consequences of the things she said and the things she did; but it was imperative somehow to shout him into loving her, taunt him, abuse him into it (a Pyrrhic victory but a victory nonetheless) – warts and all, boils and all he had to love her and yet, of course, she couldn't let him love her like that – her desperate pleas wrapped up so beautifully the recipient could only stare at the paper in appalled fascination. 'What's wrong,' she blurted out, 'is you sitting there like a stuffed dummy, never opening your mouth, never saying anything. You're incapable of any form of communication at all. Aren't you?'

'I'm gonna do the washing up.' He turned away with a sigh and bent to pick up the plates. That was not what she wanted, not what she wanted at all. She pounded after him into the kitchen. 'I don't want you to do the washing up. I want you to open your mouth for a change.' The sight of his curved back, his slightly round shoulders bent over the kitchen sink angered her even more.

'What d'you want me to say?'

She froze, mid-air, on the little step. The hag had risen – full glory, from the dead – and there was nothing to do but ride it out on that old nag of a nightmare until the sun sank into the west, burnt out; the bread was digested, acid and all; the bed was remade and remade and remade.... 'Well, if you don't know that,' she practically spat, 'you're even more stupid than I thought you were.' It was what he hated most of all – to be called stupid – it offended his male brain, his precious male brain that skipped and danced over puzzles and logarithms, tangential equations and algebra.... And he was going to go....

She felt a fear clutch at her heart – for he was going – going to the bathroom where she heard him urinating through the thin, thin speckledy walls....

He was going alright – to the banister, picking up his coat, checking for his wallet....

'That's it – run away as usual – spineless bastard. You're pathetic – you can't face any sort of confrontation can you?'

There was really no doubt about the fact that he was going – down the stairs, at a run, two at a time, desperate to get away from her, the door sliding open with that strange shush shushing noise and...

'If you go, I'll break every one of your tapes.'

... he was gone with a bang of the glass front door, with the finality of a hammer at an auction.

She stood, a little dazed for a moment, then began wandering aimlessly from room to room as if to reassure herself that they, at least, were still there; or to be utterly convinced that *he* was well and truly gone. Sometimes she went after him, depending on how she felt and what she was wearing – though one time she'd chased him into the night, barefoot, pyjama'd, in the bleak midwinter (that was before her mother had died. It had been going on, she thought now, even then) and never felt a thing. Everything that remained of him (being a tangible reminder of his absence) became a source of irritation; and she glared at the crumpled tea towel he always left on the kitchen table and the unwashed dishes in the sink. He didn't even have the grace, she thought, to finish the washing up; and with a movement full of exaggerated disdain and an exasperated tut escaping her lips, she hung the tea towel back in its rightful place on the coat hanger hooked to the kitchen door handle. Two sausages sat, one burnt, one undercooked, congealing in glistening fat on a little side plate and her eye lingered on them quite solemnly for a while as if they might contain the secret of the universe and any minute now spill the beans; though in the end all they seemed to convey to her was the fact that the stove, like everything else, was fucked. She was fucked, the world was fucked, everything in the fucking flat was fucked – she felt a faint sense of relief in the expulsion of breath and repeated several times: 'Everything in the fucking flat is fucked.' The fridge, the cooker, the effing bloody Hoover – stingy bastards, purple trousers, kerchief wrapped round her neck like some sort of Parisian, going on about snails, sitting there in their monstrous spectacle, that cancerous building that seemed to sprout a new tumour by the month... raking it in in their bakery, raking it in ONLY BECAUSE they economised on everything from paper bags to currants. Two, she'd counted in her last scone. And even they had sunk to the bottom. She stared morosely about her, at the painting from Athena that Helen had given her years ago, wondering why she'd kept it so long – probably because it reminded her of a time when everything seemed conquerable, even bad taste; the filthy-rimmed curtains Mrs M had put up (Parisian style no doubt, so no one could see in but you could see out); the peely, patchy, speckledy-hen walls (looking as if they'd been spattered in piss); the mousetrap filled with tempting delicacies – morsels of cheese, peanut butter, ravioli and anchovies (apparently they couldn't resist tinned anchovy); and the infestation of grime that twinkled and winked from every crack and cranny as if to say 'Come and get us if you're hard enough'. She wasn't. She gave the fridge another dent for good measure with the toe of her boot, went into the sitting room and threw herself in a little heap on the sofa.

'The gnome has gone out carousing,' she muttered hysterically to herself after a few moments' silent contemplation of the gas fire which glowed with coal but never sank to embers. 'The gnome has gone out carousing – cheers mate, thanks a lot' (she toasted an imaginary partner mid-air) – 'and the ice queen has to wait, WAIT WAIT WAIT in a freezing flat, for his return.' It was always the same. There was no point thinking it could be any different. He just couldn't face confrontation, couldn't face it at all. The slightest bit of agitation and he was off like a scalded cat. The only person you could rely on in this world was yourself. She fed herself a few medicinal green drops from her old-as-age-old, stone-encrusted bottle labelled 'How not to get Hurt', 'How to Survive' (there were many other bottles, colourful, haunting, glass-blown bubbles with hags and queens, suns, moons and genii in them, but they were uncontrollable) then stoppered it up with a sigh. He wouldn't get away with it. She expected it of him but he wouldn't get away with it. It crossed her mind to phone his mother, which she'd done once or twice in moments of high dudgeon, recounting the episode with a terrible glee, putting herself in the best light for all she was worth.

'Yes, I provoke him – no doubt about that – but nothing justifies his going out for six hours at a time and coming home drunk. He just will not stay put and have it out.'

'That's right,' his mother always said in her pretty, lilting Welsh voice. 'He's deep, tha's what it is. Always was.' (It had made her laugh when she'd first heard that. He was about as deep as suet pudding, fizzy pop, lemon meringue pie. There was nothing deep about David; he just didn't know how to communicate.)

She ran over a few choice lines in her head, rehearsing an eloquence she didn't feel and yet, as she did so, she found herself getting angrier and angrier; the more she justified it all in her head (in an imaginary conversation with his mother) the more irate she became; and all the long-forgiven memories (or so she thought) of things he hadn't done, should have done, promised to do, promised not to do, popped up one by one, fresher than daisies, yanking up the well-settled earth of her head. She stuck her tongue in her cheek in alarm – a rash would come up now no doubt or some sort of boil with all the stress he was putting her through.... The blood, trapped inside so long, seemed to race around her body, chock-a-block with poisons, toxins, evil little nasties... she got up, went over to his collection of tapes and CDs piled up on the floor, selected one with a discerning eye (one she didn't much like) and, taking the camping mallet kept in the corner of the room (from their one unfortunate camping expedition to Pembrokeshire where they'd been kept awake all night by a dog called Guinness), she hit the tape quickly with three fierce knocks.

Violence, as always, was heady, unstoppable, like wine or a dam bursting. He is grovelling, she thought, and smashed the tape again harder, one, two, three times... turning her face aside so as not to get splinters in her eyes, though it might perhaps have looked as though she couldn't bear to look.

'THAT THAT THAT for his promises! THAT THAT THAT for his lies..!'

She saw, in her mind's eye, under all the yanked-up earth, the small china horse she'd been given as a child and her own squidgy fingers breaking its knees (that genie was shapeless, nameless, unpredictable as a bottled sun); and the thought of the china horse with its little broken knees and her very own father having to glue them back on made her for some reason even angrier and with a final sweeping arc (which could have been the arc of a rainbow) she brought the mallet down on the little tape's head.

'THAT for running out on me!'

She sat back on her heels, a little calmer, and surveyed the wreckage. Black spools, like guts, glittered in the light of the gas fire and her own shadow, enormous, hunched above it like a hag being roasted in the flames. She felt a faint sense of pity for the broken object in front of her and a momentary feeling of shame overcame her. Still, she thought, with renewed indignation at his exit, if that's the sort of thing he's going to do, that's the sort of thing I'm going to do; and she lay the implement down beside her handiwork for all to see, as a serial killer might leave his calling card, or a cat leave rats like trophies for his master. In the sitting room. With a camping mallet. Miss Scarlet. As a child she'd only ever wanted to be Miss Scarlet, Barbie, or maybe one of Charlie's Angels.

Stretching herself out on the sofa, she toyed again with the idea of ringing up his mother, went so far as to reconnect the phone; then switched the television on quickly in a play for time. She flicked the remote aimlessly and licked her teeth nervously, rather as if she were thumbing through a magazine in a dentist's waiting room. Images shot out at her: a big black bear being thrown, like an old rag, onto a rubbish tip, somebody measuring its paw with a ruler, music in the background – mournful, melodious; a long blond-haired man walking up and down in the snow, then a close-up of his cell and an object (handmade, cobbled together, indescribably odd) of feathers and leaves. 'To remind me of freedom and the passing of time,' he smiled, his face splitting open like a rotten watermelon. Marly licked the smooth edges of her teeth in dismay and sped rapidly past fast cars and washing powder to a clandestine affair going on in full view. Here was reality! Similar to her own yet not quite her own; and she sat glued to it for half an hour or so, allowing herself to be engulfed in a familiar miasma of tittle-tattle, intrigue, intimacy and enmity and the undeniable pleasure of watching human beings being human.

Sometimes she forgot that soap-opera characters were imaginary, and when she remembered felt almost cheated; other times she watched the news as if it were a film, waiting to see what was going to happen next. It was a world of many realities, they really should have said, the fizzy sweets and the fortune fish, where you could pick and choose from a pick n mix of imaginary facts. Jelly beans AND sherbet dip? You'll make yourself sick! I'm going to see America through the drive-in movies – and in the end all that was left was imaginary facts. I think therefore I am, someone had said, but you could think yourself into oblivion and then where would you be? There were not enough selves, that was the thing, to fit all those realities, unless you smashed yourself to smithereens with a camping mallet and sat about all over the shop – your lungs doing the bends in the bubble gum, your heart in the jelly beans, your feet in the sherbet dip, your liver laminating in acid drops and your soul wrapped up in a black jack (Is that what God did? Did he exist as a whole in pieces: as himself in all those realities? One in all, all in one. Jesus, your dad must be fucked, David had said.) – the only witness to your existence, a vivisectionist confectionist! Everyone needed someone to bear witness to their existence – that's why Helen rang her up all the time, imparting every detail of her fiendishly complex love life – to prove she existed, keep record, pass the memories on (in case she forgot and forgetting was like never existing). Memories: those arbitrary jostling moments like shapes through a glass darkly, the polyfilla of days; picking your nose up Jabba's house on a rainy afternoon; catching ladybirds in the playground with a girl called Jacqueline (who ate the whole of a tangerine, peel, pips, pith and all); a tea shop in Wales out of season; Stokesy shouting 'parson's nose'; and a priest saying night when he should have said light or was it the other way round – that proved you existed in the past, that got you up to where you'd got to. Unless, of course, you didn't want to remember and that was another matter entirely. That was when you buried the nameless in numberless graves. (Dogs dig graves for bones too, and then they excavate them. You love resurrecting corpses, David had said, and it was sort of true.) Our father which art in heaven, hallowed be thy nameless souls on the point of departure by torture from the Khmer Rouge. You destroyed all photographs (for what hadn't lived, can't have died or been killed); converted old wedding rings from something purely symbolical to something purely functional; melted down old memories like skin to lampshade, tooth to coin; pawned the good clock that hid the mouse that wound you up that went tick tock tick tock TICK TOCK.... She wondered when the lovers would get found out. Any minute now by the look of things. That was the trouble with soap operas – everything was discovered, everything found out, every big or little secret inevitably revealed (whereas in real life you had to live with their concealment); and they focused on the consequences of the things people did as opposed to the consequences of the things they didn't do. Things you did got their own punishment or reward in time; it was the things you didn't do or the things you did too late, that held you accountable in your own head, they were the real terrors. Ghosts of if only setting up realities of what could have been, should have been, in place of a reality that was.

I'll ring her up, she said to herself now. I'll ring her up! And the words flitted about her head like a Clouded Yellow. I'll ring her up in a minute. I'll ring her up right now. She even went so far as to begin dialling the number then changed her mind and put the phone down. She sat hugging her knees for a moment then leapt up and went through to the kitchen to fix herself some porridge and orange juice. She sliced an orange open with the bread knife and the juice spurted everywhere, like blood, all over the place, trickling down her chin and the speckledy-hen wall. Wasn't there a wailing wall somewhere in the world, stuffed full of prayers and oaths, curses and scarab beetles...? She waited for the porridge to 'moither', watching over it like a broody hen with a wooden spoon. 'If those walls could talk what a story they could tell' – that was a line from a play or the post office maybe. What about if they could wail? What did that say about the souls they protected? She scooped the porridge into a bowl, drank the juice in one full tilt, tapped the wall (just in case) and went back through to the sitting room. It was unforgivable! Leaving her to fend for herself in a freezing flat, a soul in limbo with nothing to do but wait for his return. She'd show him who was boss. She'd shake him down to his complacent foundations. She'd play cards; she'd play hardball if that's what he wanted (You play cards, he'd said once; and she would too: Queen of Diamonds, red and glittering, icicle bright and snow-queen deep, hard as nails, blood like orange juice, distiller of poisons – agrimony and meadow saffron if she had to....) She ate with her head bent over the bowl and wiped her mouth with the back of her hand. Right now. This minute. She would. 'Hello Anne,' she practised out loud. 'It's me.' No good. Try again. 'Is that Anne? It's Marly.' I will too, she muttered, putting down the bowl and getting up to go through to the bedroom where she took a quick, vague, myopic peek in the round porthole of a mirror on the wardrobe, as if checking her appearance was some sort of prerequisite for a meeting on the telephone. She fiddled with her hair for a moment or two. No doubt Michael effing Angelo would be piping up in the background as usual, like some sort of flautist off-stage, behind the scenes. He never actually came to the phone, just sat there listening in, butting in like an old ram with lumbago, from the Sistine Chapel of his easy chair. She'd swipe him off it alright. Gout? No wonder. He thought his heart was packing up if he so much as picked up the Hoover. The only thing he was good for was a stew with brown sauce. She'd had a dream once, where she'd found him gobbling rosaries in front of the TV, slapped him in the face and confronted him with the words: 'I suppose David gets his evasive tactics off you then?' (He had to get them somewhere.) Occasionally, when she really wanted to hurt, she asked David how long his father had been out of work; and he replied just as nastily: 'About as long as you!' The difference was, her illness was real – invisible maybe, but real. (All really real things had to be invisible. It was the imaginary stuff you could touch.) She wasn't bald and she still had two tits, and people might imagine it was all imaginary; but it was real alright, as real as anything else you couldn't see, plain as a pikestaff if you cared to look. Michael effing Angelo, on the other hand, got the sack on account of Dai Melon's grouting and it was all over for him, finished, kaput – canticles, shining lights, incense and all.... He was practically glued, now, to the television set; he grumbled about footballers and he wouldn't do 'women's work'. She didn't see why he couldn't apply himself to cosmetics with Revlon now in the valley. There wasn't much difference between paint for walls and paint for faces... wailing walls, wailing faces... Anne slaving away in the pharmacy all day.... There wasn't much difference, come to think of it, between her own mother and David's, though Ivy never wore nail polish or ski pants in the sitting room. The only time Ivy wore ski pants was on a trip to Switzerland as a young woman.

'Bend ze knees, Ivee,' the ski instructor had shouted. 'Bend ze knees!'

Her friend had joked: 'It's like slipping on perpetual banana skins'; and they'd drunk *Glühwein* in the evenings. (It was a memory she'd treasured and passed on.) After that she'd got married and gone downhill for good. Ivy ever slipping on perpetual banana skins, between Scylla and Charybdis, rocks and very hard places, with knees that never bent underneath the weight, toes that never curled up (or saw paint) though they were the very last thing to go cold.

She studied her face in the mirror with a certain amount of critical detachment, peering this way and that in order to catch a glimpse of every single crack and cranny, gleaming like diamanté from the planes and surfaces of her skin. 'I love myself,' she practised out loud, a modern-day Narcissus with a modern-day mantra culled from spiritual gurus on spiritual TV shows. 'I am perfect,' she uttered, knowing how powerful words could be even if you didn't believe them and struggling with the yawning gap between what she said and what she felt. There seemed to be nothing but gaps. Gaps between the world inside and the world outside, the internal world and the world of the mirror; and the little word 'but' linking the two. I love myself but... I'm perfect but....

(The world inside did a sort of macabre dance when you said out loud that you were perfect.) 'But' was the bridge between what you were and what you wanted to be, what others thought and what you knew, what you did and what you said, what you thought and what you felt, what you thought you should think and what you really did... nothing but gaps and the little word 'but'. 'But' was never-ending. 'But' was the bit of skin between pork sausages in a row, separating one from the other, yet linking them all together. 'But' was the point of struggle, place of resistance, hesitant, fragile, easily ripped. 'But' was a woman (of a passive disposition), a tug of war of unequal sides, an unbalanced equation. 'But' was guilt, fear, duty, doubt. 'But' was the spot between a rock and a hard place and Ivy should have been Ivy But...

'It's about accepting,' Terry had muttered, but how did you accept the unacceptable? Like David running off for hours on end, leaving her to fend for herself with nothing to do but peer in the mirror... she'd show him. She didn't need him. Men had wanted her before; they would do again, as soon as she was back on her feet. She might be full of buts but she didn't have a single gap between her perfect teeth; and she had a goblet neck, so Imran had said. She hung on grimly to the compliment like a trapeze artist losing his nerve. It was worth something, surely, to be told you had a goblet neck. Unless, of course, he'd meant goblin. Gobbling even. His English had never been that good and then again it might very well have looked as if she were gobbling when he presented her with that cashew nut and the peculiar remark about their genitals becoming friends.

'What d'you think about sex?' he'd asked her the first day they'd met, his bulbous eyes bulbing, shiny shirt shining, tight trousers tightening.

'Well, I don't see anything wrong with it,' she'd replied, grimacing, 'if people really love each other.'

And then that business of dropping a nut down the back of her neck as a pretext for undressing her and she hadn't really wanted to but... she didn't really like him but... men were half order, half cajole ('give me your lips,' he'd cried in the heat of the moment) and women were nothing but gaps and buts.... She pressed her forehead against the cold glass and her breath cut off the world of the mirror. Let him drink himself silly down there at the pub. She couldn't care less. Let the shrouded outside scream and shout. It didn't affect her now. She would float like a balloon to the top of the room and watch him down below doing his little thing. Let the blackbirds sing a chorus of buts. Let the stars brush their pearly whites and the moon yawn discreetly behind the back of his hand. Let Felix the next-door (and very conceited) cat clean his whiskers under the window and prink for pilchards in the dew. She wouldn't wait up. She would remain quite calm, get on with her life; and simply go to bed.

By the time the key turned in the lock she was wound up to a pitch of such intensity she could barely think straight, let alone lie in a position that convincingly looked like sleep. She'd forgotten how loud a drunk could be: puffy little breaths, snorts, trips, farts, burps, hummy little skips – he'd had a whale of a time by the sound of things whereas she... He seemed to take an age getting up the stairs and she lay there stiff as a board, hard as a poker (like the soldier in the fairytale who couldn't bend for toffee, couldn't change his nature), clenched as a nutcracker and there he was doing his own little nutcracker suite, slide guitar, air guitar, legato scales around the room. Oh, Tchaikovsky, what have we got here? A drunken little man who could do with a metronome.

The lights blazed on and the bright outline of objects fizzed beneath her eyelids.

Oh, aren't we precise? Laying your money belt down beside your keys in the basket full of chinking coppers that should have been taken to the bank long ago, but then, you're such a dope; placing your watch just so on the bedside table... God, what a reek! D'you think you're going to sleep with me tonight? Fat chance! In your dreams! How do I know where you've been? You might have been chatting up a girl behind the bar, thinking she was more fun than I could ever be. What was she like? Bacardi and coke? Silky sheeny stockings and mascara'd eyes? Did you impregnate her on the sly and me none the wiser, thinking you could come home right as rain, nice as pie? (They say it happens all the time.) Are you sick in the head? You can't see straight, fumbling and tumbling like a little mole on crutches, tripping over sonatas at the edge of the bed in your dirty great boots that should have gone to Doctor Barnardo's long ago but then again, you're such a dope... (And mine like a water nymph's... what sort of a match is that?) Oh Tchaikovsky, get a load of this: a clarinet quintet on legs making a dash for the littlest room. Oh Ludwig B, cup your ear to him if you dare: symphony number two down the lavatory pan with apparent gusto, with feeling, with a bombardment of staccato noises and no consideration whatsoever for the neighbours. You turd. You shit. Sometimes I wish that you were…

'Where have you been?' Out loud, fully fledged, following him into that stinking, rotting sarcophagus of a night.

'What?'

She tutted in exasperation for she knew he'd heard, of course he'd heard; he was simply stalling, playing for time, waiting to judge her responses, mood, inclination, attitude – as if he didn't know, sozzled to the eyebrows as he was. 'Where have you been?'

'Out.' A defiant slamming of the lavatory seat, a slight swaying under the hot tap.

'Out where?'

'Anywhere,' a dab of the towel and a parting shot, 'to get away from you.'

She stood stock-still, stung to the quick, then turned and followed him almost robotically as he charged through to the sitting room. 'Fuck off then, if that's how you feel. Go away and stay away. You obviously don't give a shit.' She stopped in the doorway, trembling like a Victorian ghost in the white cotton nightdress that seemed to shrink a little more every time it came back from the launderette; he was staring at the mangled tape and swaying a little in the dirty yellow light. He looked the picture of dejection. And drunk, she reminded herself. And drunk.

'Every time you go off I'll break another one of your tapes.'

'Fair enough,' he said quietly.

Even now, she thought, stepping into the room, even now it could all be over, if he would just turn and take her in his arms, throw himself down on his knees and apologise for leaving her, leaving her alone for hours on end when she was alone all day – ill, out of work – and promise never to do it again, promise never to abandon her, never forsake her, never hurt her, never stop loving her; but he stood there in front of her, swaying before her very eyes, a little dishevelled, a little tired, reeking of God knows what and emanating who knows where.

She smiled, a reflex action, a nervous tick, and began pacing the room. 'I rang your father. He says you've got to ring him back. He says you're a silly little boy – that's what he said. You're a silly little boy and he's coming to take you home.'

'Course you did.' She watched him slump, like an old man, onto the sofa and pass a hand over his eyes as if to blot her out. Somewhere outside came the sound of glass breaking; and a cat howled eerily, spookily. His head moved wearily in acknowledgment of the sound.

He takes more interest, she thought angrily, in a cat than in me; and she ran over to the phone and shook it grimly in front of him. 'You've got to ring him back. You've got to ring him back.' She went shrilly on and on, gauging his reaction all the time, but he remained blank and indifferent, barely looking at her. That was the other thing – he never believed her. Never believed she'd rung his parents, never believed she'd leave, never took anything she said seriously. Everything was a joke, a bluff, just a lot of hot air, just Marly being Marly. She picked up the receiver, started dialling the number, then stopped at the last digit and put the phone down with a silly smile.

'He says you're an idiot, says you've always been like it. He says you're an idiot and he's coming to take you home. Mind you, he's an idiot himself, a total waste of space.'

Something flickered in his eyes. Oh, she'd lit something now alright. 'He is though, isn't he,' she carried on, brutally working the knife in. 'Bloody useless, just sits watching the television all day. No wonder you're like you are. Your whole family's dysfunctional....'

He stared at her with eyes full of hate. 'I'm going to bed.'

'Oh no, you're not.' She ran over, pushed him back down on the sofa. How easy it was. He was strong but she was stronger. 'You're going to sit and listen to me for a change. D'you know what it's like? D'you know what it's like, huh, being left for hours on end…?' She seized his bullish neck between her twiglet fingers and, feeling a surge of power rush through her, began ramming his head against the back of the sofa. 'D'you know what it's like, huh? D'you know what it's like?' How easily he submitted. How easily she mastered him. So close to the fire and yet not a flicker of flame in retaliation – in fact there was almost fear in his eyes. He was in her control, he was in her clutches; and she almost despised him for being there. 'You're spineless, you're pathetic, you run away from everything. You can't drive, can't swim, but you can drink yourself silly alright can't you, you stupid bastard.' She kept ramming his head against the back of the sofa, barely knowing what she was saying, filth pouring out of her mouth, tears pouring out of her eyes. 'You're a piece of shit. You're nothing. You make me sick. You…'

Suddenly, without warning, in one drunken, fluid movement he brushed her aside as if she were a gnat and stumbled past her out of the room, cursing and muttering under his breath. She heard him clattering about in the kitchen for a moment; then the bathroom door shut and bolt violently.

She picked herself up and examined her knees in the dirty yellow light. One was a little scraped and she blotted it with the hem of her white Victorian nightdress. The magnetic blue butterfly stared at her from the radiator, upside down as usual as though tricked by gravitational forces, its wings heading for earth. (Sometimes you flutter up, he'd told her, and sometimes you flutter down.) The cat howled eerily once more, somewhere beyond the windows, beyond the town even, somewhere out in space. She lay her head down on top of her knees, her anger slowly diffusing into a vague sense of unease and then, as the intensity of the silence penetrated, outright anxiety.

She leapt up, ran into the kitchen and hammered on the bathroom door. 'Open the door. Right now. Don't you dare lock the door against me – this is my house. Open up. This minute.' She pressed her ear up against it (a double door, for hygiene apparently. It's regulations, her landlady had said a little primly, Parisian style no doubt.) She heard the taps running like the sound of a distant waterfall and faint murmurings and groanings above it. She banged again. 'Open up, for Christ's sake, open up.' And then, a change of tactics: 'Let me in will you, I need the toilet. I need the bloody toilet for Christ's sake.... I care about you,' she added. It sounded hollow even to her own ears, too much of a turnabout, too much of a ruse.

An expletive, drunken, drawling but clear as a bell came through the speckledy-hen walls, splotched with dried orange juice like stage blood. The orange gaped like a face off its hinges and the porridge bowl sat with the wooden spoon still in it.

She sank to the floor, sliding down with her back against the door until she was sitting on a level with the bin liner that stood for a bin; a pale pink flower blossoming on her hem; and her left big toe just inches away from the temptingly delicacied mousetrap. It stank to high heaven, reminding her of lunches Ivy had given her as a child, of ravioli on toast topped with cheese. Always topped with cheese...

'I love you,' she screamed through to distract herself from the pain – and this time she meant it, at least it sounded like she meant it. 'Let me in. I love you, David. Please… let me in....'

The bolt drew back and the door swung open. She scrambled through.

He was sitting on the edge of the bath in a cloud of steam, looking as if he might evaporate himself at any minute; his shirt beside him on the floor; three bright lines on his arm; and the bread knife clasped in both hands as if it were a sword, as if he were about to defend himself against some invisible foe. His body shook; his face was tight, distant; he looked like a little boy whose world had just shattered.

She knelt in front of him, placing her hands over his. 'I love you,' she murmured softly, prising his fingers loose from the blade – stiff little piggies about to go to market – then throwing it quickly into the sink. She turned off the taps, picked up his shirt, moving the upper part of her body slowly, gently, careful not to startle him, careful not to betray the slightest hint of impatience, disapproval, disgust, keeping up a soft pitter-patter all the time as if he were a child or a nervous horse. 'There, that's better: I couldn't hear myself think with all that racket. Phew, it's like a Turkish bath... it's like a Turkish bath in here.' She opened the window just a fraction of an inch then took up her position again crouched in front of him, tilting her face up in an effort to meet his eyes; but they slid away from her, furtive, ashamed. She felt a surge of fierce, protective love gush up in her and she alternately clasped his knees; chafed his hands roughly, mercilessly; scolded him lovingly, fiercely; rolled her eyes, playing the fool; grinned from ear to ear like a clown. 'Oh, you're an idiot. Well, you are though aren't you? What are we going to do with you? Honestly... I don't know. You...'

His eyes lifted in response to her antics and it gave her the courage to make a joke about his torn and bleeding arm. 'A couple more lines, a squiggle and two dots and you'd have a bass clef.' She giggled, pointed hysterically, wildly; their eyes met; he smiled weakly, gratefully in return.

'I love you.' His voice was gruff, fragmented, as though it had been torn from the depths of him.

'I know.'

'I'm sorry.'

'I know.'

She crouched in front of him, squeezing his hand and staring at his face though her mind was filled with the three bright lines, bobbing, fizzing, fermenting below the surface. It would all have to be gone into later, she told herself, this sickening, appalling, ridiculous act. She would have to understand quite clearly this pain made visible, this inflicted hurt out of her control, out of her dictates, that had brought a new chaos, she felt sure, to their lives. She would have dipped her fingers in the cuts (like the saint who delved in Jesus' wounds) to see if they were true; but for now she was patient in denial, willing to play the game, play the bluff, play the lightheartedness of bass clefs and Turkish baths... the rest would all come later. They would pay for it all soon enough, their credit cards of bitterness and recriminations. It would all come soon enough.

For now she knew her role a little too clearly; his dry sobs a sharp rat-a-tat on her subconscious and, taking him in her arms, she took him to bed.

# Eight

The road to hell is paved, they say, with oh so many good intentions. Marly had never understood the phrase before but she thought she did now – it meant you had to follow through on the good intentions, there had to be a logical sequence of lights, camera, action; thinking, speaking, doing – no room for gaps, no room for buts, no room for deceit (though deception for her was a matter of course). The fact that she was the abuser stuck out with the awfulness, the truthfulness of bone through skin; and in an attempt to take responsibility for this unpalatable truth she fumblingly mumbled out loud to herself: 'I *am* the abuser, *I* am the abuser, I am the *abuser*,' trying the words out for size, rolling them around in her mouth like a sour old wine, ready to spit them out at a moment's notice leaving only a temporarily bad taste on her tongue. (That's what you did with unpalatable truths, you rolled them around in your mouth for a while then spat them out; you allowed them to skim the surface of your mind like swallows over the Nile, though they plunged later, deeper, harder, of their own accord and the heart was never ready to receive them, the heart never had time to prepare.) It was a little like when Ivy had died and she'd practised out loud: 'She is *dead*. She *is* dead. *She* is dead' as if it might make a difference because *those* words, those particular words had a flavour of one of her own lies about them; a ring of deceit, of escaping, of

93

getting out of things; and indeed for several months she hadn't dared say to anyone 'she is dead' not because the sound of it made the fact more real but in case they caught her out, tripped her up and replied a little astoundedly, a little sharply: 'What on earth are you talking about? I saw her yesterday weeding the garden, in her pale blue shorts and gold charm bracelet.' That would have spelt the end, it would have meant the whole thing really was a total figment because as well as a golden melodious harp, silver whistle, sprig of white heather and mother-of-pearl star, the gold charm bracelet also had on it a tiny penknife, perfect for deadheading and stripping petals; and as a child she'd watched her mother using it many times, in their small, walled garden, with venomous abandon.

The whole business had been gone into ad infinitum: it was something or nothing, a release, just a scratch, it would heal, there would be no lingering memento of their argument. There had been other cuts and lesser arguments (and cuts, she suspected, she didn't even know about – I fell against the wall at work, he told her once. Fell against the wall, my foot!). It was hard to reconcile his happy-go-lucky nature with these acts of self mutilation (it didn't fit into her picture of him as her rock, her stalwart, the vice that held her as she reshaped and worked on herself) and she traversed the dichotomy tentatively, shamefacedly. What had she done to him? What had she done to the shy boy with the wide smile, who wore his Tony Hancock t-shirt back to front, ordered pizzas, brought her flowers, played the guitar and made her laugh? She hadn't meant – of course she hadn't meant – and then came the gaps and the buts. She was ill, she was depressed, she couldn't help the violence – it gushed out of her like warm blood; it sprouted, mutated, catapulted, escalated; changed direction cool and easy as a zephyr breeze.... He, on the other hand, could control how he reacted – there was no need to go plunging a knife in his arm the way Ivy had plunged it into the flowers. (She saw the act as a bow against strings, to the sound of Rachmaninov – it was always Rachmaninov.) It showed, moreover, a distinct lack of respect, for if he couldn't look after himself, he could never look after her. If he wavered they were both in the soup. He was meant to be a safe place, a buffer, taking the knocks, taking the scrapes for her sake; not taking her anger and running with it, doing a whole nine-yard little sprint of his own! That wasn't the deal, that wasn't the deal at all. It displeased her to think he could hurt her by hurting himself, though she consoled herself with the fact that she hadn't actually wielded the bread knife.

Her intentions were good, her intentions were honourable – she was almost sure of that. It was simply a question of transforming intention into action, of bridging the gap, of not being fazed by the chasm at her feet. It would take some time of course: there would need to be a set of practical little steps; a succession of right choices one by one by one; a detailed and disciplined planning; a putting of theory inch by inch, hour by hour, week by week into practice. She must stay aware of the danger signs: take the barometer of her moods by the hour; consult her mental workings like some old almanac; nip the badness in the bud before it flowered; hide the old hag's pointy hat and broomstick not to mention flaming cauldron; catch herself on the downward slope before she snowballed out of control. She must bear in mind at all times that he was a precious vessel, a beautiful thing to be cherished, respected, handled with care. She would mend her ways. In the middle of an argument, she would shout out a word like 'Holocaust' in an effort to bring perspective to their small, pathetic domestic crisis. In the middle of an argument, she would think of something humorous they'd done together months ago, waggle her tongue, thumb her nose in an effort to defuse their small, intense domestic crisis. In the middle of an argument she would think of her mother dying, of stiff upper lips, of pulling-up socks, of living for the day and cutting ties with the past. (Though how on earth did you do that? What were the nuts and bolts of it? Did you take all your stuff to the jumble – her used-up scent bottles; how could she bear to part with them? Did you shave your head and reinvent your life? How did you prevent yourself re-piecing the jigsaw again and again and again when it was so easy to say 'There, there, that piece goes there: the outsize molar, the wart on the nose, the pointy, whiskered chin.') In the middle of an argument she would take deep breaths, count to ten, remind herself there was no hag, that she was the hag, that she was responsible for everything she did and that she and she alone could reach across the gap, could stop herself detaching and sailing like a balloon to the top of the room.... She would get some ointment for his arm, she would feed him home-baked delicacies until his chin sank into his neck: arctic roll, treacle sponge, trifle, meringue, upside-down pudding. She would roll out pastry with a milk bottle. She would wash her hair, make the bed, spring clean the flat, trap the rats, cut out the old and dirty mould, sparkle up the windows, elbow grease the stove. She would make plans, make lists, write out her dreams, collect stamps, Toby jugs, anything she fancied, dig out her old poetry book from school and read aloud the way she used to; listen to David playing his guitar – patiently, good humouredly; comment favourably on his performance in bed at night, lying awake beneath the stars and the pigeons on the chimney. She would deceive reality into thinking she was well; her soul so very old and half dead with despair would galvanise itself just a little; and she would rise – wouldn't she? Couldn't she? Like a phoenix from the ashes. She would let the littlest chink of hope in – not a new blinding dangerous sun but a crescent moon perhaps. A piece of crescent moon would do, for now, to hold on to.

And those moments – those moments of wonder (that would all come true) would stand in her memory like fixed stars – all alone, self-contained, still seeming and yet spinning with infinite quiet motion; there, soft, in her memory, stars to chart a course, a life by. (Amazing how they lived for billions of years, waiting for man to tinker his way through the Ice Age, the Stone Age, the Bronze Age, the Rocket Age, until the moment he was able to look through his telescope at that star looking back, saying cheese and exploding.) This moment. This feeling. This forever-now eternity.

After the downpour everything is glowing, trembling, catching rainbows. She points out a skylark (so she says), a strangely-coloured stone, a bit of graffiti, a bend in the stream. They laugh unrestrainedly at nothing, at everything, everything yet nothing touches them. They linger hand in hand, stroll, smoke the breeze, catch the rays of an Indian summer in a little old park in England on a Sunday afternoon.

Benches are full: occupied by dozing, impervious grandfathers, umbrellas, packed lunches, bags of conkers, sodden scarves, skateboards and footballs and faces under newspapers, behind headlines, doting mothers, feet splayed, with babes in arms; but they manage to find one all to themselves in the middle of the flowers. (Picking flowers she'd been taken. He'd swooped right out of the blue and carried her off – it is well to remember; and for a while there is an urgency, a slight desperation in the way she cranes her neck, tilts her eyes, opens her mouth a little too wide in gasps of excitement, surprise – she is living on borrowed time. She must drink it all in, every second full gulp; cram each moment into her mouth for when she has to return.... He, at least, is happy to forget that one day she will have to go back because for him each day is freshly stamped, new created, with the dew still on it; he is grateful, simply, for one of her smiles.)

How the birds sing after the rain! The sun has opened everything up: a Dulux dog steps out of the clouds, light streams through the trees in 'Beam me up Scotty' columns, shirtsleeves roll up, smiles come out to play. The tiny carousel is going full blast in a corner of the playground, pulsating to the music and the screeching chains of the swings that are going full swing. Rival gangs of boys on bikes eye each other warily over the monkey bars: do spins, do skids, show off, do wheelies, do 'Bet I can, Bet you can't, Bet I can infinity,' no hands, spit gum, chuck petards. A little girl blue hula hoops all alone on the grass and a tiny helmeted boy on a minuscule bike careers past shouting obscenities. Everyone is out, taking the air, as they must have done in the pleasure gardens of Vauxhall and Ranelagh in the eighteenth century. A gaggle of girls teeter and giggle a little way away from a pride of young males, lounging, indolent, aloof for now – though they will pounce, come in for the kill with the dusk. (Parasols in Georgian times were also no defence against young bucks leaping fences into the 'dark walks' in the dark.) A ruffled-up couple startle up behind the hedge at the snap of an approaching twig.

'I always wanted a Grifter,' he announces suddenly out of nowhere amidst the flowers, his mouth twitching at the tiny helmeted boy who is circling the girl, now, in hula hoops of his own, still shouting obscenities, 'but my parents couldn't afford one. My dad kept threatening me with a Bomber but in the end I got a second-hand Commando!'

The sun glints down on the flowers, on her skin, on the screeching chains of the swings, on the ice-cream man getting cabin fever in his van, on the tiny carousel going round and round. She could stay here forever, in this park, in his arms, on this bench, which is a rock in a maelstrom of colour. The painted horses plunge and dance, throw their riders off onto shadows complex as Byzantine artwork on the ground. An energetic dad kicks a football too high at his large, too slow, unprepossessing son. 'Too slow,' he barks horridly, his dreams clearly thwarted. 'Too slow.'

'What a fate!' she smiles back at him, not sure who she means but thinking how wonderful it must have been to have parents who wanted to buy you a Grifter but couldn't afford to... and suddenly he is telling her small, arbitrary, nonsensical things, things she has tried to wrestle out of him over the years... here, now, in this park, on this bench which is a rock in a maelstrom, he is giving them up to her quite naturally, freely, of his own accord....

How the smell of Cardiff in the morning is so distinctive because of the brewery; how he loves the rain, the hills, the valleys of Wales; how he likes to walk in cities at night; how his grandfather (who always kept Mackeson's stout and porridge oats in the cupboard) had died knowing his grandson had got to university; how his sister went through a stage of mixing ice cream and cherryade; how a little boy at primary school had eaten crayons and counters, pissed in the hatstand and told him a virgin was a woman who hadn't done it; how he always thought ghosts were like photographic negatives, borne out of certain climatic conditions; how he'd dragged his parents round museums as a child, boring them half to death....

These words pouring out of him one Sunday afternoon (what a strange, earnest little thing he must have been) in the golden light of an Indian summer (she was quite safe here in that warm golden light) in a park in little old England on a bench which is a rock in a maelstrom of colour....

The blue roans, dapple greys, dark bays and palominos snort, cavort, prance and bow, graceful as ballerinas; and the flowers (asphodels, surely, asphodels which grow in the Elysian fields) nod drowsily in the sun.

(Oh Hades, whispers the breeze.)

They make their way through the grubby streets in the light of early morning. Nobody in their right minds could possibly be up yet except the blackbirds, the postman, the lonely street-stall hawkers; and he, scorning the stale warmth of the sheets, cosy teapot, egg-and-bacon Saturday morning treats, strides ahead intrepid, resolute, arctic explorer in his own mind no doubt, Strider, Gandalf; hobbit more like with those feet of his clumping along in his worn-out boots. (Why didn't he ever take them to Doctor Barnardo's?) And she, lagging behind, a little irritated, a little tired, fighting the scarf about her neck, old receipts and shopping lists blowing about her pockets, her toes so cold she could snap them off like twigs. 'Let's get up early,' she'd heard him call through the grogginess of sleep, 'let's get up early and wake up the flowers, the way you used to....'

That was a long time ago, she'd wanted to point out to him, and even then... but she didn't have the heart to and so now, here she was, in this grey, freezing mist, struggling along past 'Valhalla', 'Bedouin Cottage', 'Heart's Rest', past the Darenth stream slipping away silent as a secret, in the deep, crisp, even steps of her ha ha Lord and Master.... It must have been like this on that first day, in that first dawn of creation – the world a silent, freezing greyness ready to be lit, ready to be spoken. Had He drawn them forth one by one, spinning them out of his lonely breath in Latin, Double Dutch, Romany, Yiddish, Cantonese? Did his echoes go forth and multiply, down the Grand Canyon, up the Zambeze, round Cape Horn at a rate of knots? Did any disappear off the Marie Celeste (though the table was set, the feast in place) enticed underwater by the sonar of dolphins and humpback whales singing? Did any get lost in space, still hurtling round and round, holding their breath, orbiting the angels and the barrier of sound?

He'd taken a risk – ripping her out of warm oblivion the way he did. She met reality hard; he should know by now that she met reality hard. It was only in dreams, she'd confessed to him, that she could escape the confines of her stopped-at-the-doll's-house body, her lank hair, marshmallow eyes; only in dreams did she set out on walks with the hazel stick her father had cut down for her as a child; only in dreams could the past be redeemed, could she play God with her soul, make wishes come true, do cartwheels, backflips, do the splits, shoot goals in netball in bionic slow motion, her limbs free and easy, her mind clear as water; only in dreams could her anger set itself free to soar harmlessly, twist the air, skim slow toads and blue irises, power stations and church steeples; only in dreams could she absolve herself.... It could have gone either way – he was too well aware of her sudden hostilities, surprise turnabouts, slow steps to compromise, random bursts of aggravated violence, not to have known that it could have gone either way. She had lain suspended for a while in the weightlessness of limbo, in the space between two moments, waiting for something inside to protest;

Zillah Bethell

but the tender warmth of his voice, carefully packed haversack, cheese and onion rolls, bottle of squash, the way he nudged her gently but firmly into her clothes, even the tilt of his chin, all brought her down, touched her heart, told her he was taking her with him whichever way the dice fell, whichever way the wind blew – hat, broomstick, warts and all. And just for once and just because... she would let it be, let it happen, like that strange, sad, slow dance with the hands, the eyes closed, where one partner leads, the other follows. Ebbing and flowing. She would follow, eyes closed, flow.

They pass, like ghosts, out of the town; and it recedes into the distance like some ancient oil painting put out to weatherbeat, to mature under apple trees the way Van Gogh did it. They have never been this far before on foot – it is an adventure, it is altogether different from the park and pretty cottages with their year-round tulips in vases behind windows, their crazy paving and garden gnomes that sing in the rain, fish for trout, wheel barrows, crouch on toadstools – though they hardly dare so much as breathe if you ever care to approach. Everything real here is imagined in this strange, surprising mist that cons you into non-belief then conjures an epiphany out of a stone, startling and absurd as a pigeon out of a hat, a silk handkerchief: nettles tall as soldiers; fireweed out of blackened earth; the grave of Anna Czumak (who suffered much in this life) marked by a smattering of frost, like icing sugar, and a simple wooden cross (like the lines of crosses on Caldey Island where the monks have slipped back into the soil that fed them and gave them essence of gorse and heather, which they bottled in perfumes for the tourists that come to their gift shops for sachets and pot-pourris, fudge

and ice cream, never the crosses and the stillness);
a fox in the pose of fantastic Mr Fox, waiting for his
picture to be taken by the sun: two yellow eyes,
foreleg raised, a greasy gibleted grin on his
chops…. Not a sound. Not a sound except their
voices and their footsteps which have acquired a
new freedom in this rock-strewn land – home to
wise owls, little grey rabbits, secret voles and lonely
tramps sleeping rough under midnight, starlight,
moth and bat-soft light. Not a sound except her
heartbeat keeping a new rhythm to the jigging of the
haversack on the back of the man she could no
more part with than she could fly to the moon…
this strange, surprising notion in this dawn just
breaking; this truth just being felt.

The leaves in the wood are almost blinding – it is
difficult to know where to put their feet. The climb is
slow and ponderous with many turnings in order to
catch their breath under pretext of admiring the
view; many jokes about rations, miles to go before
they can eat, levels of physical fitness; many antics
on the red-gold slippery leaves, leaping and skating
with the abandon of children, of cartoon characters;
many mock heroic savings of worms and snails from
puddles and pools…. She is glad he ripped her out
of warm oblivion to meet this new day which is just
like one of her dreams. They have decided the top is
Lothlorien and they must reach it before the light
comes over the hill and into the meadow otherwise… otherwise… but she cannot think of anything
bad enough to happen. Nothing in this world can
catch her today. It is enough just to walk, look about,
feel the blood flow crimson round her stopped-at-
the-doll's-house body. It is enough just to be far
away from the town; feel the sadness kept at bay by
the sound of a robin singing, his smile, the sky. No

need to call their names one by one by one in Latin, Double Dutch, Romany, Yiddish, Cantonese. No need to stand in fairy rings, blow dandelion clocks, spin widdershins round blue moons and hollow trees at noon, clutching sprigs of white heather, golden harps, a silver tin whistle, mother-of-pearl star. No need to step a foot beyond the confines of her soul – stay still for they are here, in her heart, in her eyes, in her smile, in her hair, in her sudden surprising laughter, their frail, transparent wings fluttering in and out of her fingers, like eyelashes against a cheek, like a butterfly kiss. Wherever you are they are there. They are combing their hair in pocket mirrors of dew; Chinese skipping with gossamer rope and blades of grass; threading old moonbeams into their clothes; posting their mail in woodpecker holes; sweeping their mushroom and mulberry homes with dustpan clouds and feather brooms; catching the rabbit warren underground tube – for Camden Town and Primrose Hill; some are waking up the flowers – a little chore for them like cleaning their teeth – and after all these years, after all these storm-blasted, wasted years, these years of futility, pain and despair, she can hear them whispering back through the soft grey mist; she can hear them whispering back to her over the years: 'campion, speedwell, periwinkle, wood myrtle. Silene dioica, Veronica chamaedrys, Vinca minor...'

He feels it too. She is alive again. The lines have gone from her mouth, from her eyes. She is like the girl he first met, her tall neck shimmering over the crowd, far above the rest. There is a possibility of hope, of happiness in the soft blue irises of her eyes. He is magically transformed in those eyes.... He is her rock, her shelter; he will protect her from the wind and rain, the storms and snows. She will grow old in his arms.

He has stood by her in the dark places and now he is taking her into the light. At the top of the hill they will see the new day, the new beginning. He takes her hand. She is ready.

'World Number 426' it had said on the box, 'Fragile' – though it looked tough as old boots to her. She shakes it gently just for fun and just to watch it settle again, the snow falling soft as enchantment on the small white house, the small green lollipop tree.... Outside is pitchy black except for the fireworks going off nineteen to the dozen, illuminating the heavens, the moon, a stray trotting dog and their own small corner of the street. The flat is warm and cosy, smelling of lavender, marigold soap and shampoo; and dimly lit by a pink scented candle (in tribute to the night), the landing light over the stairs and the anglepoise lamp glowing over the settee where David sits reading a thriller, her own small jumble of pens and paper, lists and library books piled high on a cushion at his feet. This is the time she likes best – when the day is almost done, the dirty dishes washed and stacked; and she has just stepped out of the bath, her face and hair squeaky clean, her old pink dressing-gown tied about her waist, padding about on slippered feet, putting things in order, setting things straight, with nothing to worry about or look forward to but sleep. She places the snow world back on the window ledge and peeps behind the curtain, watching a rocket tearing up into space, a waterfall cascading over the town in silvery drops, a giant yellow moonflower bursting out of the lake to blossom in an instantaneous death.

'They sound like Rice Krispies,' she remarks at his reflection, fingertips wiping the pane already misted up with breath. 'I liked Snap best. The boys were Crackle and Pop. Snap was the cutest of the bunch, I think, and wore a stripey scarf.'

His reflection grunts, looks up, smiles vaguely, goes back to its book; she grins inwardly, wondering whether to tease him by telling him the ending, having read the last page, but deciding instead to leave him to it: the undercover federal agents, bombs and assassins, the girl called Cheyenne who rode her man, did all manner of extraordinary things to him and was in fact a spy. (It stuck out a mile – the way she cried, looked away furtively, worked in a bank. No girl called Cheyenne would ever work in a bank!)

A couple pass by, hand in hand and loitering, stopping now and then to stare and point at the fireworks; they seem so small down there on the street, underneath the spacious sky and everlasting stars. Sometimes she is overwhelmed by the smallness of things, her own life dwindling and shrinking to something less than an atom, her mind and body melting and dissolving like a boiled sweet on a radiator, like sugar in tea – though not tonight! Tonight it is all beautiful: her life, her love, the man and woman hand in hand, the stray dog trotting homeward, David reading his thriller under the glowing lamp, for they are all connected, united, wrapped up in a destiny majestic and trivial as a moonflower bursting out of a lake.

She scrambles up onto the sofa, tucking her feet underneath and arranging the cushion within easy reach. She is full of plans and she jots them down one by one on a little scrap of paper: jobs to apply for, trips to be made, skin regimes to try, books to read, music to listen to, a hundred-and-one little chores about the flat; childish dreams and ambitions to fight for. A smile hovers moth-like about her lips and now and again she dips at random into one of the library books, mouthing the words of a sentence she likes or writing it down on a separate piece of paper under the heading 'Spiritual Growth'; her mutterings and exclamations of excitement and surprise entirely lost on David who carries on reading regardless.

'"A man cannot stand in the same river twice." Hmm.' She sucks on her pen, thinks for a while then painstakingly writes it down in her open, angular handwriting. She turns a page. '"If you want to know the ending, just look at the beginning."' She repeats it louder for David's sake, half thinking it may be pertinent, half teasing him. '"If you want to know the ending, just look at the beginning."'

'Ah.' He smiles vaguely without turning and then, hearing her laughter, looks up. 'What?'

'You...' she ruffles his hair with a smile that belies the look of reproach in her eyes. 'I tell you what... you know when I was in the bath....'

'Yeah.'

'I could swear I heard Ratty scampering about in the kitchen.'

'Probably.' He shuts his book and a playful gleam enters his eyes. 'He was trying to get a gander at the fireworks through the window. His little feet were hopping about near the cookie jar. I heard him squeaking "Send 'em up, Mister! Send 'em up!" I says to him, "Look here now Ratty. There's this beautiful bird what lives in this flat – beautiful bird she is – and she ain't too keen on your meddlin' ways." Well, he did something then, I won't say what it was but it wasn't nice, it wasn't pleasant – got me dander up a bit to be honest. So I says, "Whoa there little fella, whoa there now. I'm a giant peace-loving sort of rat, but you're starting to stress my head up." He got a bit uppity then, started weaving about the table aiming little kicks at the cookie jar. I took it to mean he was goading me on, egging me on to give him a pop, so I stepped up to the table – eye to beady eye we was – and I don't exactly know what happened but the next thing I knew he had me in a half-nelson. And, well, to cut a long story short... he's got the run of the kitchen.'

'How come I didn't hear any of this?' she enquires dryly, raising an eyebrow.

'You were too busy lathering yourself up and whatnot. Besides, the whole conversation was conducted in Italian.'

'Italian? You can't even speak French!'

'*Je suis... je suis une voiture.* Oh 'eck.'

'Oh, go and have your bath!' She lobs her old pregnancy book at him and he dives off the sofa and out of the room in what is presumably an assassin-type roll.

'Poor old Cheyenne,' she shouts after him, puffing out air to stop herself grinning. 'Dear oh dear, she dies in the end, doesn't she. Poor old Cheyenne.'

'Spoilsport!' he shouts through from the hallway, pretend glum fashion. 'Spoilsport!'

Stretching herself out in his warm, vacant space she goes back to her books and her lists. These words. These words that will transform her life if only she can believe hard enough. These words, these lists, these bits of dreams on paper like caraway seeds in cake; if only she could utilise them, swallow them down in soups and stews and cassoulets, string them bead-like onto a necklace, tie them up with her laces and hair, imprint them on her very soul in delicate silvery lettering. These words, how they tempt her into a future, twinkling with vistas of hope and happiness. These good, fine words that will banish the bad from the dark, grey lining of her soul. She scribbles them down as fast as she can, for the more good words she knows, the more the bad ones will fade and disappear – it stands to reason. It says so, more or less, on the back of the book: *Transform Your Life in Five Easy Steps.* No need any more for doubt or despair. No need to escape into childhood books where good and bad are washed down with ginger beer and midnight feasts, lacrosse and the French mistress Mademoiselle Dupont, baked apples and ponies that win rosettes at Wembley for the show-jumping class and Best Turned Out. Those words are of the past, of solace, retreat. These words, these good fine words she is reading now are the magic incantations of the future. Her future. Her cake filling up with caraway seeds.

David whistles in the bath, topping her dirty water up with more hot and she smiles and listens for a moment or two, her tight cold heart expanding a little in this soft, safe, bright night where the fireworks are flying over candyfloss crowds with a snap, crackle and pop. It is quiet apart from that, sealed up in their cramped little rundown flat where the rats play Monopoly under the pipes and the yellow-green mould draws sunflowers on the ceiling (though by next week, even tomorrow, they may be manholes or hollyhocks). But not tonight! Tonight they are sunflowers bursting with life, and she jumps up suddenly in her old pink dressing-gown, kicks off her slippers and dances across the room, her shadow gigantic over the walls and astride the pin-tacked world map. She stops before it, closes her eyes and twirls her finger just for fun and just to watch it land again on some ancient green island in blue paper seas, some black dot on the horizon of a foxing yellow continent, some unknown destination in a faded pink metropolis; then goes spinning back like a top across the room to peep behind the curtains at the smoke-filled night and shake the snow world just for fun and just to watch it settle again in a blanket soft as cocoa-filled dreams and deep as a sleep of enchantment. David is singing, now, in the bath; she takes a pen, leans over the table and writes in her gratitude diary:

1 World Number 426 is just fine.
2 I will transform my life.
3 Cape Hope it is then. Cape Hope first and then the world.

She stops, suspended for a moment as David's voice comes bellowing like a foghorn out of the bathroom.

'A room with a view and you,' he sings affectedly, deliberately – she knows it – to make her smile.

'And no one to worry us
No one to hurry us...'

She changes her mind for number three, crosses it out and writes instead: I love D very, very much.

The fireworks go out with a chitty chitty bang bang, stream of red arrows, snap, crackle and pop blaze of glory; and darkness descends once and for all on the little flat.

# Nine

David approached the house with trepidation. No lights were on. He'd rushed up East Hill like a bat out of hell, checking his watch every second or so, worried in case she was fretting, fearful, waiting for him – the meeting had gone on so late. To make matters worse he'd stopped off at the flower shop on Watling Street and the old woman had taken an age wrapping up the flowers, snapping off the stalks with her red swollen fingers. 'Are they for me?' she'd cackled once or twice; and he'd smiled a little despairingly and entered into the thing: 'Not tonight, I'm afraid. Not tonight.' And then: 'Is she bonny?' 'Oh, yes,' he'd replied, 'she's bonny alright.' And she was. He'd give up the world for her if he had to, and she knew it, which was probably why she treated him so badly. Not even married yet and henpecked half to death... he wondered what sort of a mood she was in tonight. No lights was a bad sign, no smell of dinner cooking in the oven. He was surprised how much that annoyed him, after all there was often no dinner – the rats ate better than they did. But after such a good spell it was all the more distressing, frustrating to see her regressing, reverting to type. He sighed and entered the cold, dark silence, almost creeping up the stairs in the thick boots she hated, laughed at, the roses in one hand, his briefcase in the other. He felt a somewhat shambolic figure with his windswept hair and shabby jacket, his shoulders drooping forward a little under a sudden feeling of weight. The meeting had gone on so long and nothing had been accomplished, nothing was ever accomplished. Just meetings about meetings about meetings transcribed into minutes about minutes about minutes. Old Bilberry had the right idea, perching himself by the door like that, ready to make a quick exit. He felt, more often than not, like a cog in a machine, a machine that was at worst corrupt, at best useless, churning out homogeneous little people like pork chipolatas; rendering anything you did ineffectual. Just a cog, just a clown. 'Are you the clown?' the Head of Department had asked him once in a dream. 'Are you the clown, Mr Morrell? Are you the clown?' Too young to be taken seriously, too old to live as irresponsibly as he might have done – if he had dared to, if he had ever dared. He wasn't sure now that he had ever dared.

He switched the landing light on with his elbow, put down his briefcase and went into the sitting room. There she was on the sofa, curled up in a little ball, spines sticking out and at the ready he supposed. He took in as much as he could as quickly as he could: unopened junk mail, bills, letters, a subscription to a donkey sanctuary – he smiled a little wryly at that, the way she spent his money willy-nilly on good causes – two dirty mugs, lunch plate, television point on, CD point on, her pregnancy book folded up at her feet, red sleeping bag over pink dressing-gown over listless body, atmosphere thick enough to cut with a knife, nothing moving in the room except those eyes. Those eyes. He turned and glanced out of the window for a moment in order to prepare himself. A double-decker bus rumbled by; brightly lit and brimful of people going home. Home. He blinked, faltered, turned with the flowers.

'What's that you've got?' she suddenly demanded, her curiosity getting the better of her.

'For you.' He knelt, smiling, relieved, pressed them up to her nose. 'God, that meeting dragged. Would you believe they still haven't sorted out Application of Number. Bilberry did his usual thing, of course.' That usually nettled her, the way Bilberry buggered off halfway through meetings with the paltry excuse that the traffic got bad near Croydon, but tonight she remained unmoved.

'*I've* eaten,' she replied with emphasis, her violet eyes opening a little at the scent of the roses, the left one swooning away the way it did when she was lying or surprised by something. It was amazing, he thought, how her eyes spoke the emotion her face and voice did not. The rest of her could remain still as a statue while the eyes collected, reflected everything – like that book about the tosser who went round opium dens, his life going into a picture. She was like a person trapped in a glacier, only the eyes ever wanting to get out.

'It'll be cold,' she muttered as though reading his thoughts before waving him away to the table. 'You better put them in that,' she added unnecessarily because there only ever had been one vase in the flat. He plonked them in a little askew, arranging them clumsily, carelessly on purpose; and she hemmed and fretted from the sofa, asserting herself with little sighs and oh dears and 'no no not like that' and 'I think they need something smaller'. She was pleased though, he could tell, her bossiness just a facade, just a disguise to hide it. He smiled, took off his jacket, went through to the kitchen.

The place was a tip. It looked at first glance as though a bomb had hit it, though on closer inspection it was simply a surface disorder: things left out, tops off bottles, crockery and saucepans piled up in the sink, banana skins, orange peel, teabags on the draining board. He rolled up his sleeves and set to work, methodically putting things away, tidying things up, washing and drying a couple of plates, turning the oven on to heat the dinner up, keeping an ear open for sounds of movement in the sitting room, waiting for the roses to tempt her out of inertia. She wasn't as bad as he had feared. She was somewhere in the region he defined as the cobwebs and the blues. The cobwebs and the blues weren't all that serious. He could play a song on his guitar about the cobwebs and the blues. He rinsed two glasses and chopped some garlic for the garlic bread, and by the time he had the riff down pat in his head the sofa was creaking, her feet padding over the floor and, yes, there she was by the table, her head bent over the roses, muttering to herself about the length of the stems.

'They're all wonky,' he heard her cry in dismay. 'What kind of simpleton cut them all 'culiar like this?'

'Culiar – the abbreviated word was an offering, a titbit, a sign that she was almost herself again, almost at peace with the world. He thought of the old woman who'd leapt from the back of the flower shop, scaring him half to death and cackled like a ghoulish parrot: 'Is she bonny? Is she bonny? Is she bonny?' He poured himself a drink, leant back against the table and watched her across the landing, her long blonde hair falling over her face, her delicate, sensitive fingers guiding the flowers into place. She must have felt his eyes upon her for she turned suddenly and came to the doorway, holding the vase in front of her.

'That's how you do it,' she smiled triumphantly, her face lighting up like the double-decker bus, the roses sticking out all higgledy-piggledy, some tall as poppies, some short as buttercups. He held an imaginary camera to his eye and snapped her there, framed in the doorway, his goddess in blue jeans under an old pink dressing-gown, clutching a Grecian urn of flowers to her chest.

He nearly choked on a kidney bean when she started going on about old Bilberry. The roses had exhilarated her apparently. She was chewing fast, her face flushed, the words coming out in a torrent.

'God, he's a meddler though, shooting out halfway through. How does he get away with it? Doesn't anyone complain? How old is he, for God's sake? Didn't you say he had a sports car?'

'Coming up for retirement I should think.'

She tipped her head back to laugh, her teeth gleaming. 'Don't they call him the Honey Monster? Don't the students call him the Honey Monster? Why is that? Are his shoulders up all hunched? Maybe that's why he needs a sports car – to fit his shoulders in. You'd think he'd whizz back to Croydon in a sports car.'

'No idea. You know what students are like. There's this one kid, Gary Cooke, nice kid actually, wouldn't hurt a fly. Said Bilberry should have his own canteen. He said the way Mr Billerey eats a bacon roll, he should have his own canteen. Puts him off his food!'

'That's appalling. Have you ever seen him eating? Have you ever seen him eating in the canteen?'

'Well, no. I can't say I've made a particular study of his masticative habits! I mean, you know, I may well have got a glimpse of him nibbling a mint imperial in the staffroom, but I can't say it did anything for me.'

'You should though. You should offer him a sandwich tomorrow for lunch.'

'Oh yeah, I'm really gonna do that, aren't I. Oh, hiya Alan, d'you want a bit of my corned-beef sarnie only my girlfriend wants to know if you dribble when you eat.'

'Well,' she said laughing, 'I don't know how he gets away with it, though. I mean, it's only in teaching that that would happen. You wouldn't have that happening in business. Can you imagine my brother going off halfway through a business meeting?'

'No,' a little irritatedly. He almost wished he hadn't mentioned old Billerey, not if it meant bringing up a comparison with her brother. Her idol. Her square-jawed action man comic book hero who earned a six-figure income, collected ambassadors and sent her postcards that said things like: in Tunisia on business. Just had a massage and a swim! It needled him the way she held him up as some sort of yardstick; and he ate sulkily for a moment or two, staring at the bills and the donkey sanctuary subscription at his feet. 'You're not going to do that again are you? Which one are you going to adopt this year? Mustapha or...' he kicked over the magazine... 'Chocolate Brownie – found in garden shed in pitiful condition, amidst pitchforks and garden shears, two teeth missing.'

'Not sure yet.'

'I think you prefer animals to people,' he teased, spearing a kidney bean with vicious intent.

'Animals can't defend themselves. Like children.' Her eyes began to fill with tears. 'Old Bilberry's got a tongue in his head, hasn't he?'

'Billerey has,' he agreed.

It was always the same, he thought, chewing on grimly, watching her put her knife and fork together, her unfinished plate down on the floor, her turning on the waterworks like that, at the drop of a hat. Her so-called compassion always ended up coming back to herself. It might start off with a mistreated horse, an abandoned baby, a boozing old tramp, but it always had the knack of getting back to Me Me Marly, one of her own little crises. Her empathy, her sensitivity to the sadness of others, he had always felt, was at root a selfishness, a sadness about herself. Still, he wished he could give her a year's subscription to a donkey sanctuary, buy her the wretched sanctuary, buy her a horse to ride, a yacht to sail, a house far away by the sea with an orchard full of apple trees. All he had was his love and his tales of old Bilberry and the students, his make-believe stories of fairies, feathers and Quality Street. All he could do to amuse her was elaborate on his mundane prosaic little day, make a joke about the rats, play a song on his guitar. He felt quite keenly that it wasn't enough, that it never would be enough.

'At least I managed to get some reports done before the meeting,' he stuttered after a while at her savage little profile. 'It was a job knowing what to say for half of them.

You know that girl, Karen Lang, the one whose assignment consisted of four blank pages and a graph, the one who gives really long-winded excuses for not turning up – I didn't know what to say about her so in the end I said she was very unique.'

He was startled by the violence of her response: withering scorn when he had expected a pat on the back. 'What a stupid thing to say! That's the most stupid thing to say. D'you know what the word means? Everybody's unique. You're unique. I'm unique.' Her voice trembled. 'It doesn't make any sense at all to say someone's unique.'

He back-pedalled furiously. 'Kindest thing to say... absent... on drugs.'

She muttered something as she rose and began pacing the room, still muttering under her breath like a kettle about to boil, a volcano about to explode. She fidgeted about the place, picking up books and tapes then throwing them down with dismissive little cries of 'what a load of rubbish, what a load of crap'.

He noticed that the objects were those belonging to him and he stared at her in dismay. 'What's wrong? What's the matter now?'

'Nothing's wrong. Nothing's wrong. Why should anything be wrong?' She paused before the vase and pulled out a flower. With a funny little smile she waved it in the air, wafted it about under her nose, stuck it behind an ear; he smiled back nervously in order to placate her and also because she did look quite strange bunched up in her old pink dressing-gown, a rose stuck behind her ear. She looked like one of those fat Russian dolls that contain countless versions of themselves underneath and it crossed his mind that if he unravelled the old pink dressing-gown and tore off the beaming, superior mask he would find another little Marly and another and another, still beaming and superior, until at the end, in the very centre, a little wooden heart the size of his thumbnail or, worst of all, no heart at all.

'You're all the same,' she bawled out suddenly, making him jump. 'You're all the bloody same. The problem is, you pretend to be different, but you're just like the rest of them. You're all the same, every single one of you.'

He tried to pinpoint the moment when the conversation had turned but as usual he could not; and he was almost too weary to bother racking his brains about it. Something had gone 'ping' in her head, something had flipped in that subterranean little soul of hers and there wasn't really any point in trying to figure it out; he simply sat there waiting, metaphorically and resignedly fastening his seatbelt. In the old days, before the car had fallen to bits, she would have pelted off in it at a time like this like some sort of nutcase, revving up the gears, breaking the speed limit and screaming at him or out the window at anyone else who would listen: 'You men like action films, don't you... but you can't take it in real life can you, you sick fuckers!' In the old days... in the old days. Strange but it seemed like only yesterday he'd heard her shouting: 'You men can't take it in real life, can you!' It was always something to do with men. Men was a four-letter word for her and God help him when it suddenly dawned on her again that he wasn't simply a rather portly and jocular extension of herself but an individual in his own right and, worse than that, a man. He felt the sarcasm rising in his throat and he clenched down on it by staring out of the window with casual indifference, though inside his stomach was tight as a knot. It was unjust somehow the way he worked, loved her, and she sat there with her violet eyes brimful of hate. He watched the 376 rumble past en route to Bluewater and Gravesend; he wondered if the people on board were looking forward to going home, going to the pictures, after a hard day at the office or the factory. It seemed later than usual and he glanced at his watch, wondering where the time had gone and she, on the attack as always, came down on the movement like an eagle-eyed ton of bricks.

'Well,' she shouted, flinging a rose in the air, 'if it's so fucking boring why don't you go back to your reports.'

It would be so easy, he thought, to walk a straight line to the horizon, never looking back, to get on a bus and see where it took him (the way he'd done as a child – though he'd only got as far as Port Talbot and his Nana and Gramp had had to come looking for him).

The violet eyes flickered over him in tones of hatred, anger, disgust. He felt something choking up inside, some little thing inside choking to death. He loved her and she hated him. He loved her and she hated him. The roses were flying around the room now as she really got into her stride.

'Be nice to get a bit of sensitivity for a change instead of these stupid things.... Sitting there like a stuffed dummy. Why don't you go back to your reports if everybody there's so *unique.*'

He saw her as though through the wrong end of a telescope, a tiny pink figure waving her arms in the air and stamping her feet; the roses falling over her like the snow that fell in the glass snow dome on the window ledge; and her voice came to him muffled, as though she spoke from the depths of a cupboard, from the realms of Narnia where a little boy looked on eating Turkish delight. He looked on – a little boy eating Turkish delight – as the film unfolded before his eyes. A horror film, he soon discovered, in black and white mainly, though sometimes seen through a red-coloured lens. Close up the girl looked quite terrified, her dark eyes swooning away a little as though she were genuinely surprised by something (a clue perhaps to the monster's identity), her long, delicate fingers shielding her face, her mouth opening wide with no sound coming out of it except in sudden bursts – like when you're swimming underwater then come up for breath. You never saw the monster's face though sometimes you heard his voice like vinyl on the wrong speed, caught a glimpse of a whitened knuckle, saw his shadow on the wall, giant, merciless, in pursuit. There was a lingering shot of one of her slippers flying through the air, then coming to land unceremoniously on the stripey settee: Exciting. Alaska. Snow Powder Land. The words jumped out at you like some sort of clue: Exciting. Alaska. Snow Powder Land.... There was a zoom in on her tangled hair in kidney beans and rice (kidney beans and rice all over the carpet), then a montage of lightning shots from topsy-turvy angles: trampled roses and the ceiling, bloodstained feet and tear-stained cheeks. That's when you saw his hands. His hands closing in about her neck, her shadow fluttering moth-like from wall to painted wall, helpless, aimless, out of focus.... The little boy ate the Turkish delight quicker and quicker until he felt quite sick.

Afterwards he saw it all through a violet-coloured lens; and he, a blundering fool, beating the life out of her. Afterwards he stood before her, his arms dangling loose by his side, astonished and bemused and quivering from head to toe like the giant peace-loving rat that he was.

# Part three

# Larger than gods,
# louder than gods

# Ten

She pressed Terry's bell with a frenzy that startled her then stepped back to wait. Her head was all to pieces and every little piece was bouncing off something like a small rubber superball, the sort she'd played with as a child. Erasmo the Plasmo had been her favourite – a pink mottled one she'd bounced off chimney pots, flower pots, bus stickers and car windows, much to the distress of her mother, the lollipop lady and several green-fingered neighbours. Now it was her head that was doing the bouncing – off the sun, the walls, the screeching tyres along the road, Terry's far, far, far too red car taking up most of the driveway. He'd have an answer for it all no doubt, sitting there in his black leather chair, chewing on the dead wood in people's heads, cleaning up on all their shit so to speak; he'd say it was due to a lack of this that or the other (serotonin, oestrogen, endorphins – take your pick), that it was all part and parcel, that everyone was a pattern in the same evolving tapestry – as if the earth itself were jigging and jiving to the rhythm of one gigantic heartbeat. That would be a thing to be sure, if it were true, though it wouldn't do *her* much good and it didn't seem to explain why some people flew like eagles and other people groped like moles. Or perhaps it did. There were karmic obligations to consider apparently, according to the library book she'd been reading. Marly didn't know what a karmic obligation was exactly but it seemed a bit much that you couldn't start off with a clean slate, that you had to cart about all the baggage you'd kept from a life lived as Joan of Arc, a blue giraffe, Winnie the Pooh. One of Ivy's green-fingered friends had said that Ivy must have done something very bad in a previous life to have ended up the way she did – all tumours and missing bits. In the last few months of her life her body had taken on the appearance of a great fat creature sucking on different sized gobstoppers; or maybe she too had been filled with a hundred and one little superballs all desperate to escape, bouncing off her artery walls, ligaments, tendons and disease fractures. 'What did I do wrong?' she'd said to Marly once, in the middle of a still, creeping night, her own life creeping not so gently to its end. Ah, then, what could you say? What could you begin to say at the end? That the life had been well done, the few mistakes easily forgiven, a daffodil grown, some roses pruned, a few good seeds well planted? 'Nothing Mum,' she had replied, hedging her bets. 'You did nothing wrong.' 'To be continued' they put on gravestones in some parts of the world – and now in America, the latest trend. One life just a scene in an unfolding drama, a side character in a motion picture (though side characters, David always said, were by far the most interesting). But what if you never fulfilled those karmic obligations and kept incarnating in the same old torturous shell, the blood recycling for ever and a day in that one gigantic heart, while God looked on, killing himself laughing at all the energy he was saving. What then?

They'd tried valiantly to forget about it – after the initial and very bitter recriminations, shamefaced apologies, avowals and denials, realisations on Marly's part that she had nowhere else to go, they became excessively polite to one another. 'Did you have a nice day?' she'd ask him when he came through the door, like something out of an American movie; and he would reply in conscientious detail that Anton the French teacher had been found drinking spirits behind the bike sheds, that Ross Newman's belching continued undiminished, that plans for the Christmas pantomime were a complete wash-out already because no self-respecting or disaffected student would dream of signing up for it. They spoke to each other like mature, sensible adults – no code, silly expressions, put-on voices or malapropisms. They even took pains to use each other's full Christian names – a sign that all was not at all well with them; they discussed the news, the weather, the world at large, and the tenant who was moving in to the downstairs flat bit by seemingly endless bit. 'He brought a chair today,' she'd say to David over supper. 'How much stuff d'you think he's got?' He'd already de-loused the hallway carpet, a little to Mrs M's irritation. 'Fumigating the vestibule floor, if you please,' she'd sniffed at Marly, accosting her by the front gate on her way to the bakery. 'No doubt he can see extra termites through those optical lenses of his!'

They circled each other as intimate strangers – a strange little dance of sidle and sidestep – like some tribal display from Papua New Guinea in which, by all accounts, there is a great deal of hot air and inebriation, a lifting and lowering of paradise feathers and a ferocious drumming of sago skin drums. 'The lifting and lowering of paradise feathers is,' according to her library book, *Fond Recollections of a Gentleman Traveller*, 'a kind of now you see me, now you don't affair where the true personality is glimpsed for a moment beneath the mask of betel nut juice and zephyr flower petals (though these are more commonly used by the women in nail decoration), the sago skin drumming a potent if rather tedious reminder of the ever-threatening thunderclap, the wrath of the gods.'

They felt their way through every moment, pressing and testing it for strength and elasticity, made polite noises, said please and thank you, peeped from behind their paradise curtains, then retreated. They spun and danced, circled and fanned, still peeping and retreating, as the sago skin drums pounded hard in their hearts like far-off distant thunder.

The rain had helped – it gave them something to talk about. It had rained and rained every night until dawn and then it had rained some more. People were up in arms about it; the government, it said, was looking into it, poring over satellite readings and meteorological forecastings, even the Prime Minister had come out and looked about. Homes in Kent were flooded by the dozen, the Cotswolds were covered and the Thames that kept rolling from Bluewater down to the mighty sea was almost fit to burst her banks. There were dire warnings of natural disasters, 'Revelations' chapter sixteen, greenhouse gases and Noah's Ark. A student who signed himself '9T9 Flake' covered the pale blue tower where David worked with jaunty, colourful umbrellas; a skull and crossbones and doom-laden slogans, which the class felt morally obliged to discuss. 'Forget impending doomsday,' David had had to chastise them, 'and get back to Calculus!' Leaves blew the tracks quite clear of trains and those who ventured onto the buses found themselves stuck in the early hours in the middle of Land's End, having finished *War and Peace* for the first time in their lives. Sea winds got up and, finding nothing interesting to do out there in the Atlantic, picked up speed and gave the cliffs an almighty wallop. Chimney pots toppled off, windows shook in their panes and the nights were the sort of nights when past lives came back to haunt you. Seagulls screamed inland from the edges of waves, took over Piccadilly Circus and Trafalgar Square, and laughed their secret laugh in the Dartford park. Marly kidded herself she was living on the coast and David smiled for he loved the rain, no matter what, with or without an umbrella – it reminded him of the hills and valleys of Wales. They called a truce in all that rain (where hidden things emerged and other stuff got washed away) though inside she still raged.

The 'may our wishes come true this month this week this afternoon' receptionist ushered her in with that dreadful smile of hers and the words 'Terry won't be two ticks'.

Marly went into the empty room, shook the droplets off her raincoat, prised a few wet tendrils from the sides of her cheeks and wiped her glasses. There was a smell of ginger and garlic drifting in through the walls and open doorway and she imagined June's blueberry head bent over her wok, frying up shallots and noodles for Terry's lunch. She'd heard her say to him once, a little sharply: 'You've only got to add the dressing, Terry, while I take the dogs out.'

He'd seemed a little put out – as if he didn't much like the thought of having to do the dressing while she took the dogs out and Marly had wondered if he was as much a gentleman in his private life as he was in his professional. She didn't really care what he was as long as he helped her; she'd found him in the *Yellow Pages* and blindly put her faith in him: this thin vitiligoed figure at the end of the bar in her last-chance saloon, the only visible raft – apart from David – in the middle of her shipwreck. And she clung on to him through misgivings and paranoia, hell and high water; something more primitive than hope kept her clinging.

'Lovely weather,' he smiled, looming in the doorway like an angular lamp post before coming forward to greet her, his thin arms open wide. She was always a little embarrassed by these embraces, fearing that up close she might be somewhat repulsive. 'Where does it all come from, this rain? The mountains, the sea?'

'Both, I think.'

'We should put a sheet on it!'

'Ha Ha.' She watched him settle himself in his black leather chair, pick up a pen and paper. He showed her a poem someone had photocopied for him that morning by Kahlil Gibran.

'"Let there be spaces in your togetherness,"' she read out loud. '"Let the winds of the heavens dance between you." That's nice.'

'Yes. He was an extraordinary fellow, though, apparently: vagabond, womaniser, drug addict!'

'He wasn't!'

'Yes, apparently. He probably wrote that when he was high on heroin, LSD!'

Marly giggled. 'That's the thing, isn't it, you read all these lovely things and then you find out what they're like. Coleridge was an opium addict, you know.'

'Was he? I didn't know that.'

'We did *Kubla Khan* at school. I remember the teacher saying he was an opium addict... I like this though: "the winds of the heavens dance between you..." I suppose that's how a relationship should be... not in each other's pockets too much.' (That was something David's mother had said to her on the phone – that she thought they were in each other's pockets too much.)

'No, that can be a bad thing. How are you getting on at the moment, you and David?'

'Alright.' She wanted to keep off David. He wasn't the one with a skinful of rashes, head full of superballs, body full of blocked-up blood. *He* was alright: he slept, went to work, made his jokes, scoffed his grub and now – since the worm or rather giant sloth, as she rather acidly put it to herself sometimes, had turned – used his fists.

'We had an argument the other day,' she rushed in before she could stop herself, '...it got a bit violent. I flipped, got into a rage... started throwing things.'

'What was the argument about?'

She paused for a moment. She wanted to say it was a word, a look, but it sounded so stupid and it wasn't that really; it was never the thing itself. It was like that play where they joked about people getting divorced because of a salad or some word. It was never the salad or the word; it was the way you ate the salad, garnished the word with a look, a gesture, hid it, bartered with it, kept it hostage under the pillow in exchange for sweet FA nothings.

'Nothing really, it never is about anything... it's just I always feel like I have to look after myself... that the only person I can trust is myself. I go very cold, detached....'

'You trust David though, don't you?'

'Yes, rationally I do... I mean: I know he's potty about me. He's never given me any reason not to trust him. It's just that... well... he's a man.' (*You cudgel, Miss Marlee, you cudgel the keys. Think of the breeze, of air, of fingers of forked lightning running through your pretty hair. Can you play Kinderscenen, Scenes from Childhood, Träumerei, Dreaming, Lullaby or Frightening? Horrorwitz played Dreaming for every finale. Horrorwitz played splay-fingered like you.*)

'It's not just men.' Terry swivelled in his chair and stared at her with his bad gangster face as if she'd somehow wronged him. 'It's a human trait to think the grass is greener. I've sat here for nearly twenty years and I've heard stories from women and from men and I can tell you it's a human trait. I don't care if you're a vicar, it doesn't mean you can be trusted. No human being is one hundred per cent trustworthy.'

'Oh don't say that,' Marly said lightly but meaning it. It wasn't what she wanted to hear. She wanted to hear that some people were different, exceptional. 'Sometimes I see it all laid out and it's fine, you know, children, a little house, very secure... and then I get scared, think it'll all go wrong. I see couples in the supermarket with kids and it all seems so impossible... seems so impossible that I could ever do that.'

'You see the rainbow for a moment and then it's gone.'

'Yes, that's it, that's it exactly. And then at other times – when I'm really bad – I don't think like that anyway. I'm just grateful to be looked after, to be fed.'

'You're lucky you've got someone like David,' he said gently, 'who's going to be there.'

'Yes, I suppose I am.' She thought of the boots kicking her in the ribs, the boots that should have been sent away many moons ago to Dr Barnardo's. 'I suppose I am.'

His beaky nose dipped over a new sheet of paper as he wrote in his forward-sloping writing, curling up his lower case stems, no doubt to prevent disease creeping in or perhaps some sudden heart attack. Everything was quite caricatured to her today: the picture of the girl in the shape of a cross, her green eyes bulging like gooseberries, the children sniggering behind her back, smiling at her crucifixion; the figures on the vase on Terry's desk, having a ball in perpetual motion, chasing each other round and round, almost seeming to be doing the goose step; and the book of dreams described and analysed Victorian style, laid out on the window ledge. She wondered if it had anything under 'shrinking kitten': sometimes she had a dream of a tiny kitten, harder to find than a needle in a haystack, though when she did she always realised it was far too tiny to exist. The doorbell went suddenly, making her jump and Terry raised his head to stare gloomily out at the black car squeezing past his far, far too red one in the driveway. 'They're always trying to sell me the *Reader's Digest*,' he muttered irritably and Marly smiled weakly in return. 'The problem is,' he added, his eyes trained on the black car, 'you leap ahead and imagine the worst.'

'I do do that, yes,' she agreed.

'Which when you come to think of it,' he sighed, 'is a terrible waste of energy. We don't know what's going to happen... we only really have the moment.'

'That's true,' she murmured though it went against the grain. What if the moment was too bad to live in; then what did you do? The moment stank! The moment was overrated. You could only live it second by second whereas dreams could be spread quite thinly over the day like margarine or Philadelphia, memories crammed into a minute. And how did you live in the present anyway, with all those past lives ganging up on you?

'I've been reading a book,' she began conversationally, as he delved in his suitcase of poisons, 'about past lives.'

'I see.' He always said 'I see' like that, his head very straight when he didn't want to commit himself or come down on something like a GP or a politician. When she'd first asked him how long it would take to be well he'd coughed and spluttered, hummed and haa'd and said he was sounding like a politician and she'd had to reply that he was a bit.

'My mother's friend, Maureen, said my mother must have done something very bad in a past life to end up the way she did.'

'That was a very irresponsible thing to say.' The bottles clinked as he searched amongst them, his long, twisted fingers rooting around remedies for bee stings, athlete's foot, syphilis and gingivitis.

'No, but anyway, she kept getting these messages from Ivy in heaven. Apparently my mother wanted her to get a plant for the rhubarb patch, so she went off and bought a plant but when she got back the car boot wouldn't open. She kept bringing back these different plants but the boot wouldn't open for any of them. In the end she got this huge white rhododendron and the boot opened for that one so she concluded that was the one Ivy wanted for the rhubarb patch! It was huge, beautiful, very expensive – about thirty quid apparently.'

'I see.' He kept his head very straight but his mouth appeared to be twitching.

'David said that she's going to get very sick of Ivy's messages from heaven if they cost her thirty quid a time!'

'You're much better you know,' he smiled from his chair, taking two brown envelopes from behind the book of dreams. 'Daily' he wrote on one, 'Wed & Sat evening' on the other, curling up his lower case stems again to prevent some virus getting at him or maybe an airborne pathogen. 'From where I'm sitting you've got much more energy than you had, say, a year ago.'

'Hope so.' She shuddered to think what she'd been like, say, a year ago.

'You're really pretty good now.' She watched him lick

the top of the envelopes, his tongue darting in and out like the honeyeater she'd seen on a TV documentary – or was it an anteater? She shuddered a little and he looked her full in the eye. 'How's the job, by the way?'

'Okay,' she replied, smooth as silk. How easily the lies came up to her lips: white lies, black lies, pink elephants can fly lies. (*A nocturne, a variation, an invention, an étude. Chopin, Schumann, JS Bach, Mendelssohn Bartholdy, even Debussy.*) Anything to fit in, shift the guilt, protect herself or please someone else. He'd seemed so keen to see her well and she hadn't wanted him to think his treatment had been altogether unsuccessful. Always so eager to please a man, young or old, fat or thin, except David, of course, who was far too close. Besides which, it had become a little embarrassing to be unemployed still after nearly two years... and so the little job of dental receptionist in Gravesend had come along quite suddenly, out of the blue, out of the backside of a bright pink elephant.

'Any root canals recently?' he joked.

'Oh no, not for me,' she laughed hysterically, licking her gums in apprehension. 'One thing I have got is perfect teeth... which reminds me, it worries me not using fluoride....'

'Oh, you don't need that. They use that stuff in rat poison. Anything left over they shove into toothpaste.'

'You don't use it then?'

'Oh no.' He shook his head vehemently.

'And you're alright?'

'Well, these are dentures....'

Marly stared at him in astonishment, counting her teeth with the tip of tongue in agitation, not sure whether to laugh or cry.

'... But I lost them way before, after the radiotherapy.'

Ah yes... when he'd nearly died near Wormwood Scrubs. She smiled at him sympathetically. 'My grandmother refers to hers as teeth not made by God!'

He laughed and patted her arm. 'You'll be alright,' he

said reassuringly. 'Keep off the sweets, cakes, chocs, colas... you haven't got a sweet tooth have you.'

'No, my mother had though, at the end – I think it was the steroids. She kept a bag of Maltesers and marshmallows in a drawer by her bed.' (*That cake is a magnum opus, he said to her once in sleep. Did you make it out of tripe? Did you measure the constellations? The teacup rattled on Scott Joplin's nose and there were always crumbs on his top wet lip – the remains of a half-eaten digestive biscuit. Doing the Cake Walk, Sunflower Slow Drag, Elite Syncopations and Peacherine Rag. My heart stopped beating, did an intermezzo....*)

'We're going on holiday next week,' he remarked pleasantly, helping her on with her raincoat, 'to Ireland. Looking for leprechauns!'

'That'll be nice.' She felt a giggle rising like a hiccup in her throat, the way it had done long ago in school assemblies, detentions, always at the most inappropriate moments and she pumped his arm extra hard so as not to give herself away. He ushered her out through the stained-glass porch, his blue eyes twinkling like a merry widow's sapphires and she grabbed his hand again in delight, the giggle opening up into a red hibiscus flower. 'Hope you find one,' she laughed as she squeezed her way past his far too red car; and he smiled back and said he was absolutely counting on it, laughing and waving back at her until she was out of sight.

(*fingertips creeping ri... tar... dando.*)

# Eleven

'He thinks you're vain and obsessive,' she said to herself, standing in the queue at the job centre. The video showing today was *How to become a Bus Driver*; the sound was turned off and the buses kept going round and round on a little screen above her head. 'And compared to him you are – a man who'd lost his heart and teeth near Wormwood Scrubs.' What a fate for anyone – to have lost their heart and teeth by twenty-one! No wonder he'd never got to New Zealand; just ended up in his big white house behind his far too red car, eating the good stuff June prepared for him and consoling himself no doubt with the fact that other people's heads and bodies were as screwed up, wonky and buggered as his own. Accepting it all – reality, fate, the rubbish God cared to bestow – out of trepidatious timidity. Trepidatious timidity – she knew about that; she inched herself forward a few steps in the queue and stared angrily at the man in front of her. 'Look at him looking,' she almost shouted to herself, 'at that woman in the pinstripe suit!' She hated the way men looked at women and hated it even more if they didn't look at her. In the old days they would have done before... before...

'Those eyes,' someone had cried admiringly once, on a train, on a bus, under the bedclothes perhaps, 'don't need anything.' Did David know he was with a woman whose eyes didn't need anything, not an inch of kohl or a dash of mascara? It was imperative somehow that he know, that he be told. The fewer compliments he gave her the more vociferously she voiced the compliments of others. He knew all about Imran and the cashew nut. She'd regaled him with every last detail of his silken curling moustache, his shiny shirts and the lines he'd written in a poetic trance about her goblet neck, soft bright heart and dancing peacock steps. 'The problem with him,' David had said a little drily, 'was that he needed a television; he obviously had far too much time on his hands!' Funny man. Funny man. Weren't they all such funny men! Look at him looking at that woman in a pinstripe suit. Human trait, my eye, there was nothing remotely human about men. 'Shall we go to Swan-Sea?' Imran had asked her, twirling his curling silken moustache and defrosting a chicken at halfway past midnight in an effort to seduce her. 'Shall we go to Swan-Sea?' Trepidatious timidity. She'd go now, like a shot, if she were well. Everything was do-able if you were well: riding Appaloosas over the Andes, racing alligators up the Blue Danube. Fly away, said a voice more than once in her head, when you have got through the chrysalis stage. She was saving up time in a savings account and when she was well she would spend spend spend it, though Terry had said she must live for the moment, face the here and now of her reality. Funny man, funny man – sitting there in his black leather chair, chewing on the dead wood in people's heads like a ruddy woodworm, burrowing into their cobwebbed and creosoted secrets. No wonder he went off looking for leprechauns, he probably thought if he made a wish they'd give him back his heart and teeth. The secret of life, he'd confided once in his room where dreams were tied up in books and books were tied up in dreams, is to find excitement on your own doorstep. Marly didn't know if it was the cry of a wise man or a defeated one. To find excitement on your own doorstep. How on earth did you do that?

'Too true,' the man was busily saying to the woman in a

pinstripe suit. 'They have six men now to do the work of twelve – that's how I did my back in. No one would help me lift the tyre. They were all too busy having their tea break.'

'Oh dear.' The woman's eyes were completely glazed over and she flicked an invisible speck from her sleeve. She hadn't been out of work long, Marly thought. There was still too much of a clean sheen about her. Give her a few months and the suit would go, the heels would go, the highly coiffured hair would go and by next spring there would be nothing to show but dark roots and last year's wardrobe. And she would be glad, moreover, to talk to a man who'd done his back in lifting a tyre.

'There aren't many people,' the man added mulishly, staring about at the empty desks in the review section. 'They must be all on their tea breaks!' He glanced at his watch and tutted in exasperation as if he had an appointment. There was no appointment, Marly decided. It was simply the final act of defiance. There was nowhere to go and nothing to do but you didn't want to be held up nonetheless. It was like being kept waiting at the door of eternity – the good lord might be off doing the rounds of Jupiter, Neptune, up Uranus, playing chess with an archangel or toasting his crusts in the light of the moon; but you wanted him to get a wriggle on and open up so you could go through and sit blissfully on the other side of the door. She wondered whether her mother was sat waiting blissfully somewhere in Paradise, the way she'd waited in hospital waiting rooms to be led into smaller waiting rooms to wait to be led into smaller waiting rooms until at the end she got to a room where a doctor the size of a pea carved her up into missing nonentities. There was waiting and there was remembering and there seemed to be nothing much in between. Marly had waited most of her life though she wasn't quite sure what she'd been waiting for: waiting for life to begin, for death to end, for the bell to go, waiting for her favourite television show, to be rid of the wart on the end of her nose, for David to come home, in queues at desks, at checkouts, at interviews, in the early hours for the dawn to break, for the clock to strike midnight and she be transformed out of a pumpkin into something truly audaciously great or at the very least something reasonably okay (like the newspaper cutting about Mr Right. How you had to make do with Mr Reasonably Okay!) Living in a subjunctive case, in a future-perfect tense and speaking out of parentheses – like Michael effing Angelo who butted in on the phone from his easy chair like an old ram with lumbago. Waiting for the fanfare and the parades that had passed long ago or were still to come in a gleaming tomorrow, though Terry had said they were here right now in her ear this very minute if only she could hear them – silly fool, looking for leprechauns in Ireland of all places.... Why doncha just look in the mirror, mate. Save the trip!

'Next please.' The voice sounded harsh and a little impatient and Marly almost stumbled over to the empty chair, past the poster of the girl with the biggest smile in Britain, having recently landed herself a job. Unbelievable! She dumped her rucksack down on the floor, pulled her chair close and smiled an innocuous smile at the woman with the bunched-up mushroom hair.

'Have you got your card?'

'Oh... yes... ' Marly scrambled about in her pocket, pulling out her mother's old shopping list, one of David's handkerchiefs and a few ancient receipts in the process, while the woman drummed her nails impatiently on the desk – they were red today and diamond-encrusted as though she'd fallen from the sky, scraping stars as she went. Marly stared at them a little aghast as she handed over the dog-eared card.

'Have you contacted at least three employers in the last week?' the voice began in peremptory fashion. Most of the advisors had the grace to appear bored when they went through the list but the woman with the bunched-up mushroom hair did everything 'most emphatically' by the book, jotting down ticks to Marly's answers and scrutinising her face as she did so.

'Yes.' (Tick)

'Have you visited the job centre at least twice in the last week?'

'Yes.' (Tick, eagle-eyed look)

'Have you consulted local, national and international magazines, journals and newspapers?'

'Yes.' (Tick, sliding glance)

'Have you sent your CV off to employers on spec concerning work?'

'Yes.' (Tick)

'Have you liaised with relatives and friends concerning work?'

'Er no, not this week.' It was best to fake honesty at some point. Being superhuman wasn't entirely convincing or believable. The art of lying dictated that one or two threads of truth had occasionally to appear.

The woman's pen paused over the tick and her face went zing as if she'd stumbled on too much mustard in her ham sandwich or gobbled down a red-hot chilli too quickly. 'You must leave no stone unturned,' she admonished, 'in your search for employment. When you've been out of work as long as you have, you're eligible, briefly, for almost anything.'

'No... er... yes,' Marly muttered vaguely. She was often quite vague in the job centre. At first it had been a ploy, a ruse – if they dismissed you they didn't notice you, if they didn't notice you they couldn't judge you – but now it was all too familiar a feeling to have a brain like a bowl of porridge – home-made, no treacle – and to take each thought day by day, step by apathetic step.

'It says here the Limes never received an application from you.' The blood-red nails drummed like stars over the keyboard. 'Nor did Argos... nor did the Crayford Nurseries:

138

Roger Short, Manager of Shrubs, says he most emphatically did not receive an application from any M. Smart.'

'Oh dear,' Marly replied with genuine sadness, though she knew quite well she'd never applied for any of them.

'Do you have an explanation?' The woman's eyes almost seemed to be popping out of her head in disapproval and the mushroom bun was starting to wobble, 'briefly, for why your forms did not arrive?'

Not briefly, thought Marly, staring blankly at her hands, her feet, the buses going round and round, the powdered creases in the woman's face. 'The post is bad,' she mumbled at last. 'Several things have gone astray. My father wrote to me once, I think, but it never arrived....' The girl smiled mockingly from her clean white poster and Marly's heart shrivelled up in her long dark raincoat.

'I see.' The voice seemed to suggest that it wasn't born yesterday and didn't suffer fools gladly but something in Marly's face must have softened it a little for it changed tone and added almost kindly for once: 'Would you like another form for the Limes – the post hasn't yet been filled.'

I bet it hasn't, Marly thought, galvanising herself in defiance. Nobody in their right mind would work for a psychiatric institution where old women flitted about like peculiarly faded ghosts in search of the parade and the man in furry slippers. 'Okay,' she responded nevertheless (knowing better than to say no) taking the form and cramming it soullessly into her pocket.

'We have another opportunity here,' the woman with the mushroom hair added brightly, obviously changing to her softly softly catchee monkey routine. 'Softly softly catchee Marly,' David had whispered to her once, pushing a tendril behind her ear, 'cos she's a little monkey!' 'Cleaner required, part-time permanent. £4.20p/h. Previous experience of buffing machine an advantage.'

Buffing machine! Marly smiled weakly. It seemed the most likely thing in the world, the way the woman said it, to have experience of a buffing machine. 'Okay,' she said again, nodding her head and watching the fingers race like stars over the keyboard, conjuring constellations of Orion, the plough and...

'Ambient replenishment? Local supermarket. Must be a team player.'

...little bear scything round your Venus Colossus. Stacking shelves – she'd done it before in a downtown upmarket supermarket, ghosting out with a moonlit trolley piled high with Fairy liquid, loo roll, shampoos and dog biscuits, freezing her hands off in the freezer section and gunning prices onto tins of Pedigree Chum and pineapple chunks – before it was all computerised. It had been quite a satisfying job (though she hated shopping) like stocking up the larder, just her and her trolley up and down the rows and aisles and solemn little piles of groceries awaiting their fate....

'That's all for now.' The woman's eyes were on the next 'next please' and her mushroom bun bobbed a dismissal. Marly almost felt tempted to bow and salute the way Pegleg Pete did to the cars, waving his handkerchief like a magic trick; but she turned with her rucksack and marched to the door, past Bernie Mungo grinding his teeth beneath the bus video; and she imagined he probably thought that the buses would take him right the way over the warm and oily azure seas to the land of mangoes and coconut trees....

It was still raining outside and a howling gale was getting up (dishevelled, in his pyjamas, finding only burnt toast for breakfast), swirling grit into people's eyes and litter about the streets. Marly noticed the woman in the pinstripe suit crouching down beside the wall and talking into a mobile phone; she desperately tried to eavesdrop but all she could catch above the rain and howling wind was 'New York' and 'shopping trip'. 'Bah!' she thought, pulling her hood close and taking refuge in some kind of crazy moral superiority, 'What

an egregious thing to do. Why doncha just shop right here in
the precinct dear, save the trip!' She cut across by the Daisy
launderette (Fresh as a daisy, that's our motto. We get things
squeaky clean... blood, chocolate, stains, vomit. Have you
heard our Daisy...) wondering why she felt so excluded. It
wasn't that she wanted to be like the woman with her
wretched suit and mobile phone... and then came the gaps
and the buts... it was more the fact that the woman belonged
to something or seemed to belong in any case whereas Marly
belonged to nothing, not even herself. You had to belong to
something. Everybody had to belong to something. Even the
gentlemen and old ladies congregating in the shrubbery per
diem for a whiskey mac and packet of nasturtium seeds
belonged to the park, that bench, the rocks and the trees. She
stared with vague unease at the people milling about her,
splashing through puddles, putting up umbrellas; some stared
back surprised or annoyed, some laughed at the scarf
wrapped right around her neck. 'It's not that cold,' a man
shouted with a titter in his voice and she smiled back, glaring
inside. 'You judge on first appearance at your peril, my lad,'
she muttered in her thoughts and in her father's voice, purple
fingers winding up the grandfather clock in the attic. 'You
judge on first appearance at your peril, my lad!' You could
stare and stare but it didn't get you anywhere; you couldn't
see, really see, beneath the bright cagoules and pastel
umbrellas, the layers of skin and layers of deception. The
human being, in a single psyche, could contain the seeds of a
beautiful flowering plant as well as the seeds of a killer. There
were acres of room inside to pretend, to be, to live or to die,
to count yourself a king or queen of infinite space, to be
afraid, to be loyal, to be brave. An old man with a stick could
be a war veteran, a tax dodger, cab driver or a burglar and you
couldn't tell from the outside. The bodily form took on all
manner of disguise; sometimes the body reflected the mind
and sometimes it expressed what the mind denied – like the
man who'd opened his mouth to scream at Gallipoli and

couldn't shut it months later. Stuff lurking in the mind came out in the body, according to Terry. It was easy to scoff at Pegleg Pete saluting the cars or Waltzing Matilda feeding the ducks but how did you know what was going on on the inside? Inside he might be saluting his lost comrades, she feeding the five thousand. Pain made manifest, spilling out in little wiggles, odd behaviour, strange compulsions and disease. Marly had struggled to understand the half-choking language of her own body over the years, her body that had stopped at the doll's house; and no doubt her body had struggled to understand the half-choking language of her mind – but she didn't know which came first or what came where. All she knew was that she didn't belong to her mind or her body, that she was pared right the way down to the bone and somebody in her place was walking through the park, sitting down on the bench by the memorial for the dead, conducting this endless monologue in her head and wrapping the scarf right the way around her neck though it wasn't all that cold – the man was right – in an objective sense.

The grass had a flattened silvery quality and the leaves were brown where the river had left its mark. The flower garden looked quite wrecked – just one or two bright stems braving the rain and howling wind – she imagined the gardener's woebegone expression, standing in the falling rain, her arms full of dying flowers – and a couple of magpies croaking over a crisp packet, no doubt trying to spy the free gift inside: toy soldier, plastic ring, luxury break in the Bahamas for two, if only they could cram all their *objets d'art* in a single suitcase. Pigeons fluffed and coo'd underneath the library's eaves, deafening the silent readers trying to read in the silent reading room; the seagulls were nowhere in sight, having been seen off by the purple-necked Coo Crazy Clan, or pulled back to the angry waves by something stronger than tides or moon. Marly huddled inside her long dark coat on the soaking bench, feeling the rain drumming over her head. There was something reassuring about the rain; it gave you an excuse to go home and sip cocoa in front of your favourite television show, put your feet up, paint your nails, stoke the fire with chestnuts, glowing coals and melting marshmallows; it gave you an excuse to be a small insignificant self, to be pared right the way down to the bone because compared to the wind and the rain you were pretty small and insignificant.... Marly blinked and blew away the droplet of rain that always collected at the end of her nose, noticing out of the corner of her eye an old man and Labrador dog hobbling in her direction; she turned with sudden interest to the memorial for the dead, gazing at it with a feigned and abstract attention: somebody had hung a plimsole around the soldier's arm – it dangled like a peculiarly elegant handbag – and a fat black moustache had been scrawled above his lip. She wondered if it was the work of 9T9 Flake but she couldn't spot any trademark umbrellas depicted on the statue's torso; just knee-length leafen boots the river had left in its wake, giving him the air of some elfin warrior king – Elrond or Celeborn – about to descend on Lothlorien....

'Pity we can't export it!'

'Yes,' she said automatically, turning in surprise. He'd crept up on her stealthy as a cat – hobble or not – or Gandalf carried on an invisible Shadowfax. The Labrador dog almost collapsed at his feet, panting like a grampus the way very old dogs do, even when they're sitting quite still.

'Some countries haven't had rain for years,' the man went on sombrely, peering at her with an aggrieved eye from under his cap. 'They can't get their agricultures started at all.'

'It's a terrible shame,' Marly agreed, taken aback and wondering why the dog was dribbling onto her boot. She felt a little sorry for it and bent over to pat it on the head.

'Make a mint, we would, if only we could export it!'

'I'm sure we would.' Marly nodded vigorously, trying not to smile at the ridiculousness of the situation. The man's cap was quite drenched and he fingered the brim with a blackened nail. 'You'll catch a chill like that,' he added. 'Come on, old girl.' She thought for a moment he was talking to her but the Labrador dog started heaving itself, leg by shaky leg, to its feet and they lumbered off up the path. 'I expect I will,' she called after them, a little annoyed and getting up because it seemed a bit odd to stay sitting after that. She wanted to bring the old man back, invite him home for a cup of tea so they could talk all day to their hearts' delight about rain and agriculture; but every second's delay sent him closer to the bustling town and she remained quite rooted to the spot, staring at the plimsole and fat black moustache, wondering what to do and where to go.

In the end she turned and made her way upstream along the same old route beside the Darenth, her coat billowing out behind her, her hair flying about all over her face. She just wanted to escape, to be left alone, to be able to live her life. He just couldn't accept her sitting in the rain like that. Oh no, he had to poke his nose in with his Catch a Chill Love and dog that looked like it had run a marathon. Exporting rain, my foot! He'd probably had the joke lined up for months, waiting to spring it upon the first person he could. Ha ha, funny man. Weren't they all such funny men? Couldn't they see she was close to the edge? Couldn't they see she was close to the precipice? 'I am a wondrous thing,' she cried silently at the dark birds huddled in the boughs of trees that swayed and squeaked like cats on the prowl, 'so full of goodness I could burst like the Thames.' It was best to say the good things. Replace negative images by positive ones, Terry had said, though inside she still did a sort of macabre dance when she proclaimed to the universe that she was good to the brim. She felt ashamed that she couldn't apply herself, couldn't get herself a job, couldn't even get up in the mornings when there were countries that couldn't get their agricultures going. She felt ashamed that there were refugees when she was clothed and fed by a man that loved her, though he used his fists.... Bad, rotten, riddled with guilt. A little old rotten thing packed away for lunch in cling film a long time ago... not worth living for, not worth fighting for... she stared from under her hood at the stream swollen up with old fish bones, sodden secrets, dead leaves and shiny bottles all heading for the locker of the oyster-lipped Davy Jones. There were many streams and many secrets, they really should have said, the fizzy sweets and the fortune fish and all of them led to the human heart, all of them led to Davy Jones' locker.... If she put him through hell and he came through it meant that she was worth living for. If she put him through hell and he came through it meant that she was worth fighting for. She'd put him through hell over the years and he'd come through with flying colours until now, until now. She was justified now in provoking him. She was justified now in provoking him by the way he reacted. Wasn't she? Wasn't she?

The rain stung her cheeks as she stepped gingerly around the old oak tree that had fallen in the bad November storm. It lay there horizontal to the ground, balancing on its crippled branches; its raw, jagged stem seemed to stare at the sky in mute supplication. The grand old matriarch had toppled at last one night when the lightning illuminated the heavens. (How are the mighty fallen, her grandmother was wont to gum-ble, poring over old photographs and tarnished silver spoons.) Little grubs, bugs and fungi teemed over her torso, despite the rain, getting their hands on what was left of her. The tree cutter would come soon, chop her into pieces and take her home for firewood or maybe a bedside cabinet or two. What a fate for a tree that had withstood aeons and aeons or what a relief, depending on your point of view – gone in a puff of smoke, just ashes on the breeze, or to be transformed into something that stood on a Persian carpet or parquet floor behind twitching lace curtains, never moving a muscle. The leaves on the grass looked like pieces from a jigsaw puzzle:

Autumnal Scene on Sunset Boulevard or Fiasco in a Windswept Park. It seemed terribly sad to Marly that the old oak tree had fallen – it seemed like a portent, a symbol, a sign that something bad was going to happen, a break in the continuity of things, a rupture with history – and how could you ever break from your own history? She hated change, not because she liked it where she was but because she had a horrible feeling that change could be for the worse; she could never quite believe that change could be for the better. As a child she'd jumped off buildings onto breakneck cardboard boxes with her daredevil, tomboy friends but as an adult she quailed at the thought that a tree had fallen in a bad November storm.

The old Canterbury road was busy as always and she had to wait a while before darting across in a gap and sliding down the bank, her boots skidding over the wet mud. It was calmer by the lake and she pulled her hood down the better to look about her. One or two fishermen were hiding under their black umbrellas or inside their green tents doing God knows what; and the rain pitter-pattered softly over the trees, the leaves and the wooden slats of the tiny jetty before sliding silently into those strange concentric circles on the lake. (What a lot of bangles the river gods must have.) She made her way along the gravelly path, hopping over little puddles, dog shit and bulbous roots as she went. It was always the same... every day, every day... circling round the same old lake as she circled round the same old thoughts in her head. Just a variation on an old refrain. Violin strings. Theme by Paganini. Yes she loved him. But not enough to take the risk. Yes he loved her, more than anyone else ever did but did it make up for the fact that he used his fists? Past *Harlequin* and *Albatross* trussed up in tarpaulin by the rotten old boatshed. She'd never actually seen them out on the water, they just lay there trussed in tarpaulin, propping up the rotten old boatshed and what a foolish name for a boat *Albatross* was in any case. Come to think of it, she'd never seen any boat out on the lake, just endless rows of fishermen round the edge, holding their sullen rods over the moody water. The silver birch trees shimmered as always in the rain, their wet bark like canvas or naked skin, their branches entwining like a pair of Siamese twins sharing the same fetal heartbeat.... She'd learned to lie still and quiet as a mouse. She'd learned that he was bigger and stronger than she. She'd gone to him for comfort after he'd hurt her, though it was he that had hurt her. When the person that loved you hurt you as well you had to pretend it was somebody else. You, me and number three. Same old refrain in a different key on a theme by Paganini, Elgar, Saint-Saëns and Edvard Grieg... she felt the rain wash over her face and watched the strange concentric circles ripple and disappear. It was a bit like the butterfly effect. A butterfly fluttering its wings in Tobago could affect the state of Afghanistan, Vietnam, the Arctic, even the gods might feel a fluttering near to their hearts if only they could feel hard enough. Lungs, gills, butterfly wings, all rippling to the rhythm of the one gigantic heartbeat. That fisherman over there touched water that had brushed past dolphins, clouds, maybe great freighters, deep sea divers. It was all connected. She felt a vague sense of peace at the thought that it might all be connected, the joy and sadness collected together and that it would all pass and it didn't matter; and the trivial point of her life would end and something else would take its place. Every argument they had was The End though they always began again – and it didn't matter and it would all end and then begin, variation on a same old theme.

So why did the anger cut through her like a dagger? And why did it matter right here right now? You couldn't just sink away into death, the mind revolted at such a step. You clung on to life for better or worse, whatever the cost you kept on existing in the hope against hope (for hope was hard to kill) that something better lay round the corner. Killing yourself was a complicated affair – you couldn't just hack away at your wrists or pop a cyanide tablet down your neck like they did in the war movies, you had to get things in order, set things straight, get on a clean pair of pants at the very least for when they found you. (They used a mop to get that woman out of the lake at Crayford. The note just said: Can't stand it any more. Thanks. Cheerio. Don't forget to feed the cat.) She'd discussed the options with David: the Roman way, overdosing on pills, jumping off the Dartford bridge and helium balloons. They'd seen on TV how to die by helium balloon and David had laughed and said you better not change your mind halfway through and try calling for help cos your voice would come out all squeaky! She smiled at the thought of his jokes and his laughter, his warm strong body and the solidity of his spirit that kept her centred, kept her rooted. Her rock, her velveteen rabbit... he was like a Christmas bauble, a beautiful, golden Christmas bauble at the top of the tree and something quite perverse in her head, something quite unbelievable made her want to smash it to pieces, smash it into smithereens. She didn't know why. It was some kind of reflex action. She hurt him so he hurt her back and then she had to hurt him again. Just variations, escalations, endless rings and butterfly...

'You're pushing him to the edge of his limits,' his mother had said in her pretty lilting Welsh voice and she had replied, 'Oh dear, am I really?' though inside she had thought well goody goody gumdrops, maybe now he'll know what it feels like to be rock bottom, at the edge of his limits and he might have some sympathy for me for a change. She didn't actually believe he could ever get as low as she – he didn't have the constitution for it. Eat, drink and be merry was his motto; and she saw him in her mind's eye as one of those cross-legged, beaming buddhas, all stomach, crinkly eyes, double chins and cheesy grins. 'You're just a little Bacchus!' she'd said to him once, putting him down as always and a little pretentiously, though she didn't even know who

Bacchus really was. 'What what? You're kidding. I most certainly am not,' he had cried, eyes wide in mock reproach. 'Bacchus was a fatty with no knickers, wasn't he!?' And she had replied, 'Exactly, that's my point!' and they had laughed and laughed till the tears streamed down their cheeks.

She crept under cover of the trees, up the bank and out of sight of the fishermen with their prying eyes and sullen rods – she didn't want anyone else telling her it wasn't all that cold. She would go by the way of the horses. She didn't always go by the way of the horses because, for a start, they weren't always there – the gipsies spirited them away at night for months on end and then they suddenly appeared again one bright fine day, tethered to their spikes like goats; and staring at the M25 with their wall eyes, their white eyes, their frightened eyes and their oh-so-very-human eyes. And then again, she couldn't always bear to look at them, their moth-eaten coats, scraggy tails and ribs sticking out all over the verge. At first she'd thought of going to the pet shop and buying them bran and oats to feed them up a bit but then she decided it'd be worse for them when she went away to live by the sea which she would do soon enough with or without David. They would stand there waiting for her and she would never come. Best not get their hopes up. Better to live without hope if you could. As a child she'd cared for a pony called Zany who'd slept in a stable of soft golden straw. She'd fed him Maltesers and blackberries in the summertime and he'd nodded his head up and down when he ate them as if to say thank you very much; sometimes he spat them out! Once, the girl who owned him told her to get him some sugar and she'd come back with a packet of granulated. 'Lumps, you silly fool,' the girl had shouted. 'He's not having a flipping cup of tea!' In the dark recesses of her mind Marly had hoped the girl might get leukaemia, like Helen's cousin, and then Zany would be up for grabs. It didn't happen like that though; instead the girl just got bigger and bigger until she burst out of her jodhpurs and little riding jacket and got rid of Zany in exchange for a great big showjumper; it was rumoured Zany had gone for slaughter. Better to live without hope if you could... the sound of cars got louder in her ears as she approached the spot where the caravan always sat, its great big wheels like chocolate Wagon Wheels, its green-painted sides with the cream and silver chrome dancing horse and the piebald that stood, tethered to a wheel, sway-backed and staring at the sky. Her heartbeat quickened as she stepped across the rain-soaked grass, holding her long grey skirt up high and peeping through the trees in the hope of seeing some shape, colour, pattern, movement... ah yes, there he was, old Magpie as she called him, tethered to a wheel and staring at the sky as always, the green-painted sides more chipped than ever, the cream and silver chrome dancing horse yellowing with age. A grey pony stood a little further away, tethered to a wooden spike stuck in the ground, his body hunched up against the wind and cold rain. A dog barked sharply and Marly froze mid-step until a man's voice silenced it; the grey pony flinched and startled at the end of his metal chain. She felt sick with disgust and her bare fingers trembled on the barbed wire that separated her from the road and scrubby verge. She'd seen them riding their horses one cold January morning, red-cheeked and wild-eyed, careering madly over the scrappy fields around the motorway, whipping their horses over little boulders, thistles and tree stumps, bare-backed and high-handed and she hadn't been able to tell whether the horses were happy or simply frantic. The grey pony stumbled along the muddy track of his own strange carousel, straining to get at the grass that lay just out of reach. Even from where she stood she could tell he was stick thin, neglected, stunted by a windswept thornbush and no doubt full of tapeworm, ringworm, sweet itch, you name it.... He suddenly stopped and looked in her direction over the motorway – which must seem to him like a roaring river full of cars that swirled and snapped like crocodiles – stared for a moment as if he could see her through the trees then dropped his head again under the weight of the chain that went like a noose around his twiglet neck. The tears streamed down with the rain on her cheeks and she took off her glasses and turned away, trudging back the way she came. When would he get to his warm golden stable; that little lost grey pony? When would he get to his fields of praise?

# Twelve

She fixed herself some scrambled egg and a cup of tea, flopped down on the sofa and turned on the television. Three hours to kill before David came home and ten minutes to go before the Oprah Winfrey show. It was still raining outside and quite cold in the flat so she pulled the red sleeping bag close about her legs, balancing the plate of scrambled egg on her knees and the cup of tea on the upturned cardboard box (put out many months ago to pack away her few remaining possessions for when she went to live by the sea – with or without David). If the worst came to the worst she could get a bus to Bluewater and look around the shops – that would while away an hour or so. She didn't much like the shops – too much stuff, too many people and you had to beware the beauty counters – but she liked to follow the little river map on the floor, read the poetry on the walls about old father Thames who kept rolling along down to the mighty sea, and look at the statues carved out on the ceiling of gods and goddesses and strange mythical beasts. 'That unicorn's real,' David had teased her once. 'It's stuffed, from a museum,' and she'd almost believed him for a second! Sometimes they walked hand in hand just looking at everything, pressing their noses up to the glass like a pair of street urchins; sometimes they went to the cinema. She hadn't seen many films before David, she'd preferred reading books because in books you could see what you wanted to see whereas films were right up there in your face and you couldn't even pretend that the heroine looked like you! Now she loved the hot and stuffy popcorned darkness, the people all crammed together, crunching and swearing and giving little running commentaries on the film. Once they'd seen a film and the old man sitting behind had kept asking 'Has it begun yet?' He just sat there the whole way through waiting for the film to begin. That's how he got through a ton of popcorn and ice cream – just waiting for the film to begin, though it never did for him. It must be like waiting for death, Marly had thought, when you're as ancient as he; life was the adverts, the popcorn and the ice cream; death was the feature film.... She sipped her tea, stared at the rain and wondered if the Christmas rush had started. Quite possibly. It seemed to get earlier and earlier every year – soon no doubt they'd have jingle bells dashing through the snow in the middle of the summer holidays. The Dartford town centre already had its Christmas lights up and the shops were merrily belting out the merry Christmas tunes. Last year Santa's grotto had opened up on October 5th – she'd made a mental note of it because it had seemed so foolish. You could even get Christmas crackers in the January sales for the following year though you might not live that long, you might not even be here. (No wonder the old man in the cinema was confused. Come to think of it, he'd probably been talking about Christmas!) She understood the feeling though, of getting things done earlier and earlier – occasionally, when David went home to visit Anne and Michael effing Angelo, she ended up having her supper at 4 o'clock in the afternoon! If she'd had a cat she'd have put him out for the last time at 11am, the poor thing. Give her a few years and she'd be buying her crackers in the January sales with the other bargain hunters, just to be sure she had them in time, safe and tucked away in the cupboard under the stairs with the dusty fairy lights that never seemed to work and the second-hand bits of old wrapping paper she thought might come in useful. (How very much like her mother she could be.) 'My life's just an old Christmas cracker,' David had muttered last year in his Harold Steptoe voice, after too much rum punch and too many mince pies, 'tear me apart and all you get is a bad joke, silly hat, plastic moustache and bangless bang!'

The Oprah show was on. They were doing a quiz about relationships – very simple, just five easy questions, yes or no answers, the expert said, and you would know if he or she was the one. Marly leaped up, grabbed a pen, paper, library book and cushion to lean on, flopped back down on the sofa and peered at the television, listening for all she was worth.

'Is he reliable?' the expert began, standing next to Oprah Winfrey and articulating very clearly.

Oh yes, thought Marly. He was reliable as mud, predictable as sticky toffee pudding, banoffee pie. He was reliable alright.

The man paused for effect and looked around at the audience as if he could tell they were ready for the next one. 'Does he satisfy you sexually?'

Er... yes, after a fashion, in a manner of speaking, more or less she supposed that he did though she wasn't much bothered about that sort of thing; it was more important to her that he treated her right and she could tell him pretty much almost anything.

'Do you feel that you fit together?' the man went on quite solemnly as if he were singing his way through a psalm.

What d'you mean 'fit' Marly shouted at the television and Oprah smiled back at her, cool as a cucumber in her long white flowing gown. For heaven's sake, man, what on earth do you mean by 'fit'? Fit together like a jigsaw puzzle? My arm here, his leg there, the wart on the end of my nose in the middle... Golden Couple on Sunset Boulevard? Domestic Harmony at 120A East Hill? She reached the crease at the bottom of his chin and could rest her head in the crook of his neck if that was any good, in that sense she fitted him, strangely fitted him.

'Has he stuck by you through thick and thin, through the valleys and the shadows, the bad times and the testing times?'

She sighed and supposed that she had to admit he'd stuck to her like superglue – though sometimes she'd wanted to prise him off and now he was starting to use his fists....

'Would you be unable to cope if he wasn't around?'

Of course she wouldn't be unable to cope. Who on earth did they think she was? She could cope on her own easy peasy lemon squeezy – and she would have to soon enough when she went away to live by the sea with or without him. (But you have no financial capability, he had said when she'd raised the question of leaving.) Anyone could cope on their own if they had to, it was simply a mindset, a hardening of attitude. Of course she wouldn't be unable to cope....

'Hallelujah, count your scores!' the man suddenly cried in apparent jubilation. One or two people tittered, others cheered (they were always cheering on the Oprah Winfrey show) and Oprah's teeth gleamed in delight. 'If all your answers were NO then I have to tell you you're with the wrong person.' The relationship expert shook his head, suddenly sorrowful. 'What are you doing with this guy? You're on crazy street with Mr Crazy and you gotta get outa there.'

There were several groans from the audience and Oprah smiled sympathetically. 'We've all been on crazy street,' she said gently. 'We've all been there.'

'Sure have,' the expert agreed.

'You just gotta get the crazy bus outa there!' she quipped.

'You betcha!'

They smiled at each other under the lights then turned to the audience. The expert was about to continue when the camera shifted to a middle-aged woman in the audience who was standing up to ask a question. She was shaking nervously under the spotlight and seemed particularly excitable. 'What if you got the bus outa there and ended up back on crazy street with another Mr Crazy? For twenty year I been...'

'Just keep riding those buses ma'am,' the expert said quickly, smiling broadly. 'Ride 'em all the way along to Kansas if you have to. There's some real nice folks live up there.'

The audience erupted into spontaneous applause and the woman sat back down looking dazed.

'Well now,' the man continued, stroking his moustache, 'if you got a coupla NOs then it may well be you're with the one before the one, if you see what I mean.'

'No I do not,' Marly shouted again at the TV. You could go on forever and a day like that: the one before the one before the one before the one.

'And if you got one NO or less...' he paused again for effect.

That's me, thought Marly in suspense.

'Then I suggest...'

'What, what?' she cried, leaning forward and almost knocking over the empty cup on the cardboard box. There were one or two stifled whoops and hollers from the audience.

'I suggest that you...'

Oh for goodness sake, man, get on with it.

'Book the church!' he cried at last, punching the air with his fist. 'Book the church!' The audience went wild – throwing slips of paper about the place, cheering, hugging each other, stamping their feet.... The expert kept punching the air with his fist, egging them on. It was obvious the whole thing had gone to his head. 'Just take that crazy bus round to the minister's house,' he shouted, 'and book that goddamned crazy church!'

It looked like Oprah Winfrey was trying to calm him down when they cut to the commercial break.

Book the church, Marly wrote on the little scrap of paper, giggling to herself at the expert's antics. She doodled a heart and a childish D 4 M then scribbled them out again in embarrassment, her nose almost touching the page it was getting so dark in the flat. She wouldn't go up to Bluewater, she decided, after all, what with the Christmas rush and everything it would be too packed. She would stay right here, quite quiet in the flat, listening to the rain drumming on to the roof and waiting for David, perhaps a snooze in the red sleeping bag, another cup of tea, an afternoon film. She spun herself round until she lay lengthways along the settee, propping her head up on a cushion, turning off the television and closing her eyes. It was a relief to know that she didn't live on crazy street and David wasn't a Mr Crazy (though he used his...). He might not be a Mr Right but he was at the very least a Mr Reasonably Okay. (Was that what Terry meant by accepting?) How could she ever have doubted it? Had she been blind? It wasn't too late to turn it all around. It wasn't impossible that she could be well. If they went away to live by the sea who knows what could happen. They might even get married in a crazy church – she could see it now: Michael effing Angelo ridiculous in a top hat, Anne with her painted toenails and her father... well, her father wouldn't come but they would be married nonetheless in a church full of flowers and prayer books in Ariel boxes (at Ivy's funeral the prayer books had all sat in Ariel boxes) and crazy Roman candles that lit up the stained-glass windows – what a lot of scrubbing the choir boys must do. They would go this very weekend and pick out a gown at the bridal shop in Bluewater, with the other young couples that sauntered by, the girl always dragging the boy by the arm and saying 'Isn't that dress beautiful?' and the boy saying 'No, I think it's horrible', not having a clue what she meant, not having a clue what lay in store. Amazing how you got swept away by the dream – you'd practically take a gnome up the aisle for the most beautiful dress in the world; and yet you'd give it all up for the greatest man on earth. David wasn't the greatest man and nor was she the greatest girl but they might do very well far away from the little grey wounded street. If they lived in a cottage on top of a cliff with roses round the door and honeysuckle creepers; a cottage with a washing machine and cookery books, wooden floors and patchwork quilts and a gate that led to the path to the beach.... Ah yes, there she was, racing down the cliff-top path, picking flowers as she went with no Hades in sight, just acres and acres of clean white beach where David sat building sandcastles with a sturdy robust little boy with roses in his cheeks. The sky so blue as if it had just been washed by an enterprising set of little angels – what a lot of Ariel they must use... her hair, her skin, her eyes so clear and bright, her legs so tanned as if she'd just stepped out of a TV advert, the three of them strolling hand in hand, catching the rays and counting the seahorses on the waves. How they plunge and dance – she points them out to her son – graceful as the Ballet Rambert. How their manes glitter up in the sun, like lots and lots of granulated sugar... she is mixing them bran mashes in the kitchen full of cookery books! She is teaching the boy to play Bach and he plays – how strange – with purple fingers. She is sleeping safe and warm and tight underneath the patchwork quilts for there are no sad ghosts here. Only happy ghosts haunt the cottage with the roses and the honeysuckle creepers.

She woke up with an hour or so to go before David came home. It was almost completely dark in the flat and she groped for the lights, feeling her way into her slippers as she went. There were sounds of thumping from down below and she figured Jason was back already though normally he was quiet as a mouse, peering through his optical lenses no doubt or stroking his golden fleece. She turned the radio on to drown him out and set to work about the flat. She would have it spick and span for when David came home... he would be so pleased. Her mind was quite clear after her short nap and a vague sense of contentment still clung to her. They would soon be away from this little grey street! She polished and dusted, hoovered and hummed, occasionally breaking into song along with the radio when she knew the words. She just did things that needed to be done, without thinking or feeling and it was good to act without thinking or feeling: she repositioned the rat trap, dusted a small ornament, rinsed out a peanut butter jar. She prepared a little pasta sauce (à la David) with lots of mushrooms and onions, courgettes and tomatoes – just the way he liked it. She dug out the Limes application form from her bag, settled herself at the table and meticulously read through it. The anglepoise lamp got quite hot against her cheek as she strained her way through the questions, putting down answers she thought they wanted to hear and struggling to fit her large unwieldy writing into the small spaces; though at the end there was a great big space to fill and she didn't have a clue what to say.

'What qualities do you think you would bring to the job?' She sucked her pen, stared at the walls, nipped back and forth along the tiny corridor to check the pasta wasn't boiling over and still didn't know what to say. In the end she wrote: 'I have great sympathy for others,' and then, to fill the space: 'My grandmother is very old and my mother died in traumatic circumstances.' It was a fair point to make, she felt. It showed she had an understanding of the mad, the flawed, the senile and the useless (she being all four)! She knew their fear, hopelessness, dissolution and constraint. She sealed up the envelope, put it on the chair to post then went back to her random little acts of cleaning. She bustled about quite merrily, spotting one job to do after another and another. The more she did, the more she spotted what needed to be done; but it was good to act. They would soon be away from this little grey street! Her future sparkled up at her like a bright new shiny pin as she fluffed and hummed with her dusters and dishcloths.

He eyed her warily as she foisted the letter upon him, almost poking him in the ear with it. She was prancing up and down in front of him, obviously pleased as punch with herself.

'I'll probably get an interview,' she jabbered, 'not that I want one of course. I did it to get them off my back really. They said I must leave no stone unturned in my search for employment.'

'Too right!' he agreed drolly.

'Manager of Shrubs at Crayford Nurseries said he never got an application from me.' She made a face. 'D'you think I'll get an interview?'

'Probably,' he smiled. Not that it mattered much if she did. She often had interviews but she never actually got to any of them. The colour of the building or some small incident on the way sent her on a wicked impulse home again. Once she'd travelled halfway across the country for an interview and come straight back, later on ringing the people and telling them she'd been involved in an RTA. Her acting abilities were unsurpassed. She was born to deception, he reckoned. She'd got the phrase RTA off a TV programme about doctors apparently.

'Terry's off on holiday, you know, to Ireland.'

'Is he indeed?' He poured himself some orange juice, topping it up with cold tap water.

'Looking for leprechauns!'

He chuckled. 'I bet he does, really. Hunts 'em down and puts 'em in his remedies!'

'Silly,' she giggled, her violet eyes bright with excitement. A little too bright, he decided, though he was pleased to see her in a good mood for once. He watched her dishing the pasta out onto a couple of plates, faffing about awkwardly with oven gloves and a great wooden spoon, her cheeks flushing up with the heat; and it tore at his heart to see her trying to perform this unfamiliar housewifely little task. In the end he took over from her, fearful lest she burn herself and end up blaming him for the evening; and she accepted quite gratefully, standing studiously at his shoulder for a moment before prancing off round the room again, making small flourishing motions with her arm at the sideboard, the cooker, the kitchen sink as if to say 'Da daaah! What d'you think about that?'

'Wonderful,' he kept saying, nodding and turning his head in amusement. 'You have done a lot of cleaning.'

They carried their platefuls through to the sitting room and sat down on the settee. Marly carefully placed the TV magazine on her knees to protect her legs from the heat before balancing her plate on top of it. It was a habit, David now realised, that had always annoyed him because more often than not she ended up spilling her food all over the magazine and the pages stuck together with dried-up gunk and sauce. It wasn't that he cared much about hygiene himself, to be truthful, but something about those stuck-together pages depressed him a little. There wasn't any need of a rat trap, he thought, watching her, with that TV magazine!

'What have you been up to then?' she enquired suddenly, her voice quite upbeat and dynamic sounding.

'Oh, you know... work.'

'Yes, I know that,' Marly replied a little irritated, wondering why men were so useless at detail. Ask a man the colour of his mother's eyes and he'd probably look at you askance, stumped. 'But what did you do at work?'

'Well, from 9 to 11.15,' he began painstakingly, 'I had my A level class, then I had a fifteen-minute break where I did a bit of marking, had a quick pee, then I had to take a GCSE group from 11.30 to...'

'Yes, I see,' she interrupted hastily, realising she wasn't actually interested in the detail. 'Terry showed me a poem this morning, it was really nice... "Let the winds of the heavens dance between you..."'

'What's that mean then?!'

'Look, I know you're a mathematician and all that but honestly, listen: "Let the winds of the heavens dance between you." What d'you think it means?'

'I dunno. One of 'em's suffering from flatulence?!'

'Oh yes, very good.' She blew out air to stop herself grinning. 'I'll give you the winds of heaven in a minute.'

'Winds of hell more like!'

'Ha Ha.' She blew out air again and little bits of pasta shot out all over the floor and TV magazine.

David stared at her, pretending to be horrified. 'Dear oh dear, I can't take you anywhere.'

'You never do, mate, you never do!'

They munched on in happy silence for a while, their reflections mingling and glimmering in the newly polished TV screen. He sensed a suppressed excitement about her – it was in the active stillness of her body, the too-bright violet eyes. She was hatching a plan, an idea, a surprise, he was certain of that. He had a surprise for her too – he smiled in secret anticipation of her reaction – but he would wait his turn. Wait for her, as he always did, to pour her strange little heart out to him, dark and fast as Ribena.

He didn't have to wait long. After a few more mouthfuls she turned her vivid, almost glowing face towards him.

'We'll have to start packing soon. I should think we could be in our cottage by springtime. Terry says I'm much better now…'

'Good, I'm glad.'

'…but I'll be brilliant when we live by the sea. We've got to get cracking, there's so much to do: cleaning up the flat, packing up; putting our notice in to Mrs M.'

'We… ell…'

'What d'you mean "well"?' She stared at him defiantly, wishing she could ask outright for things – not this stupid fait accompli phrasing, this badgering, this bullying – but she was scared that if she asked outright for things they would simply be refused. 'Well?' she repeated.

David laughed, a nervous laugh it seemed to Marly, a laugh that meant nothing, meant that he was simply humouring her. 'We can't just take off like that,' he mumbled at last.

'Why not?'

'We just can't.'

'Why not, give us a reason. Go on, give us a reason.'

'Well, there's my job for a start.'

'We could get jobs.'

'You haven't worked in years!'

Marly bit her lip, her cheeks reddening. 'I could work if I was well and I would be well by the sea. Anyway, you could get a job.'

'I've got a job.'

'I know, but it's here.' Marly made another flourish with her arm and this time, David thought, it didn't mean Da daah. He felt the night closing in about them and a shiver went down his spine as if somebody had waltzed their way over his grave. The friendly banter had gone; the secret anticipation inside had gone; and he struggled to regain his happy momentum. 'It'd take some time,' he said at last, desperate to appease her.

'Why does everything have to take so much time? Why can't we just do something, why can't we just go for it, act on impulse for a change? You never act on impulse.' It was all very well, she thought, toying with her food, him spinning his little stories at night just to get her off to sleep, his fairies, feathers and Quality Street refrain, but when it came down to it he hid away in his safety nets, all talk no action, typical ha ha fucking funny man.

'We can't just up sticks like that, it's expensive. We haven't got the money.'

She stared at him in surprise, her eyes narrowing, and she noticed his face was pale and clenched, the warmth of summer having left it long ago. She felt a stab of guilt followed quickly by anger. 'Why ever not?'

He read the look as an accusatory look, a look that said he wasn't good enough, didn't earn enough, didn't compare to her brother the businessman, the square-jawed action man comic book hero who earned a six-figure income, sent postcards from Italy and presented her with slippers from the Arctic (Exciting Alaska Snow Powder Land) and he blurted out unthinkingly – oh David you fool you fool – far too unthinkingly: 'Because I'm supporting you. Because I'm subsidising you all the time.'

'Oh well,' she exploded, jumping up and pacing the room, her food forgotten. 'I'm so *sorry* I'm not working. I'm so *sorry* I've been ill, I'm so *sorry* my mother died…'

Danger zone, he thought flippantly, though he didn't feel flippant at all. He felt like a paper bag was coming down over his head and he wanted to hit out at something. He wondered how much longer he could endure these stupid cycles – it felt, at this moment, he had endured them for a lifetime.

'If I'm such a terrible *burden*,' she was shouting, cramming his guitar books into his rucksack, 'I don't know why you don't *leave*... go on, leave, I'll pack your suitcase for you.'

She picked up his guitar and tried stuffing it into the rucksack on top of the books but it didn't fit and she swore under her breath. At any other time he might have laughed at the ridiculousness of it all, but it didn't seem funny to him now; he was full of dismay and amazed at how she turned on a sixpence from love to hate, how they had got back to this place again, this place of pain and hatred. He sat there, his plate on his knees, staring into space, hearing her yet not hearing her. No doubt she was attacking him, as she always did, attacking him for not doing this or forgetting to do that – some trivial insignificant little thing for years and years and years; for not loving her enough or being good enough or earning enough for them to go away and live by the sea;

for not understanding her or treating her right or having a clue about her strange little whims and obsessions; not living up to her great expectations or being a patch on that square-jawed, comic book action man; not lining his boots up at the end of the bed no doubt or wiping his fucking arse the right way probably or worshipping long and hard enough at that godforsaken temple of little Miss Marly Smart; not even being a real man but a typical ha ha fucking funny man; not loving her the way she wanted to be loved. How the fuck, he wondered, did she want to be loved? These words churning up in him; but he couldn't get them out and the more she attacked him the more they choked him up inside... so that in the end he got up, took his coat and walked away. Walked away before that vicious little stabbing thing stabbed him half to death. Walked away because he knew he might just turn on that stabbing thing and stab it back to kingdom come.

Marly stood transfixed, hand on guitar, as he pelted down the stairs. She couldn't get over the fact that he was going – it all seemed to be happening in slow motion like the time she'd crashed the car and had glided along the ice for an eternity. She shouted after him: 'Go on then, you always do – use your fists or run away. You can't face any sort of confrontation can you.' Then she pulled on her boots, grabbed the transistor radio that sat on the table and raced after him into the darkness, dimly aware on her way out of Jason knocking pictures up on his walls, making a little home for himself. Fly away, said a voice as she sped through the gate, from this little grey wounded street. She ran on tiptoe, silently, silently, because her boots had a small heel and would make a sound and she wanted to catch up on him silently silently – softly softly catchee David – that little gnome wandering off down the street, blissfully unaware of her coming. Ha ha. The cars shone crazily under the street lamps and her fingers tightened round about the radio in her palm. How she hated him for running off, abandoning her like that after all they had said, for throwing in the towel and jetting off on a night's carousing – thinking he could leave her there right as rain, nice as pie. How did he ever think she would be right as rain, nice as pie – she was evil, poison, twisted up inside and she always saw an argument through to the bitter end, he should know that by now. She ran softly past the launderette and the flower shop on Watling Street where the old woman laughed a crazy laugh and popped out at you like a pale rhododendron. She was in throwing distance now. She slowed down, came to a halt, took aim and hurled the radio with all her might at the hunched-up figure in front of her – it crashed around his feet and he jumped in shock, turned and, seeing her there in the darkness, ran up and grabbed her by the throat. One or two cars tooted, somebody shouted something and a couple passed by on the other side. His eyes were full of disgust and he stared at her unblinkingly as they stood right next to the Emmanuel Pentecostal where they might have got married in another world to this – Michael effing Angelo ridiculous in a top hat, Anne with her painted toenails and her father, well her father wouldn't come but – it was a crazy enough place, that church; its worshippers parked quite hazardously round the launderette, singing and hallelujahing their way through a Sunday afternoon (what a lot of Ariel they must...). She stared right back at him, daring him to lay a finger on her in full view of the street, daring him to show his true colours in public. After a little while he loosened his grip, let her go, turned and carried on down the street. The wind was suddenly cold. She had no coat on. She did not follow him.

# Thirteen

She was waiting for him though when he came through the door in the light of early morning. Nobody in their right mind could possibly be up still except the night owls, the barn owls, insomniacs and Felix the next-door and very conceited cat who prinked for pilchards in the dew. Even Jason had gone to bed, wrapped up in his golden fleece no doubt and dreaming of landscapes and picture hooks. It was foolish, she knew, to stand barefoot on top of the stairs like a little old vengeful Victorian ghost in a white cotton nightdress when he was suited and thick booted, drunken, drawling, brawling and crawling his way back home... but she had risen – oh yes, she'd risen alright – like a christ from the tomb, like the vapours from a malodorous old sacrificial swamp where they might once have thrown victims, horse-shoes, pork pies and gimleted goblets to appease the heathen gods. What gods? What gods? They'd let her down once too often those gods. Let 'em play their little games of trivial pursuit with suns and moons, earths and archangels, heavens and hells. She had her own little weapon right here behind her back, not to use but to threaten, to protect herself for when he saw his guitar. His guitar! She felt a faint stab of fear when she thought of what he would do when he saw his guitar. She should never have broken it, though he deserved it – music was real: it screamed, laughed, made love, went on picnics.... (As a child she'd thought she was trapped behind the bars of a musical score like some sort of Alcatraz; and one fine day they might bend like elastic and she would escape.) She should never have broken his guitar. She felt as though she were gliding on ice again as he came relentlessly up the stairs, ːǁ ːǁ a faraway look in his hazelnut eyes.

'I got your guitar to fit in the end,' she remarked almost rationally as he pushed his way past her, stinking of alcohol and cigarette smoke. 'It fits perfectly now, you'll see, so you can go now, can't you.' She followed him into the kitchen, hands clutching the knife behind her back, and watched him blundering about the place, pouring himself a glass of water, peeling a banana. There was a look of sullen resentment in his eyes and she felt a dim fury rising up in her. Who the hell did he think he was, coming back here right as rain, nice as pie, without so much as a hint of an apology, stuffing down his glass of water, guzzling his banana in such a nonchalant manner. My god, he deserved worse than a broken guitar.

'So you can go now, can't you,' she carried on in a whine, knowing she was talking gibberish, 'now that I've got your guitar to *fit*.'

The word 'holocaust' spun through her head (in an effort to defuse the intensity of their small pathetic domestic crisis) but she dismissed it with a shudder. It had no business here. It didn't belong. Nothing belonged here. Everything in the flat proclaimed that nothing belonged... which was why the mould drew manholes and hollyhocks, sunflowers, giraffes, penises, little weasels on the ceiling, like some young scamp of a poltergeist practising his artwork... which was why the rats ran riot in the kitchen, under the skirting board, abseiled down from the cornices no doubt in an effort to get at the cookie jar (He's a bachelor rat at the moment, David had laughed in the beginning, but soon he'll find Mrs Right Rat and then we'll be in trouble!)... which was why the blue magnetic butterfly sat upside down on the heater, its wings heading for earth. She stared at his raisin and hazelnut eyes, half closed as he gulped his banana and a little voice inside whispered: please just hold me, hold me and say it doesn't matter, nothing matters, the broken guitar, the sadness, evil and rottenness.... Say we can get our plane ticket out of here bareback into the waves, run away from this little grey wounded street. Please take my hand and say we can fly away if we dare to, fly away if we dare....

'You bitch!' He'd seen it. He'd seen it across the hallway, sticking out of the rucksack like the jagged stem of the old oak tree that had fallen in a bad November storm. He put down his glass and raced through to the sitting room, she following at his heels like a little old familiar, muttering inanely as she went. 'That's what'll happen if you keep running away from things.'

His eyes were full of agony, of anguish and he crouched down, almost cradling the guitar in his arms, his finger tips touching the flayed strings, bashed-up wood, fingers that had teased her hair, cupped her face. 'Fuck it all,' he mumbled under his breath, rocking back and forth a little unsteadily. 'Fuck it all, fuck it all...'

She towered above him, half guilty, half gloating to see him hurting, hurting as bad as she had done. 'It was rubbish anyway,' she muttered defiantly, leaning over him, hands behind her back.

'Fuck you!' He suddenly grabbed the guitar, making her jump, lifted it and bashed it against the side of the table; it croaked and groaned like the old oak tree must have done when the lightning struck it. He bashed it again. And again and again, almost dementedly.

'Leave it alone,' Marly ordered, furiously upset to see him continuing where she left off. It was all very well for her to hurt the guitar, but for him to come drunken drawling brawling crawling his way up the stairs and start bashing the guitar to bits, disturbing the street and Jason asleep in his fleece, enraged her almost beyond belief. You didn't shout and carry on like that where she came from. You didn't wash your dirty linen in the middle of the night for all to see; you brushed it under the carpet for the rats, shoved it deep deep down inside, put on the mask with little eyelets for the eyes (which was why she knew that the stone cold faces are the ones that are feeling).

'Leave it alone,' she hissed again, enraged at this violence out of her control. She made a grab for the guitar and the knife slipped from her fingers, clattering over the table and onto the floor with a dull soft thud... ⌒ ⌒ ... David stared at it in astonishment then picked it up... and the look in his fruit and nut chocolate eyes was unrecognisable.

Marly backed towards the door, like a little old vengeful ghost, barefoot in a white Victorian nightdress. 'Use your mouth not your fists,' she taunted him. Even when he had the upper hand she still taunted him sometimes because her tongue was the only weapon she had left. 'Coward, bully... I know you're incapable of it but try and use your mouth not your fists.'

She was gliding on ice again when he pushed her against the wall and stabbed around her head, digging up the grubby little flowers in the wallpaper. (Lightning-quick yet oh so slow.) It was a bit like one of those circus tricks where they throw knives around a woman, leaving her outline there for all to see or cut her in half into separate boxes then put her back together again. Everybody claps and cheers. It's a nice day out for the kids apparently. Doves come out of hats. Cards disappear down somebody's ear. Everybody fooled by the illusion, the magic; the conjured epiphany. How easy it was to be fooled by the illusion, thought Marly, the illusion of peace, of love, of contentment... those moments, those moments that had stuck like stars in her memory, those beautiful, soft, shining moments, they were the illusion. This was reality. This, this, this was the reality: this pain, this hatred, this fury. This was the forever-now eternity.

'You're fucked,' he shouted then in her ear right next to the flowers. (*Picking flowers she'd been taken. He'd swooped right out of the blue.*) 'You're fucked and you want to fuck everyone else up as well. It's always about you... what *you're* thinking, what *you're* feeling, never mind anyone else. Oh but then, I forgot, it's always more of a struggle for you isn't it... it's always that bit more of a struggle for you.'

She stood, dumbfounded, at these words pouring out of him, these words pouring out of him in the light of early morning, in the dim religious light of an early December morning (she was quite safe here in that dim religious light. Wasn't she, wasn't she? Fuck the gods, fuck the gods... just two simple humans battling it out in spit and blood, much larger than gods, much louder than gods.)

'You treat me like shit and then you want me to talk! Jesus H Christ, you expect me to talk after that... talk talk talk,' he almost screamed it. His voice was almost a scream. (*Sometimes music sounds like screaming. Have you ever heard Bluebeard's Judith screaming? Have you ever heard a man or a leveret screaming?*) 'You're poison, d'you know that. You turn everything to poison.'

Oh yes, she knew that. She knew about the poison. It dripped out of her like rain drips from a dirty gutter. She could fill a vast array of colourful, haunting, glass-blown bottles with her little drops of poison. Poison to eat me with, drink me with, sleep me with, fuck me with... she sank down, out of his grasp, onto the carpet, muttering a little acidly, for she hadn't quite given in yet, 'Oh don't be so melodramatic. For goodness sake, David, don't be so melodramatic!'

It was like a red rag to a bull and she watched with an almost bitter satisfaction as he charged off round the room, slashing anything in sight: his shirt, the curtains, a cushion, the armchair. Half of her watched with bitter satisfaction as he blundered drunkenly round the room while the other half sat (in a separate box) still, tiny and quiet as a mouse whispering 'What have I done to him? What have I done to him?'

After a long, long time of waiting and of silence, interrupted only by his spasms of dry sobbing, she looked up. Dawn must have been breaking for little flecks of light poked horribly through the curtains, illuminating the bare, torn remnants of the room. Her eye travelled slowly over the slashed and broken objects and every time she saw something special that was ruined she felt a sudden burst of anger bubble up then subside. She was still a strange mix of fury and sadness, each emotion chasing the other like dogs their tails, but she was at least free from physical pain. The knife hadn't touched her: it had caught her hair, pulled at her clothes but she had come out of it all unscathed, like one of those magic tricks, like the women who left behind their outline in knives. At last, with great difficulty, she brought her eyes up to David.

He sat, his shirt in tatters, at the end of the sofa, still shaking and clinging to a cushion. His stomach was streaked in blood where the knife had cut into him and a new patch of psoriasis had spread from his upper chest. (It hadn't been like that a few weeks ago. Surely it hadn't been like that a few weeks ago?) His fingers twisted an end of the cushion into a sharp point which every now and again he scraped against his left palm; his hair stood up away from his head in receding wintry curls. (It hadn't been like that a few months ago. Surely it hadn't been like that a few months ago?) Marly felt a faint fluttering of terror in her heart and she rubbed her bare feet in alarm as if to inject some energy into them, then jumped up suddenly and started pacing up and down in front of him, clapping her hands together for warmth.

'Brr, it's nippy,' she remarked jovially in an effort to bring some sort of normality back to the room or at the very least break the terrifying silence. 'My goodness it's cold!'

She was full of pity and compassion now for the man who sat in front of her, shaking and clutching a cushion. It came to her suddenly that it was her friend who sat with his stomach daubed in blood and psoriasis. Her friend! Her friend who loved her, protected her; did almost everything for her except go along with her dreams. Her beautiful, beautiful, brave best friend. (To my brave best friend, someone had written on a bouquet for her mother, though she never found out who.) What on earth had she done to her friend?

'Cor blimey, it's nipsome!' she grinned, wriggled, pulled faces for him. 'It's enough to nip your toes off, aint it?'

He managed to muster a flickering smile in response, a ghost of a smile, a faint hieroglyph of a smile; and her heart was suddenly her own again. She raced over to him, wrapped her arms about him, buried her face in the winter grey curls. 'I love you... I'm so sorry... I love you, you know.'

After a few moments' hesitation – which she noted and deep down was troubled by – he hugged her back. 'I'm sorry too. I love you too.'

'It doesn't matter about going away... we can stay here, we'll be alright here.' She was all concessions now. Now that she had broken him, brought him to his knees, her love for him was overwhelming. She rained little kisses down on his head, hard and fast as pebbles. 'We'll be alright, won't we...?'

He pressed her close, rocked her back and forth as they crouched awkwardly together on the end of the sofa. Deep shudders still racked his body and she shushed him gently as if he were a child, patting down the stand-up curls for they frightened her a little. 'There now, there now, it's alright now....'

'I'm not helping you, am I?' he suddenly burst out, clasping her tighter than ever. 'I'm just hurting you. I'm not helping you am I.'

'Course you are!' She pushed at him roughly to show him how wrong he was. 'You're brilliant, you're fabulous, you're the best!' She rained a few more kisses down on his head for emphasis, though it flitted through her mind that every time she broke him down he took a little longer to rebuild.

'I'll end up killing you,' he muttered darkly, holding her quite still, 'or going doolally.'

She laughed outright then. It was ridiculous to think of him doing either of those things, killing her or going doolally, as he put it. He wasn't the type. He was her cross-legged beaming buddha, all crinkly eyes, cheesy grins and pork pie chins. 'Don't be so silly,' she squealed, planting a stern kiss on his forehead. 'Of course you won't!'

He sighed and turned away; and she, half amused at his melodramatics, half worried about him, slid gently down onto the floor until she knelt in front of him, her hands on his shoulders.

'Look,' she began quite seriously, staring him straight in the eye, 'you've helped me more than anyone else ever could or would. Most people would have run away years ago. You look after me, you support me... you give me money, pay for me to see Terry. Without you... without you...' she stopped, faltering, then carried on. 'You're brilliant at helping me.'

He stared at her, sad-eyed. 'It doesn't feel like it sometimes.'

'Well – you – are,' she rejoined quite firmly as if she were telling him off; then dug him playfully in the ribs. 'Think of all that lovely stuff you get me... all them lovely pressies. I bet you'll be getting me loads of pressies for Christmas up Bluewater,' she winked.

'Nice try,' he half smiled.

'And think of all them lovely meals you get me... all them lovely pasta meals!'

'You hates my pasta meals!'

'Well, you know, they're alright... they aint so bad... anyways, what about them stories you tell me in the middle of the night to get me off to sleep about the fairies and little shops on the sea...?'

'You've got your own little shop,' he began in his *Jackanory* voice, his eyes lighting up, 'on the sea front. Marly's Marvels, it's called...'

'Oh no no no!' She threw her arms up in the air. 'Not the kraken again, is it? Not the kraken?'

'But you likes the kraken...'

'Well, you know, I mean I do and I don't...'

'So you've got your own little shop,' he carried on quickly, 'and you've also got...' his eyes were suddenly sparkling.

'What?' She pushed at his knees impatiently, sensing something was up.

'...two tickets to see the Lipizzaner horses perform!' he ended with a triumphant note in his voice.

'You what?' She stared at him, bemused.

'I've got two tickets to see the Lipizzaner horses perform next week in London.'

'You're kidding?'

'No, I'm not.' he fumbled about in his pocket. 'They're in here somewhere. It was meant to be a surprise. I was going to tell you earlier.'

She felt the tears start to sting at the back of her eyes and she pressed her face to his knees for a moment before jumping up and pulling him to his feet. 'Give us a piggy-back!' she giggled, leaping onto his back, and almost ripping her white cotton nightdress as she did so; and they giddy-upped round the room, Marly swishing an imaginary crop and David lumbering about stolidly, knocking knees and elbows into doors and broken furniture; their shadows mingling and entangling quite faintly on the wallpaper like some monstrous mythical two-headed beast blundering about in the flowers. In the end they collapsed in a laughing heap and he rolled her onto her back and kissed her on the mouth and his eyes were chocolate and melting again.

'You, Miss Marly stole some barley Smart...'

'What what?'

'Are going to see...'

'What what what?'

'The Wizard of Oz and the wonderful Lippi whatsits leaping and conniving about!!!'

Marly threw her arms up in the air in delight, embracing

175

the giraffes and little weasels on the ceiling, maybe one or two new blooming sunflowers. 'The silver dancing horses,' she breathed, her eyes shining up into his. 'The silver dancing horses....'

# Part four

# Arwen
# and Elessar

# Fourteen

The silver dancing horses stood waiting in the wings: ears pricked, muscles tense, skin super sensitive to the black leather boots pressing into their sides, the soft-gloved hands resting lightly on their withers. Soon. The much-loved voices whisper to them. Soon. The crowd is hushed, waiting, expectant, craning and tenterhooked; and the music has begun: a tremulous fluting, a cajoling violin. A small draught blows through from the cold dark arena, lifting their manes and silk-fine tails; bringing the scent of dampened sawdust where they will imprint their loops and curves, serpentines and figures of eight. Soon. The much-loved voices whisper to them. Soon. There is a deep inhalation, a moment of suspension; then the soft-gloved hands press tightly on the reins, the wind goes singing through their manes and silk-fine tails and the violin cajoles, cajoles....

*'All the way from the Hapsburg P... Palace in Vienna,' the compère announced, stuttering slightly, 'these horses have travelled to perform for you tonight, ladies and gentlemen, boys and girls, an equine ballet to rival Swan Lake! Prepare to be amazed at the intricate steps and manoeuvres of haute école; the acrobatic leaps and jumps of the Airs above the Ground. Prepare to be entranced by the rhythm of their dancing.... Get ready for the equestrian treat of the century, the magic of the snow-white stallions... Horse of Royalty! Horse of the Gods!*

*Horse of living legend! Give it up then, ladies and gentlemen, boys and girls, for the LIPIZZANER HORSES!'*

They step into the arena like stars out of darkness, to the strains of the *Moonlight Sonata* and the roar of the crowd. This is what it's all been for: the days, months, years of training; patient handling, soothing voices, much-loved hands; the rigorous and repetitive movements in the rust-coloured sand of the *Hofreitschule*; gruelling exercises on the lunge to promote suppleness, flexibility, speed and endurance... the good fine oats, molten shoes, dress rehearsals and stable routines; the radios and record players used to accustom their ears to fugues, rhapsodies, arias and minuets; the polished saddles, gleaming bridles, shampooed coats and varnished hooves. All for this! This moment when they step like stars out of darkness to the strains of the *Moonlight Sonata* and the roar of the crowd.

*'Their history has been a t... turbulent one. Exiled and evacuated many times from their homes in Lipizza and the Federal stud at Piber, due to war and military aggression, they have nevertheless continued to flourish and remain to this day the most noble and majestic of breeds. And the Spanish Riding School of Vienna – a masterpiece of baroque architecture designed by Josef Emmanuel Fischer von Erlach in 1735 – is still intact (despite air raids and Adolf Hitler), the only institution of its kind in the world; its purpose unchanged through the centuries – to perpetuate the art of classical horsemanship in its purest form.'*

Bred for this: this fiery brilliance, this obedience, this display. Not for nothing are they known as the Horses of Kings, Horses of the Gods, for once upon a time their ancestors bore emperors and heroes into battle, conquered old worlds without swords, discovered new ones without wings. Stamped in their blood and bone is the landscape of their birthplace: the steep-faced granite tors, limestone plateaux, snow-stencilled trees and cut-glass tinkling streams. Before they ever danced beneath chandeliers, they danced beneath the stars on frozen lakes and lagoons, the snow packed hard in their hooves. Before they ever drew strength from the roar of the crowd, they drew strength from the air and sunshine, the fearsome Karst Bora winds. Before their eyes became a part of the spotlight and camera flash, they were part of the deep transparent shining pools, the bright water in the secret ravines. Long ago their hearts pulsed to the rhythm of the seasons, the soft singing breezes. Now they pulse to Aïda, the cajoling violin.

The young stallions are the first to show what they're made of – eager to please, a little green, their coats just turning grey. It's a while before any of them will lead the School Quadrille, for they are apt to be a trifle skittish when the crowd gets overly vociferous or a camera flash is too loud; and it is then the soft-gloved hands must steady them a little, remind them they are perfectly used to brass bands, tambourines, Pavarotti going at it hammer and tongs. They glide into formation in the centre of the ring while the others drift away like smoke, pale ethereal wraiths in the moonlight sonata. Their riders salute, doff their bicorned hats; silver bits clink in velvety mouths and then they're off: flying hooves in unison over the dampened sawdust, beats in one two time like a soft flapping of wings as diagonal pairs of legs rise and fall simultaneously in a high-stepping, syncopated trot. There is a moment of suspension, a space between two hoof beats where nothing touches the ground and they are truly floating, truly floating over the sawdust ring.

*'The 'passage' is at the heart of haute école. Based on the natural movements of a foal at play, it nevertheless requires great strength and skill. All haute école training is based on principles laid down hundreds of years ago by the great master of classical horsemanship, Xenophon, and is almost*

*unchanged to this day. Even now training is transmitted by word of mouth from generation to generation – no written texts or instructions, just word of mouth from rider to rider, groom to groom.'*

All of a sudden they lose their momentum, the music changes to a honky-tonk piano and the silver dancing horses are trotting on the spot, hopping about on their toes like cats on a hot tin roof. The riders are sitting quite still but the horses are dancing about on their toes as if the sawdust itself were burning, turning their coats from fetlock to forelock a melting molten gold. Either that or invisible strings are dangling from the ceiling and the silver dancing horses are only giant toy puppets. The crowd gasps in astonishment; a child leans over in excitement, drops her ice-cream cone into the ring; it hits Majesto Deus on the nose…

*'This is the 'piaffe', sometimes known as the trot of deep inflection. Great impulsion but no forward movement.'*

…making him startle and prance out of line. He awaits the reprimand from the black leather boots, but it doesn't come; only the soft voice telling him that this is the sort of thing he must expect. Later on there will be garlands, bouquets, rosettes, never mind ice-cream cones! He feels the gentle pat on his neck. All is forgiven. As far as the audience is concerned it was just a part of the dance. He moves back fluidly into line, side by side with his playmate Favory Adonis, as they canter the length of the arena. The ground is soft beneath their hooves, soft as the meadows round the castle at Piber where free of rein and man's command they leapt over catkins and lilacs in bloom, scattered powder snow like stardust, crunched through rock crystal frost. Before they were chosen for the *Hofreitschule*… Now they race under streamers in a floodlit arena, their riders still as stone… they pirouette by the curtained exit…

# Seahorses are real

*'Lighter than a Nureyev... airier than a P... Pavlova...'*

...flank to flank, shoulder to shoulder, just as they were in the meadows at Piber...
180
270
360 degrees...

The crowd gapes; children point and cry out. They must surely be clockwork horses on an old tin musical box...

The music stops. The lid snaps shut. The lights go off and they're gone in a puff of smoke.

The *Pas de Deux* comes next, a ballet for two, one horse an exact mirror image of the other. Every trace of the honky-tonk piano has gone and the music has changed to a faltering piccolo, an eerie bassoon. Two riders come out in blue and gold Renaissance dress, their horses pale and delicate as finely wrought silver. They weave in and out of the darkness, spinning their spells of moving light, their riders still, stern and unsmiling, the horses' eyes like glass. This is a dance in dreamland where the soul takes flight, where images are half real, half imagined. It is difficult to see where one horse ends and the other begins for they move in synchronicity, reflecting, merging, dissolving into one hoofbeat, pastern, bright-crested neck. This is a dance of buried treasure, of winter and long-forgotten things. This is a song from the shining pools where eyes turn into a liquid fire, where velvet mouths are silver dipped and this is a dance in the secret ravines where hoofbeats resound. Echo. Resound. The faltering piccolo takes up where the crazy bassoon left off, playing the same refrain in a different key. Even the audience is deceived. Is it one horse or two? Is it one rider and his shadow? One horse and his spirit drifting in and out of darkness, spinning spells in moving light?

Now it's his turn. Siglavy Parhelion. The crowd has waited for him. The arena has waited for him. The world has stopped and waited for him. Siglavy Parhelion: the flying horse.

*'Performing the Airs above the Ground is the horse they call Pegasus and his master of almost twenty-five years – First Chief Rider Colonel J Lebronski. Two times Olympic Gold Medallist, Grand Prix Champion and chosen in 1992 to perform on the South Lawn at the White House, this is his last grand tour before his retirement in June. It gives me great pleasure then, ladies and gentlemen, to be able to introduce to you tonight, the great horse himself, the unique, one and only Siglavy Parhelion – better known as Pegasus, the Flying Horse!'*

He recognises the sound of the applause, even the compère's words; and he knows the music off by heart. *Gloria all' Egitto.* He places each hoof down carefully in the dampened sawdust ring and bows his strong and graceful neck in response to the roar of the crowd. It's the last time they'll cry out for him, those bright pale faces that shine in the darkness like the flowers on the steep-faced granite tors. The music throbs deep in his veins as he moves in time to the Grand March from Aïda. He always comes out to the Grand March from Aïda. *Gloria all' Egitto. Gloria all' Egitto.* Warrior! Conqueror! King!

*'The Airs above the Ground were originally used in wartime. The spectacular leaps and manoeuvres of the 'levade', 'courbette' and 'capriole' were designed to protect and defend riders in the battlefield. Now preserved simply as a form of equestrian art.'*

He moves swiftly into the courbette, rearing up on his hind legs and propelling himself forward, his forelegs never touching the ground. It is a savage attack on invisible air and the audience stands in delight. No opponent on this earth would stand a chance! These are the killing moves, the killing dance, dance of glory and spoils, blood and brutality, scarred legs and wounded knees. The drum roll clamours in his heart and breast. *Gloria all' Egitto.* His ancestors drew the chariots of gods and heroes; their bodies decorate the Parthenon frieze...

*'Such is the nobility of the Lipizzaner horse, that he would lay down his life for his master... take the spear or bullet in place of him; which is the reasoning behind the manoeuvre known as the levade.'*

...now he plays for the applause of the crowd. Dancing the dance of death to the music of Aïda. Dancing the dance of death in a floodlit arena for the bright pale faces that shine in the darkness. His master asks for the levade and Siglavy Parhelion rises up to an angle of forty-five degrees, taking the spear and invisible bullet for the man who crouches high behind his neck, clinging on for dear life to the silk-fine mane, boots wrapped tight around cream and silver hide; though there is nothing to fear here but rosettes, sweet wrappers, maybe one or two ice-cream cones!

*'And now for the capriole – originally used to decapitate foot soldiers – it is the most difficult feat a horse can perform. Very few stallions in the world are able to perform it. We are lucky that Siglavy Parhelion is possibly the greatest exponent ever.'*

He pauses for breath, awaiting command, his muscles quivering under the spotlight, his mighty heart almost fit to burst. He must give it his all, for it will be the last time. The last time they watch him fight, watch him dance; watch him fly. There is a shift in the saddle, a softly spoken word, a deep inhalation and a pressure on the bit. It is time... he has to jump. The trumpets blow, he drinks the air, his muscles bunch and he springs to the height of a man, lashing out his back legs at some invisible foe. He hangs suspended, outstretched, mid air…

*Gloria all' Egitto… Gloria all' Egitto*

Closer than any horse has ever been to the gods. Closer than Icarus ever got to the sun. He could kick over the moon if he wished. The crowd is in tumult at his feet. Not for nothing is he known as Pegasus: Horse of Kings. For a moment longer he soars, uninterrupted, then drops like a stone into darkness…

The crowd is in uproar. What on earth is going on? No light. No sound. Is he hurt? He jumped so high. They strain to read their brochures by the light of the curtained exit – the finale is the School Quadrille – a choreographed dance routine of some kind. So what is the commotion in the darkened arena? Has Colonel Lebronski fallen off and cracked his elbow? Has Parhelion's mighty heart given out at last? But no, what a relief – there he is right as rain and skittish as a two year old, leading the last dance, the School Quadrille to the tune of Smetana's *Bartered Bride*. The riders are dressed in red and gold-plumed fancy dress and only now do they break into smiles. This is a dance of life and love, of laughter and surprises, of linked arms, swirling petticoats, promises and rings. This is a dance under chandeliers in the rust-coloured sand of the *Hofreitschule* where the Empress Maria Therese drank china tea and Beethoven conducted symphonies. Timpani, trombone, bassoon, strings! They foxtrot, polka, waltz and minuet with Marenka and Jenik, the grizzly bear and Miss Esmerelda Salamanca in Smetana's rural idyll. Delightful! Rumbustuous! Dancing the dance of life and love, laughter and surprises, of cut-glass tinkling streams and soft singing breezes, of birth and death.

Siglavy Parhelion heads the final salute, Deus and Adonis quicksilver at his heels, the rest of them behind like a wave of white horses. The rosettes, garlands, bouquets are for him. Of course they are really for him. He feels the soft hand resting warm on his neck and though his bones are aching, his heart almost bursts with pride. He has flown, fought, danced once again for the bright pale faces that shine in the darkness like the flowers on the steep granite tors of his birthplace.... The soothing voice is soft in his ear, as the garlands fall, softer than the singing breezes. He understands. It will be the last time. He stands motionless facing the crowd, a silver horse carved out of the stars, immortal in their hearts and minds. He stands and faces his final curtain, bows his strong and graceful neck for one last time. By next year the alpine flowers, heather and broom will have covered his remains. His spirit will have rejoined the Karst Bora winds.

The applause went on long after the horses had gone. Marly sat, her hand in David's, and stared at the empty arena. They had disappeared like star-touched ghosts and nothing remained but scuffed-up sawdust, one or two still-steaming droppings. Everyone was on their feet; rustling about with bags and coats, hats and scarves; and the compère was rabbiting on about stalls and badges, video gala performances, tours to Austria and *The Sound of Music*...

'Not bad that, huh?' David squeezed her hand.

'Nope!'

'You know we've got to go.'

'I know.'

'The train goes at ten past.'

'I know.'

Had they raced over mountains with the Von Trapp children, away from the bombs and the Nazis? Seventy stallions, ten instructors, fifteen grooms, a bookkeeper, farrier, saddler, pictures, furniture, archives of the Spanish Riding School; and General George Patton singing 'Doh a deer a female deer, Ray a drop of golden sun, Me a name I call myself, Fah a long long way to run', on the way?

'It's ten to, now. Have you got your scarf?'

'Uh huh.'

'Bag?'

'Uh huh.'

'Purse?'

'Uh huh.'

'Coat?'

'Uh huh.'

'You know we've really got to go…'

'I know.'

She didn't want to leave this magical place where silver horses had danced over sawdust, danced their way in to her sick little soul.

'Can we stay a little longer?'

'We'll miss the train.'

'I know.'

'We really have to go…'

In the end he took her hand, and led her past the upturned seats – they really were the last to go. Already some men with badges were walking down the aisles, picking up litter and old brochures people had left.

'No respect,' Marly muttered to herself.

'What?'

'Doesn't matter…'

She turned her head for one last look then entered the drab yet brightly lit corridor. It stank of old socks and stale popcorn and posters of 'The Lipizzaner Horses: Equestrian Treat of the Century' were hanging quite askew on the walls.

'Hurry up,' David muttered at the crowd in front. He kept glancing at his watch.

'It's alright,' Marly smiled reassuringly. 'Plenty of time.'

'No we have not. Stone the crows! Get a move on folks, get a move on!'

'I might be an *élève*,' Marly giggled, squeezing his fingers, distracting him a little. 'I might be off to the Spanish Riding School. Can you see me doing the capriole?'

'Too right I can. You'd probably decapitate me head off for me!'

'I reckon I could. I can ride. I'm good at music...'

'A little too old I think, my love,' David smiled, glancing at his watch again. 'A little too old.'

A little too old. Quite possibly. A little too old and a little too fucked.

David frowned at the crowd, which was bulging now around the stalls, slowing down even more. A tall dark-haired girl was blocking the path in front, standing around with a group of friends. She was holding up a t-shirt of Colonel J Lebronski and laughing her head off. *She* wasn't too old, Marly thought, a little irritatedly. Even under the harsh, artificial light, she was shining, luminous. Her friends were oohing and aahing at her antics, and she picked up a little badge of Siglavy Parhelion and held it above her pointy left breast.

Marly looked quickly at David to see if he was looking.

He was looking alright.

Her heart turned to stone; and the magic fled her grubby little soul, not little by little in fits and starts, the way her mother's soul had fled, but in one agonising, decapitating fell swoop. He was right beside her holding her hand but she was miles away from him in her head. Miles and miles away in her head. Watching him watching the girl. More fun, no doubt, than she could ever be. 'Sweet sixteen going on seventeen into a world of men. Better beware...' Had *she* ever been sixteen? Ophelia in the school play, Stokesy shouting parson's nose when he should have shouted bravo! She'd jumped from eight to fifty in a flash of a sunbeam and now here she was, a twenty-six-year-old hag, well past her sell-by date and alone. Alone. She would always be alone. Watching him watching her. Typical ha ha ha ha man. The magic had gone; the magic had left her in a puff of smoke, a snap, crackle and pop. She dropped his hand, without a word, and headed long and low like a cat, past the girl who was sixteen going on seventeen and her group of admirers, past the happy men and happy women, bags and rustling coats; headed long and low like a cat into darkness, her face numb, her heart turned to stone.

# Fifteen

June opened the door for once, her spun-at-the-funfair hair mingling rather attractively with the stained-glass porch. A scent of orange and cinnamon wafted out with her, reminding Marly of Christmas trees and fairy lights and the small pomanders her mother had made of tangerines stuck all over with cloves like bright, round hedgehogs.

'Hello Marleeen?' June sounded surprised, as if she wasn't expecting her and Marly mentally checked her dates.

'Hello June. I'm a bit early I think.'

'Not to worry, not to worry. I've just taken him in a cup of tea.'

The 'may our wishes come true' receptionist was on holiday apparently in the Peloponnese, and June was doing the work of two.

'It's exhausting,' she smiled up at Marly. 'Worse than looking after the grandkids if that can ever be said. Little monkeys... if they haven't got their fingers in the fish tank, they're eating shoe-polish! It's the way to an early grave, I'm telling you.' She glared at Marly for a moment as if it was somehow her fault then relaxed into a smile. 'Never mind, never mind. Go on in, go on in.'

Marly smiled, a little confused at this outpouring, then collected herself and walked into the room. Terry sat in his black leather chair, staring out of the window, both hands wrapped tight around a steaming mug of tea. He looked strangely pale and vulnerable and thin, his beaky profile outlined in the chilly winter light, and Marly felt a sudden rush of affection for the old man. How long had she been seeing him now? Was it two years? Two and a half? It seemed a long time she'd been coming to this room full of books and dreams, potions and flowers, the picture of the girl in the shape of a cross and the Grecian vase on the window ledge replaced today by a flame-effect, seasonal candelabra. Very vulgar, her mother would have said. Ivy ever pristine between Scylla and Charybdis. Very vulgar. A row of Christmas cards hung on a piece of string from one side of the window to the other.

She dumped her bag down by the old piano and sat on the chair beside the stool. She felt as if she were going to cry and she tilted her head up and opened her eyes very wide, the way she did to stop herself. Her hands were suddenly shaking in her lap.

Terry sat quietly, put down his cup of tea. 'How's it going?'

'Not too bad.'

'No?'

'Pretty bad actually.'

'Yes?'

A tear squeezed out of the corner of her eye and she brushed it away fiercely with the back of her hand.

'I feel evil, all twisted up inside. Full of poison. Never used to be like this, I just want it to stop. If I think for a second he doesn't love me I go off in my head, miles away... cold, remote... a stone wall comes down. It's like I'm justified in thinking what I think, that it's only safe to be alone. That I'll always be alone. That's the truth, that's the reality. I always come back to it.'

'It's *not* the truth, it's *not* the reality.'

Marly hardly paused to take in what he said. 'We went to see the Lipizanner horses the other night in London... David planned it all as a surprise... it was fantastic... the horses were, I mean. But afterwards... I don't know... I got all jealous... I'm always looking, you see, to see where he's looking.' It was with a sense of embarrassed relief she brought this little secret to the surface and she looked away at the book of dreams, wondering if it had anything under Going back to School – she was always going back to school in her dreams – then turned quickly back to Terry to see how he'd taken it.

He remained unperturbed, the expression on his face suggesting he'd been here many times before and knew his way around the block.

She went on with a smile, defusing it all through humour. 'I'm a little owl for turning my head round to see what he's looking at. Honestly, you should see me...'

'It must be exhausting,' he smiled back.

Ironically she felt annoyed at his light response though she took it in the spirit it was meant. 'It is. And a torment. You just can't live like that. I mean, I might hear something on the radio about a man going off with someone and I'll pick a fight with David. He's probably just sitting there reading his book or whatever – not doing any harm. Or I might read something in the newspaper like 'forty-two year old goes off with seventeen year old' and I'll go home and take it out on David.'

'Poor fellow!'

'I mean, I know the more you try and control, the less you really do. I've read library books, all sorts of stuff. I understand it all in theory. I just can't put it into practice. The slightest thing and I'm back to square one.'

'Everything feeds your particular sensitivity.'

Marly nodded.

'Does David know about all this?'

She nodded again, wondering why it always came back to David. David this, David that. How he felt, how he reacted. What on earth did David matter? If you're so keen on David, she thought to herself, why don't you just have him in here: two for the price of one!

Terry picked up a scrap of paper and drew something on it and Marly put on her glasses again and leant forward to see. It was two rather wobbly circles intersecting in the middle.

'You've got to be individuals,' he explained, 'but not separate. Keep on intersecting, that's the thing. Otherwise...' He drew again. This time it was two circles side by side but not touching – 'No connection! The other thing you can get...' The pen was off again. It was as if he was trapped in his own doodle... 'is a relationship where one person is dependent on the other. Sometimes it does work but it's pretty suffocating.' This time it was one circle enclosed in another.

Subsumed in me, Marly thought, that's where he must be. Living for me entirely and alone.

'What you've got to remember is that we're all just part of a unit. There's no difference, we're all part of the same unit.'

Oh yeah, Marly thought. All of us jigging to the same bleeding heartbeat, the same bleeding goosestep. You sitting there in your black leather chair and me a despicable little Gollum-like creature. All just part of a grand design. Well let me tell you Mr Terry ha ha fucking funny man. You stink, I stink, the earth stinks; the whole grand design just stinks... 'Yes I see,' she muttered, blinking through tears. 'Yes I see.'

For a while they sat in silence, staring out at the chilly white sunshine, Terry tactfully ignoring her tears. She was surprised he let her cry, without interruption, or any attempt at comforting, but after all it was a relief. The tears trickled down her cheeks and now and then she brushed them away with her sleeve. When she'd finished, he turned and smiled, a warm, gentle enveloping smile and said quite matter of factly: 'I think you suffered very high levels of anxiety as a child.'

She stared through the window at the far too red car.

Beautiful, bright and gleaming. Gleaming more than a tooth polish advert. He must have been polishing it all weekend. Polishing it up for Christmas no doubt. The bumper was gleaming, the windscreen was gleaming; the number plate was gleaming. You could eat your dinner off the bonnet by the look of things. Fry an egg on the engine like they did in American movies, American legends. In the end she said: 'No more than anyone else I shouldn't think.' Even the hubcaps were gleaming... 'I saw this thing the other month about a kid who got bitten by a puppy. He was just skeleton and teeth.'

Terry sighed, just a faint exhalation of breath but Marly's sharp pointy ears picked it up and wondered why. He took a sip of stone-cold tea from his long-forgotten mug, grimacing a little at the taste of it and she pretended not to notice and looked over his shoulder. The Grecian vase had been tucked behind some books – the quaint and colourful figures chasing each other with bunches of grapes, having a ball in perpetual motion; and the girl in the shape of a cross peered down from the wall with those great green eyes of hers.

'We all conceal things,' he suddenly said, 'out of shame, embarrassment... it doesn't really matter unless it's hurting us. I hid this for a long time.' He indicated his wide vitiligoed arms, 'and then one day I thought to hell with it and I put on a short-sleeved shirt and went down to the garage and what do you know, the first thing a kid says is: "Have you been in a fire, mister?" I said, "something like that".'

He must mean the radiation, thought Marly. When he'd lost his heart and teeth at twenty-one in a hospital near Wormwood Scrubs. He'd been radiated from head to foot apparently, up his jacksy, his hooter, down his lugholes, any orifice you cared to imagine. Just like Ivy. Ivy had been radiated in all the wrong places. Ivy ever radiating like a fucking star. Ivy radiating for ever and ever like a glorious dying sun.

'You'll be alright.' He reached out and touched her shoulder. 'It'll come.'

She stared at him, solemn faced, touched by his gesture, his warm genuine reassurance and a glimmer took shape in her mind, like a beacon from a far-off ship at night, not of hope exactly, but of recognition; recognition that one day they might meet as equals and as friends. And an understanding too that what she had considered to be his limitations was simply an acceptance of a reality: both cruel and beautiful, despairing and hopeful. An acceptance of his place in the world and the courage to embrace it with a disciplined and determined counting of blessings. But the ship was too far off, the beacon too faint and the gap still too wide between what she knew she should think and what she did; what she knew to be absolute truths and the horror of her own.

# Sixteen

It was mayhem in the job centre. Builders were in doing the roof, and parts of the building were cordoned off with tape and red traffic cones like something out of a crime scene. Every now and then came the sound of violent drilling and muzak had been put on to combat the effect. The queue was inevitably longer than usual, reaching almost to the door; and a man was going round with a vacuous smile saying to no one in particular: 'We're a bit disorganised today I'm afraid. We're a bit disorganised.' He stopped in front of Marly and said to a point over her left shoulder: 'We're a bit disorganised today.' She noticed he had very long fingers and very long pointy fingernails and she smiled back, shivering slightly. It gave her the creeps the way he kept prowling round the queue, flashing his vacuous smile and long pointy nails. She wondered if he'd been a cat in a previous existence.

Bernie Mungo was nowhere to be seen. She gazed about the place trying to spot him. He wasn't in any of the cordoned-off areas. He wasn't wandering around looking at the jobs. He wasn't even by the door, counting his rings like lucky stars, his keys dangling from his waist like lucky charms. It wasn't impossible that he was out the front having a cigarette or out the back on a tea break. It wasn't impossible he was on a day off, but she thought it unlikely. Maybe he'd been promoted to Head of Security and was upstairs somewhere behind a desk, looking into a security camera. She hoped he was somewhere near. There was something reassuring about Bernie Mungo. It just wasn't right for him not to be here.

The queue inched forward a few steps and a bad smell suddenly hit her in the nostrils. The man in front was reeking! She wondered if he'd given up washing his clothes too. He was a large burly man in an overcoat, with very short hair and creases at the back of his neck as if he spent too much time rolling his head about on his shoulders. He looked very at home in his overcoat, like he wore it all the time. It was comforting, Marly knew, to wear the same set of clothes. She was particularly attached to her long grey skirt, blue shirt and blue anorak, whatever the weather. In truth, she was frightened that if she changed her clothes, things might get a lot worse. It had occurred to her that if she changed her clothes, things might get a lot better, but she could never take the risk. She wondered if she stank as bad as the man in front did. Quite possibly. Luckily the olfactory sense numbed itself after a while – she'd learnt that in school – the biology teacher had said that's how people work in sewers without keeling over.

The queue inched forward a few more steps and Marly looked round a little wildly for Bernie Mungo. He must be somewhere! Someone ought to shout out 'Get Bernie Mungo' and he would appear suddenly out of the woodwork, his Saint Christopher shining, like the time there'd been a disturbance in the review section. Maybe he really had been promoted and was upstairs somewhere looking through a security camera; she smiled vaguely at the ceiling just in case. The muzak was starting to get on her nerves: frigging panpipes! They always reminded her of Ireland, leprechauns and that singer her mother used to like – what was his name...? It was the same when they kept you waiting on the telephone and always played bits from Vivaldi's *Four Seasons*: the same bits over and over. It was meant to be reassuring! That man with the nails was giving her the creeps as well. He'd probably been a witch in a previous existence....What *was* that singer's name? He wore a cardigan and sat in a rocking chair, she knew that much. But for the life of her she couldn't remember his...

All of a sudden a mobile phone went off a few steps behind and a man's voice answered. After several yeses and nos he said: 'Can he lick it off a spoon?' There were several more yeses and nos and then he switched off and remarked to no one in particular: 'Sorry about that. My dog's got kennel cough. He's got to have Benylin. I don't know how because he never sees any other dogs. It spreads in the air apparently.'

Marly turned and smiled an acknowledgement. It was a great gift that, an astonishing gift to be able to strike up a conversation with no one in particular. Once when she'd been walking, she'd met a man called Ian who'd told her in less than a minute that he lived in the end cottage by the pub, worked nights, always got three sausage rolls for him and the other two lads, and walked the pub dog, Peppy, in exchange for his Sunday dinner which was cooked by Agatha who kept the kitchen immaculate. He'd told her other stuff as well but she couldn't remember it now.

The queue inched forward a few more steps and a smartly dressed woman came across and asked above the din of drilling and muzak if anyone was interested in the jobs at Bluewater. The queue metaphorically shuffled its feet. One or two people became acutely deaf. Marly found something very interesting to look at on the floor. Never catch their eye: that was the secret. If you caught their eye you were done for. It was the same with people doing surveys in the precinct, people rattling cans for charity outside supermarkets, even girls behind beauty counters. Once she'd made the mistake of looking too long at a girl behind a beauty counter who was shouting at the crowds: 'It's not your decade that matters but your dedication!'

She'd seen Marly staring and pounced on her; and she'd spoken so softly, beguilingly and quickly about pearlescence and luminescence that Marly hadn't had a clue what she was on about and found herself writing out a cheque for eighty quid (much to David's distress) in exchange for two bottles that would give her this pearlescence, luminescence etc... Afterwards, she'd thrown them out, too embarrassed to take them back, too ashamed to use them. The woman asked again a little wearily over the din of drilling and muzak if anyone was interested in the jobs at Bluewater. Everyone then became profoundly deaf. Marly's eyes remained glued to the grey stone floor. Val Doonican, that was his name. Val Doonican. The woman stood there a moment then shrugged her shoulders and went away muttering to herself. The whole queue quite literally breathed a sigh of relief.

There was a space for her next and what do you know but the man with the nails was settling himself behind the desk. Marly groaned inwardly, slung her bag over the side of the chair and tried to appear surprised when he said apologetically: 'We're a bit disorganised today I'm afraid.'

'Oh dear. Is that the building work?'

He nodded. 'The roof's been leaking. I've had to shift my quarters. It's all hands on deck at the moment I'm afraid.'

'Oh dear.' She wondered if the girl with eyes like antique beads and the woman with the mushroom hair were upstairs with mops and buckets, stemming the tide; and then she suddenly remembered it hadn't rained for days. What was he on about? She eyed him suspiciously, wondering if he was on some sort of medication. Those nails weren't normal for a start.

'So, if you don't mind, we won't do a job search today.' He indicated the queue. 'We've got a backlog as you can see.'

Marly turned, partly to look at the queue, partly to hide an expression of delight. She noticed the man in the overcoat standing by the window and staring out at the cold, bright sunshine. Even from this distance the creases on his neck were clearly visible. He must roll his head around like a bloody ball bearing, she thought.

'I hope you don't mind.'

'Not at all.' She turned back to the man with the nails, smiling graciously. 'Not at all.'

'Hold on a minute though, something's coming up on the screen.'

'Oh?' She propped her chin in her hands and leant forward, pretending interest.

'I've got some good news here... Marlene.'

'Oh?' She wondered if they were upping her dole cheque.

'The Limes are offering you a job on a trial basis.'

'What? Are you sure?' Marly was appalled. 'I haven't had an interview or anything.'

'Well, your application form obviously did the business. You're to start a week on Monday. There'll be a day of induction, health and safety etc... and then you're off.' He clicked to print out some details for her.

'There must be some mistake.'

'Not at all. Don't be so hard on yourself. It says here that you're just the sort of person they're looking for. Well done. Congratulations! Good to see the back of you so to speak. No offence like.' He waved his pointy nails and smiled vacuously.

'Thank you.' Marly took the piece of paper and got up to go, then turned suddenly on impulse.

'Is Bernie Mungo here today?' she asked quickly.

'Who?'

'Bernie Mungo.'

'You mean the security guard?'

'Yes.' She wondered how many Bernie Mungos they employed.

'Oh no. He left for Jamaica two days ago.'

The words rang in her ears as she pushed past the queue, out into the cold white sunshine. Left for Jamaica two days ago. Left for Jamaica two days ago. He'd gone and got his plane ticket out of here. He'd gone and left her behind. No longer would he stand, counting his rings like lucky stars, or wander round looking at the jobs for he was there right now in the land of his dreams, the land of talcum sand that burnt your toes, coral reefs that cut your feet, palm trees, azure seas, warm and oily mangoes. Everything was new, changing, different. Everything was new, changing, different; and she didn't like it one bit.

She nipped across by the Daisy launderette full of blood, chocolate, stains, vomit (Have you heard our Daisy scream?), picking up her pace out of sheer agitation. Bernie Mungo had left for Jamaica and she was to start a new job. She was to start a new job. How ridiculous! Just the sort of person we're looking for, my foot. No one else had applied for it; that was the truth of it. No one else had applied! She made her way into the park and her feet beat out the rhythm on the tarmac path that she was to start a new job: Dee de de deeh de de deeh. Dee de de deeh de de deeh :‖ A week on Monday was not enough time to cut her hair, wash her clothes, be rid of the wart on the end of her nose... a week on Monday was not enough time. There was never enough time and always too much to say the things that needed to be said and do the things that needed to be done. (Ivy ever dying in HA HA HA HA HA domestic bliss; and she had just sat there deaf and dumb to it.) Never enough time and always too much.

She sat down on the bench by the memorial for the dead to catch her breath, gazing wildly around for the gardener with her volatile hair, tramps with their beer cans, even the old gentlemen and ladies guzzling nasturtium seeds in the shrubbery, but there was no one around. It was very cold – crows kaarked in bare-limbed trees and a solitary fly buzzed round an old rose bush – but the little bench caught the sun and was really quite hot, almost burning. She took off her coat to bask in the heat though inside she was whirring with the news that Bernie Mungo had left for Jamaica and she was to start a new job. How ridiculous, for goodness sake, was *that*? She tapped the ground nervously with her toe, willing the gardener to appear if only to distract her. She even stood up and peered at the van parked by the library gates; but it wasn't Lizzie's Lady Gardeners with the little vinegar bottle stashed away on the dash board (in readiness for snacks, chips, pasties and samosas); it was a cleaner, whiter looking van and a pale bespectacled man was getting out of it, laden down with what looked like a load of old school annuals. People were scurrying into the library as always, from all directions, bringing back their books and records, CDs and videotapes. It was the busiest place in town, that library. She sat back down and turned to stare morosely at the memorial for the dead. Bernie Mungo had left for Jamaica and she was to start a new job. Someone had thrown a wreath of lilies around the statue's neck and stuck a red bobble hat on his head. Possibly the work of 9T9 Flake. It gave him a slightly comical air, a seasonal, cheerful, festive air, quite at odds with the desolate park. Why wasn't the gardener filling the beds full of Christmas, Santa; New Year Good Resolution flowers? Lilies were flowers of death apparently, flowers of death and eau de toilette, of Christmas talc and funeral parlours. (Someone had sent her mother a wreath of white lilies without message or card. An old admirer perhaps. It had all been very strange. Marly had taken a solitary rose.) Lilies were flowers of death like poppies and forget-me-nots. Like the poem she'd read: *Steffi Vergissmeinnicht*. Steffi forget me not. In the end all that was left was a photograph torn and his stomach blown open like a cave.... The pale bespectacled man was stumbling back into his van, still laden down with the old school annuals. He must have renewed them, Marly thought. Why not? School annuals were a great place to live. (You were quite safe with them. You could read them in bed.)

If she could have been anyone she'd have been a character in an old school annual.

She got up then and made her way along the little old path beside the Darenth. The river had slunk back into its bed for there hadn't been rain in days despite what the man with the nails had said. Still no sign of it either in the sky: the clouds were too white, too small; too high. Everything was glimmering, bright, reflecting; and the water burbled along quite merrily, giving off a little steam in the sunshine like some happy singing kettle. Marly knew that if she leant over the bank she would see her reflection broken up among the rocks and weeds, beer cans and old boots. Why had she never confessed the truth? Terry would have understood. He'd been here many times before and knew his way around the block. Why had she never confessed it? It lay on the tip of her tongue, at the back of her throat, stuck in the crevices of her stopped-at-the-doll's-house body.... She crouched down on the grass and peeped over the edge, her long grey skirt brushing the tops of frosted cobwebs like tiny silken tents or fairy trampolines. The surface reflected the side of her head, the sky; the trees. It looked like a portal to another world, some secret underwater kingdom. How easy to believe you could just dive in. How easy to be fooled by the illusion. Is that what happened to Narcissus? Had he gazed too long and taken it for real? Had he gazed too long and taken it for real?

'It'll come,' Terry had said as if he'd known what she meant. 'It'll come.'

She stood up, her knees clicking, and walked on, faster than a little black moorhen swimming. It was a beautiful day – clean and crisp – as if the window cleaner had been round with his rags and polishes, sparkling up the morning. She wondered if her mother was happy now. Had she found the land of her dreams at last, the land where all is forgiven, everything wiped clean. Was she pottering about the Elysian fields, planting her crocus bulbs, lilies and forget-me-nots? Or was she somewhere in between, a soul distressed, deadheading nettles and stripping petals with her tiny silvery switchblade?

She reached the old stump which was all that was left of the oak tree that had fallen in a bad November storm, one night when the lightning illuminated the heavens. It must have been older than the hills, that tree, older than Tiresias, older even than her grandmother who was really quite ancient. (I'm just an old zombie now, she sometimes said. Well past my sell-by date!) Counting the rings, encrusted in her stumps like lucky stars: silver, sapphire, amethyst and fire opal – each ring a memento, a year in the life of… no longer would she stand beneath the heavy boughs and shelter from the rain. No longer would she run and catch the catapulting leaves, just for fun and to make a wish. The top of the stump was perfectly flat like a dining room table, a little old mahogany dining room table. Did they come out at night and spread their table cloths, drink nectar from acorn cups and elderberry wine, have bun fights, play charades; and then, when daylight came, go spinning off into the pale white sunshine? 'Goodbye, goodbye, what fun we had, goodbye.'

(*He told me fairies wake up the flowers, calling them by their botanical names. And he told me music came from heaven with thunder, hailstones, hurricanes and snow. And for bedtime stories, he read librettos.*)

'Never get as old as this,' her grandmother sometimes said, counting her rings like lucky stars… each one a memento, a year in the life of…

I have no intention of it, Grandma. Absolutely no intention of it, though I am very old already, like Arwen, and he will have to prove himself.

How old could you get and still live?

# Seventeen

The door banged shut and she heard his tread on the stairs... it could have gone either way... he was too well aware of her, had too deep a knowledge of her not to have known that it could have gone either way. The bang of the door – so vehement – and the tread of his boots (which should have gone long ago to Dr Barnardo's) – so sullen and unloving – turned her away from him and away from her heart. By the time he came through the doorway, she was towering over him, metaphorically, in her head, beating him down to the size of a nut, though she sat quite still at the table, with her book.

'Hiya.' The voice was fake, cheerful; and she grunted a response.

'How many people does he think live here?' David threw a load of letters and papers onto the carpet. 'Honestly, how many people does he bleeding well think live here?' It was something of an ongoing joke that Jason put all letters not addressed to him at their door, and normally Marly would have entered into the discussion for Jason was a topic of great interest to her. She hadn't actually met him yet – if ever she was on her way out and heard the door open, she hovered on the stairs, giving him sufficient time to make his escape – but she knew that he did his shopping by catalogue, de-loused the vestibule floor every two weeks and sent off for offers with strange names like 'Pandora's Box'. Today she simply remarked almost indifferently: 'Maybe he thinks I'll forward them on.'

'That's true.' David peered over her shoulder. 'You've read that book before haven't you?'

'No.'

'You were reading it the other week, surely?'

'No... and even if I was, I can read it again can't I?'

'True.'

He flopped down on the sofa, picked up the TV magazine. Marly stared sightlessly at the words on the page, frustration mounting up in her. Why hadn't he asked her about her day for goodness sake, or at the very least told her about his own. Come to think of it, he never did tell her about his day and she never asked; for all she knew he never got to his pale blue tower but shot off to London on a shopping spree or went down the pub and chatted up a girl more fun than she could ever be – silky sheeny stockings and mascara'd eyes. Did he impregnate her on the sly (they say it happens all the time)? She leapt up suddenly and peered over his shoulder the way he'd done earlier.

'I suppose you'll be watching *that*,' she jeered, stabbing her finger at the description of an erotic film showing later that evening on TV.

He sighed and looked up. 'What's upset you then? Did something happen at Terry's? At the job centre?'

'No.' She was whirring with the news that Bernie Mungo had left for Jamaica and she was to start a new job but she wasn't going to tell him that now.

'The horses were good the other night weren't they,' he said then, changing the subject.

'The *horses* were, yeah.'

'What d'you mean?'

'Oh nothing,' she replied superciliously, as if he was too stupid to understand.

'Which bit did you like the best?' he went on, humouring her. 'I liked Siglavy Parhelion best.'

'None of it,' she answered, hating herself for saying it. 'It was all very unnatural… like robots. They should be left free to run on the hills or whatever it is they do.' She couldn't believe she was demeaning them like this, those glorious majestic creatures that had danced their way into her sick little soul. And she knew, for a fact, from her library book, that the horses loved their work, the performances, the attention, and when they were forced to retire often died or became suddenly old and decrepit, shuffling in from the pasture for their morning feed like senile old men.

'Very unnatural,' she repeated, a terrible sadness coming over her. It was like stripping away beauty, deliberately stripping it away. Is that how her mother had felt, stripping petals from flowers?

He smiled at her blankly, a look of dislike in his eyes. That was a triumph of a sort, she supposed, that look of dislike in his eyes.

She went on and on then, on and on and on, unable to stop herself.

'You like looking at things don't you. Typical man. Always looking at things.' She jabbed the magazine again, childishly.

'What are you on about? What's the matter?'

'Nothing's the matter. Nothing's the matter except for the fact you like looking at things.'

'What things? What things am I meant to be looking at?' He sat forward on the sofa. 'I always seem to be looking at things, I'm surprised I've got time to do anything else.'

'Well, if you can't remember it means you don't even know what you're doing, which is even worse, you just can't help yourself.'

'Go on then. Go on, tell me. What am I meant to have been looking at this time?'

She stood still, staring at the torn and tattered world map hanging off the wall. Would she ever get to Novorosysk, Corsica, Shangri-la? Of course she wouldn't. She'd end up at the Limes, feeding the likes of Rasputin, Waltzing Matilda, Pegleg Pete and Leslie Finch. How fitting! 'That girl,' she mumbled at last, 'by the badges.'

'What girl? What're you on about?'

'You know, that girl by the badges on the way out, after the horses.'

His brow creased. 'I don't remember any bloody girl by the badges. I remember there were some silly buggers blocking the way.'

'Tall, dark-haired, looking at the t-shirts.'

'I haven't got a clue what you're on about. I know I was going to get you a badge of Siglavy Parhelion. That's all I remember. And then you buggered off.'

She stared at him for a moment. Could she be so wrong? Could she be so completely and utterly wrong?

'You obviously don't know you're doing it then,' she repeated, 'Which is even worse, you just can't help yourself.'

He laughed outright then. 'You're mental, you are. Your head's playing tricks again.'

'You obviously just can't help yourself,' she insisted.

'Why do you punish yourself like this all the time?' His voice was almost pitying. 'Why do you want to hurt yourself like this? Why do you keep hurting yourself?'

'It's not me hurting myself,' she replied, feeling a little foolish. 'It's you hurting me, not me....'

She went and sat back down at the table, pretending to look at her book. 'Pervert,' she whispered, almost as if she were talking to herself. 'Go and look at all the erotic films you want to. Go and look at all the women you want to, I don't care.'

In the time it would have taken him to answer, he'd jumped up and pushed her chair back against the wall so that she sat, tipped up, clinging on to the edge of the table with the tips of her fingers. 'Is that what you want?' he shouted. 'Would that make you happy?' She could see the saliva on his teeth. 'Is that the sort of person you want me to be?'

'So you admit it then?' she muttered, taking one hand off the table to push her glasses up her nose, her cheeks reddening.

'Or do you want me to poke my eyes out? Should I? Should I? Should I poke my eyes out for you?'

Yes, she whispered to herself. See nothing but me. Wholly, solely dependent on me, though out loud she said: 'Oh don't be so stupid David.'

He suddenly let the chair go so that she came crashing down, bashing her knee on the side of the table. She flinched, shielded her face, thinking he was going to hit her, but he sat back down on the sofa, put his head in his hands.

'I can't do this any more,' he said in a voice Marly had never heard before. 'It's no good... I can't do it.' He kept shaking his head. 'It's no good... no good any more.'
She sat quite still, her knee throbbing, her heart racing, every fibre of her being intensely aware of his presence, the broken room, even the quality of the light. This little old room where they'd shared so many moments of boredom, love, tenderness, despair. She wanted to believe him. How she wanted to believe him. It was like groping in the dark for a light switch. If only she could believe him everything would be alright....

'I'm leaving you.'

The words skimmed over her like three little arrows. I'm leaving you, I'm leaving you... and in her head she saw the musical repeat sign, two lines and two dots, two lines and two dots which she always saw, for emphasis, exaggeration, without repetition of the words themselves. I'm leaving you. :‖ :‖

He went on into the silence, quickly and brutally.

'I'll clear out tomorrow night... start packing later on. It's not like it's going to take long.' She stared at him in disbelief.

'...probably best for both of us... this is killing us both.'

'You can't.'

He looked at her as though he very well could and would.

'You can't just drop a bombshell like that. Everything's alright and then you suddenly say you're leaving like that. It doesn't make sense.'

'You knew it was fucking me up.'

'Well, you were always alright the next day... whistling... playing your guitar... never communicated the fact that you wanted to leave.'

He sighed. 'I'm sorry, alright. It's not like I haven't tried. I just didn't realise the scale of the problem.'

Marly bit her lip. She'd feared man's betrayal and she had got it. This was it! She'd been right all along. Men were pigs, men were shits. Oh ho, she'd been justified alright... she'd been justified. 'You knew I had problems... got depressed... I never hid that from you.'

'We-ell. Look, I'm sorry for changing, alright. It's not like I haven't tried. I've tried for nearly six years.'

'It's like you're not accepting me when I'm ill, because I get ill.'

'But that's not you. It's not really you when you're ill.'

'Yes it is, it's a part of me.'

'Look, I'm sorry,' he repeated. 'It's not like I haven't tried... but it's killing me. D'you know I check my watch every few seconds on my way back from work... in case I'm late.'

Marly laughed then, part nervously, part sarcastically. It seemed such a peculiar remark to make and hardly relevant to the argument. 'Oh dear, oh dear, I'm so sorry... so why did you make all those promises if you can't see them through?'

He sat and stared out the window, lining things up with his eyes no doubt.

'Why did you say all that stuff about loving me, looking after me, if you couldn't see it through? The slightest little problem and you're off like a blue-arsed fly. I was alright before you came along.'

'No you weren't.' He shook his head vehemently.

'Yes I was. I was doing alright. And then you come along and say all those things and I stupidly believe them. I should have known better.'

'Okay, I'm a shit. You'd be better off without me.'

'Fine,' she agreed. 'You are. Go on then.' She kicked a letter on the floor that had obviously come from Anne and Michael effing Angelo. 'Go back to Wales – it seems to be the be all and end all for your family. Go and sit in your valley where it rains and it's safe and you don't have any problems. Go and find some happy little woman – Bronwen or Myfanwy or whatever it is they're called over there – have your two happy little kids, grow your fucking happy rhubarb... it's obviously what you want.'

He sat, his head in his hands, and didn't respond.

She shut up then for a while, fidgeted with her pen, her book, stared into space, stared back at the desk. Her gratitude diary sat beside the lamp, overflowing with anticipation for the Lipizzaner concert. Oprah Winfrey would be proud of her... all those spiritual psychological gurus. Ha ha. What was it Terry had said? You're lucky you've got someone like David who's going to be there. Ha ha. How ironic!

(*Above us the stars will shine, Radames said to celestial Aïda. Ironic as it turned out – they ended up in a crypt.*)

The ramifications of his leaving were immense – her head went into a spin just thinking about it.... She wondered if Jason was listening in, down below in his underworld kingdom, listening in for all he was worth or cooking himself a pizza or peering through his optical lenses at Pandora's Box. The ramifications of his leaving were immense.

'I know I provoke you,' she admitted in the end, tentatively, quite rationally. 'There's no question that I provoke you... but the way you react... you're worse than I am. The problem is you don't communicate, you bottle stuff up and then you explode. You can't just bracket stuff off in your head and think it'll stay there.'

He looked at her, his eyebrows raised, as if to say 'you can talk'.

'You need some sort of counselling. Maybe you should go to Terry as well. Two for the price of one!' She flashed a grin in his direction and he smiled back weakly. There was no way he was leaving her. Love you forever, he'd said. Always and forever, he'd said. Just like one of those fizzy loveheart sweets. 'I reckon you're worse than I am now. I'm getting better and you're getting worse.'

'Yes,' he uttered despairingly and she turned to him in surprise. He had his head in his hands again; and he reminded her of a little boy at primary school – the toughest boy in the school – who'd sat for a whole day with his head in his hands. Nobody could get a word out of him. Everyone tried, even the headmaster. Something terrible had obviously happened at home and he sat the whole day with his head in his hands, without uttering a word, a cry, even a whimper. He'd ended up in Borstal a few years later, for nicking cars.

'Anyway,' she went on quickly, 'you can't leave... cos I'm just starting a job!'

'What job?'

'At the Limes... a week on Monday. I'll probably be getting Rasputin's grub on for him.'

'Poor bastard!' David smiled grimly. 'You want to ask him why he goes round shouting all the time!'

Marly gave a wild exaggerated laugh out of nervous relief. Every argument they had was The End and they always began again. Why should this one be any different?

'Oh yeah, I'm really going to do that aren't I? Hey Rasputin, my boyfriend wants to know why you go around shouting!'

'You've never called me that before,' David remarked wistfully.

'Well, you are aren't you... my boyfriend?'

He turned away and looked out the window again, lining things up with his eyes no doubt. 'And you want to ask him why he wears that tiny pink haversack. I mean it's not like he can get any shopping in it!'

She giggled uproariously. Everything would go on as always, the two of them together in their little rundown flat. Everything would be alright. She jumped up, ran over and knelt in front of him, grasped his hand. 'You're not really leaving are you,' she pleaded. 'I'd die without you... I'll be well soon, I'm sure of it. You're not really leaving are you?'

:‖:‖:‖

After what seemed like an eternity, he squeezed her hand and shook his head; the grim little smile still playing about his lips.

# Eighteen

It had all gone very wrong. He didn't know how exactly or why, but he knew it was out of his control. He lay, his arms wrapped about her, staring at the stars she had pasted to the ceiling: some of them clumped together, some of them all alone. No spatial awareness, she had no spatial awareness at all. The cars zoomed past the window, their headlights criss-crossing the pattern of the curtains like laser beams. He counted the space between them. On average it was thirty seconds. He saw by the alarm clock that it was a quarter to two.

The world had spun on its axis. Everything was topsy-turvy and for all he knew he might as well have been in Timbuctoo. What was life, after all, but a series of geographical locations in your head. Marly was right. There were places to be happy, to be sad, places to visit, places that existed, whether you wanted them to or not, like Manchester or the Arc de Triomphe. You might be on safari in Kenya, she had said, and suddenly find yourself marching under the Arc de Triomphe in your camouflage jacket. Or boarding a plane to Tahiti and suddenly there you are in the middle of Manchester wearing a bikini! Was this the dark tunnel she had spoken of? This feeling that life would go on and on, stretch on into the distance like a Sunday afternoon, that if you disappeared down a manhole no one would care, notice, miss you.

This feeling of dread, of shame. Was this life? Is this how

life felt? Home? Where was it? Was this it? Was this how home felt? As a child it had felt like warmth, noise, safety, frustration; so safe, in fact, that he had declared his bedroom to be an independent state, much to his father's bemusement. Those who enter, he had written on the door, do so at their own risk! Now he might as well have written on the door: Nation at War – each of them in their own place, their own geographical location, defending it for dear life. He saw by the alarm clock it was just gone two.

He got up, gently lifting her delicate arms from about his waist. She slept soundlessly, other than the occasional whimper, like a small defenceless animal. Marly! A wave of love and pain shot through him as if someone had stabbed him right in the heart. He pulled the blanket up high around her long cold neck, left her sleeping under her bottle-top stars; and went out into the kitchen. It was cold, dark, eerily silent in the flat. He helped himself to some chocolate and an apple, munching stolidly in the pokey room. He wandered through to the sitting room and stared out of the window. The cars were going past on an average of thirty-five seconds. Slowing down. A man walked by under a street lamp, holding a beer can, and he thought for a moment it was his old friend Christopher Prosser from school. Surely not! He looked again, moving quickly to the other side of the window. Of course it wasn't! Christopher Prosser was back in Wales, never left for that matter, married with kids, had gotten very fat (according to his mother), worked in Peacocks on the managerial side. That guy was just a guy going home from the pub. Home! This was it... Christopher Prosser married with kids! Christopher Prosser who'd pissed in the hatstand at primary school and danced round the schoolyard singing:

'Dai Bananas went bananas
When his wife went off with
Butterfly Evans!'

The rhyme jangled in his head and he pressed his hand to the glass. It was very cold. It must be very cold outside. The night was very clear with a million stars... real stars. It suddenly came to him that he would go out. He would go outside and walk about. He would march like a soldier for miles and miles right through the night. Now that the idea had come to him he knew he had to do it....

He rushed around, pulling on shoes, socks, clothes, creeping in and out of the bedroom so as not to waken Marly. He stumbled down the stairs, opening and shutting the door very quietly, until he was out in the open air. Cold? It was freezing! His breath came out of his body like smoke and he beat his hands together by the gate, wondering what on earth he was doing. A car went by, full of drunks, and tooted at him, galvanising him into some sort of action. He stepped onto the pavement, took a few purposeful steps up the hill then stopped by the railings of the cemetery. He couldn't just go off in the middle of the night, leave her alone like that in the dark. He knew how scared she was of the dark. He turned, almost sheepishly, and went back down the hill and into the little lane that led to the garden. The gate was heavy, rusty as always and he tussled with it a while, cursing under his breath. It was very dark and quiet behind the houses, everybody tucked up in bed asleep. He sat on an old box and stared at the washing line, at the endless washing lines in the endless other back gardens. The streets were different here, the houses darker-stoned. In Wales the towns were hidden in their valleys, cut off almost from the outside world but a part of something because of that, belonging to something because of that; whereas here, here you were trapped in your own little cell, part of the outside yet trapped in your own little cell like rats in a cage. He could see the bedroom window from here: the frosted glass, the drainpipe, the clothes-horse Marly had inherited from her mother. Marly! He didn't know it was possible to love someone the way he loved that frail tormented creature at peace, for once, in sleep. He was scarred through with loving her. Her tight, cold body and violet eyes. Her strength and vulnerability; anger and pain. He'd just wanted to take the bad stuff away and all he'd succeeded in doing was giving her another helping of it. Another helping of the bad stuff.

He clenched his fingers into his palms, soft lily-white ink-stained fingers.... His great-grandfather had been a street fighter. He wondered why the thought came to him now of his great-grandfather fighting in the streets of Cardiff, fighting for money, for life. Only a coward hit a woman. Marly was right. Only a coward and a bully hit a woman.

The sound of carols drifted up from the bottom of the hill, mixing with the jangled rhythm in his head of Dai Bananas went bananas. He laughed out loud and his laugh turned into smoke. Never get a filthy job like mine, his father had said. Don't get a filthy job like mine son, his father had said; and the steelworks had let him go, too young to die, too old to start again, except for the endless and fruitless rounds of painting and decorating.... And now he sat, a hypochondriac, one hand on the remote, the other on his game leg. Don't get a dirty job like mine, his father had said; and he'd listened. Here he was – a schoolteacher with lily-white ink-stained fingers. Here he was a schoolteacher 'parcey que lay grandes vacances'! The French examiner had asked him why he wanted to be a teacher and he'd replied in execrable French: 'Parcey que lay grandes vacances!' The woman had given him a rather dour look and he had, inevitably, failed the French exam. Not a street fighter or a miner or a steelworker but a teacher with ink-stained lily-white fingers... only a coward hit a woman. A bully and a coward.

He'd wanted to work as a secret agent! At the age of ten he'd amused himself and his small circle of friends by proclaiming he'd grow up to be a secret agent. Not the 007 variety, but the Sherlock Holmes variety. He loved to work out how things worked: gadgets, puzzles, riddles and secret codes. He'd have worked on the Enigma machine if he'd been born in a different time. His powers of observation at that age had been truly amazing. He'd known that the horses in the picture had very human eyes and the teacher had patted him on the head and said he was a promising child. And later on the economics teacher had said he was an economist and the mathematics teacher had said he was a mathematician and his parents had come home pleased as punch! He'd even worked out at a tender age that the digits of the numbers in the nine times table always added up to nine, presented it to his father on a little slip of paper titled 'Morrell's Law' and his father had stood there shaking his head in wonderment... and now he sat with his gout, hernia, diabetes, fading eyesight, one hand on the remote, the other on his game leg. Don't get a dirty job like mine, he'd said to his son; and his son had listened.

Now they rarely spoke. Marly took up all his time: the secret code he wanted to crack, his own Enigma machine. He'd spent the last few years of his life trying to decipher her encrypted little soul, trying to unravel her inner workings though in the process his own life had started to unravel. He knew it, felt it, resented it and a fury built up inside him, though his love for her, astonishingly, remained undiminished, clear as one of those bright white stars. The sound of drunken singing got louder in his ears, mixing with the rhythm of Good King Wenceslas went bananas... sssh, he whispered out loud at the washing line, glancing automatically at the bedroom window: she would be scared if she woke all alone in the night. Just like a child. Just like a monstrous child she was with her senseless fears, bubblegum hopes, cruel imperiousness and strange innocent love. Someone had stamped their own code on her a long time ago... a long, long time ago. Some obsequious little man with a genteel charm, encyclopaedic knowledge and a genius for making one feel ill at ease. Some obsequious little man who lived in a house full of fusty old musical scores and a collection of Purple Emperors in big glass cabinets. When they'd first met he'd said to David, with a twinkle in his eye: 'I only use the metronome in worst-case scenarios,' and David had thought he's nutty as a fruitcake, I'm out of here by midnight! In truth the man was a fucking maniac. Insane. A fucking maniac. He'd given him, for so long, the benefit of the doubt... sometimes he'd wanted to go and shake the life out of the old man, leave him rotting under his piano stool but love of Marly prevented him. Love of Marly opened up everything and prevented everything. He'd thought when he first met her that his life had attained an heroic purpose. An heroic purpose at last! He would protect, cherish, defend this pale fragile monster for the rest of his life.

It was easy to love a monster, easy to become one. He'd hurt her more probably now than her father ever had. Had he come to claim the Purple Emperor's crown? Was it something you handed around, passed from lover to lover, parent to child, from generation to generation like the shape of the nose, the colour of the eyes? Could the process ever be stopped except at the jailhouse, the padded cell; the psychiatrist's couch? It was a good snug fit... how amazing! *'The truly amazing expandable contractable crown.'* It had sat on the head of that obsequious little man, the pale fragile monster's and now his. It sat on his head like he'd been born to receive it. Was this the place Marly had spoken of, the place that existed like Manchester or the Arc de Triomphe: this feeling that life was impossible, that life without hope couldn't be lived?

He got up, suddenly realising how cold he was, and stumbled out of the garden, tussling awhile again with the gate and cursing under his breath. It was quiet behind the houses and peaceful, everybody tucked up in bed asleep. The streets were different here, the houses darker-stoned. In Wales the towns were hidden away in the mist and sweet valley rain whereas here, here you were trapped under a bright arid moon that shone inexorably down on every crack in the pavement, every little secret.... It sat on his head like he'd been born to receive it. When it got too heavy what would he do with it but pass it around, hand it down. 'Give me my sceptre and my throne,' he sang at the cars which were going past now on an average of sixty-five seconds. Slowing down until the morning rush... He saw by the light of a street lamp that it was a quarter past three. He crept in to the house and quietly up the stairs in the thick heavy boots she laughed at, hated; lay down on the bed beside his fragile monster and held her close until his mind went out.

# Nineteen

Marly got up early the next morning and went into town. It was one of those bright, clear, cold days again and the sun shone down on the streets, paving them with gold. She did a little skip as she went down the hill, patting the change in her pocket. She had ten pounds to spend on Christmas decorations and she wanted to surprise him. She'd left him half asleep and rambling on about some dream he'd had of saving her. He was always saving her in his dreams.

*'There was an old guy and a young guy about to get you and I thought I'll go for the young guy first cos he'll be fastest on the draw. Bam – I splattered him!'*

Once he'd been a St Bernard dog apparently, with a barrel of hot chocolate round his neck, saved her from the ice and snow. Another time a monster had come in through the window and he'd chased him out again, stopping on the way for an ice-cream soda! He was always saving her in his dreams from one thing or another and he was always slow to wake – like a cat she'd had as a child who'd gone out hunting all night.... She laughed at the ridiculousness of him, glad he wasn't leaving.

She stepped across the little old bridge where long ago, so the saying goes, a pilgrim of a sort helped travellers over the ford. The ducks sat waiting on the reflecting water for Waltzing Matilda to come feed them or so it seemed to Marly. She pushed on down Overy Street, almost bumping into a man who was putting a little sign outside his pub which read: 'HUNGRY PEOPLE REQUIRED. APPLY WITHIN'

'Happy Christmas!' he smiled at her with a wink; and she laughed and winked back, getting caught up in the spirit of the thing.

People were bustling in from all directions, carrying their great big empty bags ready to be filled with mistletoe, crackers, last-minute goodies; wearing their novelty hats, scarves and mittens. Already the market was in full swing: *Silent Night* was blasting out from one of the end stalls and she could hear the rise and fall cries of the market sellers. She crossed with a group of people at the pelican crossing and a little boy with pink antlers on his head zig-zagged through them on a skateboard, knocking into a little old woman with a stick.

'Hooligum!' she shouted after him, waving her stick and nearly causing another accident; and he zipped round on his skateboard and flicked two fingers at her.

Marly smiled a little, zig-zagging herself through the people and the market stalls. So early and so many people! The place was buzzing, humming with life, and the sun shone down like honey, in and around the stalls, on top of the stripey awnings.

Piles of red bell peppers on layers of green crêpe, purple turnips, earth-coloured pears, coral-reef cauliflowers and great shiny apples – some red as the apple in *Snow White*, some yellow as lemons. Suspect bargain meats sat shoulder to shoulder with odour-eaters, Hoovers, tea cloths and dishwasher parts. A dog tied up to a hot-dog van! Fish, crabsticks, trinkets and badges. Bikinis, coats. (Marly did a double take: bikinis? Bikinis in winter!) Pots and pans and home-made cakes. The smell was enticing and Marly was tempted to wolf down a jam doughnut and lick her sugary fingers in the sunshine the way a little boy in front of her was doing.

'It's all greasy,' he said to his fraught-looking mother. 'Urgh!' she replied, pulling him along. 'Don't!'

The crowd barged, shuffled, speeded up, slowed down... and the sun rose up the sky like an eager alpine climber. And Marly laughed out loud again because he wasn't leaving and she had forgotten that life could be magic, the world an enchanted place to be.

She nipped into the precinct and quickly past the indoor stalls of nuts, sweets, coffees and meringues. She wanted to get to the Christmas shop and see how much she could get for her money. She knew she could probably get a real tree for ten pounds but then she wouldn't have anything to decorate it with and besides, there was something quite sad about a real tree. She decided she was right to go for an artificial one and her mind leapt ahead to how she would decorate the flat: silver tinsel on the banister, golden bells hanging from the doorways, the tiny artificial tree on the table in the sitting room, maybe one or two bright paper chains – and there would be money left over hopefully for a few tiny presents like stocking presents: tangerines, a tub of crisps, Wonka chocolate and loveheart sweets. She would hide them round the flat. She would hide them round the flat and – yes that was it (she almost stopped short in delight at her brainwave) – she would write little clues for David to work out. He'd love that. Like a mini treasure hunt. A Christmas treasure hunt. What fun they'd have! Silly funny little clues like 'Oh knickers' – and then a tangerine hidden in her socks and pants drawer. She could just imagine his reaction:

'Gee, thanks a bunch. Just what I always wanted – an orange in a pair of pants!'

But he'd be secretly delighted, she knew that. And feeling very pleased with herself she entered the Christmas shop.

An old pop song was playing on the shop stereo and a rather stout shop assistant dressed in a pink fairy tunic complete with silver perspex wings was lumbering about awkwardly to the rhythm. It was an extraordinary vision and Marly almost stopped dead in her tracks. One or two people were giggling surreptitiously in a corner of the shop and Marly smiled to herself, wishing David was there to share it – but she would report back in any case.... She went around, quickly and efficiently choosing the decorations she wanted and placing them in the little wicker basket, all the while trying to avoid looking at the shuffling shop fairy. A tiny electronic Jesus in a Manger scene caught her eye and the tag next to it read: A bargain at £199. She thought at first it was £1.99 and then realised it was £199; and was quite confounded. She decided after that that many of the decorations were a little garish and vulgar; and she took her place in the queue, putting the basket very firmly on the floor between her feet. She had to wait a long time in the queue but she didn't mind. She felt quite happy and glowing this morning like a little roasting chestnut, though the tips of her toes still pinched with cold. She noticed that the shop fairy was being led off by a man in a grey suit – obviously the manager – and Marly wondered if she was going to get a telling off for shuffling about like that or a breather and a cup of tea; but no, a moment later the woman reappeared holding a wand with a cardboard star stuck to the end of it and she proceeded to dance as feverishly as before, waving the wand in the air as though dispensing magic and wishes to the good folk entering the shop. Marly struggled to keep her composure by thinking of something terribly boring like the Prime Minister but after a while she lost control and burst out laughing quite hysterically. One or two people stared at her but she didn't mind. She didn't mind because it was Christmas and David was staying and she had forgotten that bad things could go away like they did at the end of fairytale books. And life could be fun, life was laughter, life was a great big hoax! And on her way out she smiled at the stout perspiring fairy because it was Christmas and David was staying and she knew they were going to have the best Christmas ever!

She tried to work out how much money she had left as she made her way back up the precinct. It was £3.80 by her reckoning – the decorations had been expensive – and out of that she still had to get a loaf of bread for lunch as well as the stocking presents. They could be got tomorrow however. Now it was simply a question of getting the loaf of bread for lunch. It was cold for a moment in the shade outside the precinct and then she stepped into the sun again. She bought a loaf of bread and a currant bun for David, then made her way back through the market stalls, weaving in and out of the throng.

'Glitter hats,' a voice suddenly shouted in her ear. 'Perfick for Christmas. All the way from Venezuela!'

She stopped and turned to see a white-haired burly old man holding a softly glowing felt hat covered in gold and silver glitter and dangling with candied lemon and orange peel from the brim, like an Australian bush hat.

On impulse she asked: 'How much?'

'For you, sweetheart, £2.50.'

I'll only have a quid left, she said to herself, but to hell with it!

'I'll take it,' she grinned at the white-haired man. 'It might just fit my boyfriend's head!'

He packed it up very carefully in a brown paper bag, adding a sprig of mistletoe 'just for you sweetheart'; and she packed it up just as carefully in her haversack then carried on down, across the pelican crossing and up onto the bridge. The ducks still sat on the golden water, waiting for Matilda and their waltzing daily bread and Marly, peering over, caught a glimpse of her own reflection and was startled by it. It wasn't an horrendous thing at all. Not an horrendous thing at all. She saw a tall, slim woman dressed in a shapeless coat, her long hair shimmering in the pale white sunshine. She wasn't perfect by any means, not perfect like the women in the magazines but she was real, she existed, she had a right to be happy, to be loved. Marly felt quite sure at that moment that she was real, that she existed and that she had a right to be happy, to be loved.

How the world changed when your head changed! It was a world of many mirrors, they really should have said, reflecting and distorting your own self right back to you. She'd waited too long in her little cocoon, waiting to get through the chrysalis stage, waiting to break out into a butterfly. Waiting for the world to burst open like a flower. A butterfly that lives a day has lived an eternity, someone had said and it was sort of true. Better to live one day as a butterfly than thirty years as a cocoon. She would live her life as a butterfly now, a beautiful golden, orange-tip butterfly.

(They dip their wings in the marmalade jar, her father had said for an April Fools when one sailed through the kitchen window.)

Best to forget the bad and remember the good. Be valiant, her stars had said that week, and turn your back on the past. The magic was in the choosing, choosing to forget and forgive. Love and happiness weren't just things that happened to you – they didn't just charge out of the horizon in shining armour or sit in a crock at the end of the rainbow – they were choices you made. And it wasn't just one choice. You had to choose again and again, every second, every minute, every hour, every day, every week, every month, every year.... Bad things came and went like clouds over the sun – that's what Terry said, what he meant. Bad things came but they got washed away. Only the sun remained, day after day.

The magic was back – she could feel it there in her hands – like stars and seas, sunsets and horses, glitter hats and autumn leaves, secrets, toboggans, buttered toast and cocoa. So much to see, to feel, to explore and the feeling that life had a purpose, that there was some amazingly wonderful reason for her own life and everyone else's. Marly felt quite sure at that moment that there was some amazingly wonderful reason for her own life and everyone else's. The magic was there in the palm of her hand and all she had to do was keep a hold of it. She almost ran up the hill, clutching the haversack in front of her, her thin arms wrapped tightly about it as though she were carrying a child. She would sneak past the house and up to the churchyard, have a sit down on Umfreville's tomb and write out the clues to the treasure hunt. Yes, that's what she'd do, tiptoe quietly past the house in case he was up and looking out for her, write down the clues on Umfreville's tomb. Oh knickers was the first one – a tangerine tucked away in her socks and pants drawer. Maybe something like Dr Barnardo's for the second – a tub of crisps stuck in the toe of one of his boots! She could just imagine his reaction: 'Gee, thanks a bunch. Just what I always wanted: cheesy crisps for two!'

What fun they'd have! Little stocking presents hidden all over the flat, silver tinsel, glitter hats, golden bells, mince pies and marshmallows roasting on the gas fire's fake flame. The magic was back – like starlight and gasoline rainbows, funny films and old school annuals, Christmas and bonfire night – the world an enchanted place to be.

It was quite hot in the churchyard for a winter's day: the horse-chestnut trees seemed to swoon in the haze and silver snail trails mazed the tarmac. A ginger cat lay twitching on Charles Messenger's grave, losing one of his lives in a dream or playing out a scene in a Tom & Jerry cartoon. Marly dumped her haversack down on the smooth, flat tomb of Umfreville and squinted up at the sky. The sun glimmered and gleamed like a great golden bauble and the stone was warm beneath her hands. She dug out her biro from the bottom of the haversack and a few bits and pieces to write on: the back of her mother's old shopping list, a few curled-up receipts, an unused brown paper bag; but instead of writing out the clues to the treasure hunt she found herself writing a letter to David, in fits and starts – saying the things she wanted to say, had never said, felt she ought to say: how they must stop the endless hurt and endless recompense, about her guilt and gratitude, how she had never understood the layout of his heart, too busy navigating her own.... Now and then she paused to think and looked about her at the graves: angel wings tottering heavenward, stone crosses teetering backwards, black and gold marble, glinting and dangerous, a rail-guarded tomb protecting, no doubt, the bones of some illustrious family – the Miskins probably – they had a street named after them (where her landlady lived) and a theatre.... A few open, granite bibles where several poor unfortunates had obviously been bored to death reading a psalm, a grassy mound in the shape of a bolster, the mischievous spirit having stuck a pillow in the earth and gone off on some mad escapade or other, and a wonky, ancient, sunken thing that proclaimed his owner had turned once too often in the grave.... A flower pot sat upside down on J. and A. Firminger's little plot and Marly got up to straighten it, noticing how young the man had been when he died. What a span of years she'd lived after the death of her sweetheart. What an awful burden of years. Loving husband, beloved wife, dutiful daughter, treasured one now sleeping in Jesus and other strange euphemisms. Gone but not forgotten to the lord's kindly besom....

She almost dozed off for a while, stretched out on the tomb of Umfreville, the scraps of letter in her hand. The sun bore down on her upturned face, fizzing and flashing beneath her eyelids in a kaleidoscope of colour, a light-fantastic show, though the tips of her toes still pinched with cold. She heard a magpie yackety-yacking somewhere behind her ear and she said out loud a little ironically: 'Hello Mr Magpie, how's your wife?' then smiled to herself. She must break these stupid superstitions and obsessions. She must break through the walls and tunnels of her mind. 'Look at it twice,' David had said, 'and you've got yourself two for joy!' She sat up a little dizzily at that but the magpie had disappeared and she came face to face with a robin perched on Firmingers' flower pot. His eyes were like little black, glistening raisins and he cocked his head and looked at her from one, then the other, as if he didn't know which to believe. He chirruped and poked around the flower pot for a moment, pecked at a cobweb that glittered in the sun like a small lace handkerchief then flew off over the wall into one of the gardens that ramshackled up to the bottom of the cemetery. Marly collected her belongings, carefully placing the fragments of letter in an inside pocket of her haversack – a scent of newly baked bread and currant bun wafted up at her and she decided it was time for lunch. High time for lunch! She slipped the haversack over her shoulders and strode out of the churchyard, past the ginger cat still twitching at a Tom & Jerry cartoon or losing one of his lives in a dream.

The town traffic roared in her ears as she sped down the hill, and the too-big daisy ring jogged up and down on her chest. Perhaps a gold ring didn't make you more invisible after all; perhaps it made you more real. Perhaps a gold ring solidified things... Marly Morrell had a bit of a jingle to it. They would be married like Arwen and Elessar, she would look astonishing in her mother's dress, stars on the sleeve. Honeymoon in Greece, Paris, Las Vegas. And they would have children. Of course she would be able to have children. A boy and a girl, John and Candelabra. What a name for a little girl Candelabra would be! She would give them braces and ballet lessons, take them rollerblading in the park, to the zoo, the aquarium. Invite their friends round for tomato soup and cheese on toast. Pick them up from discos far too early to be cool. And they would grow old together, she and David. Hand in hand they would set off on that last strange journey: taking picnics in the car, pottering around amidst the rhododendrons and the archives of their lives, finding each other all over again in a new disguise.... She saw it all stretching into the distance like a beautifully embroidered tapestry, a brightly painted collage…. She didn't need a rose-covered cottage on a cliff, didn't need to run away like a sailor to the sea, didn't need to take a plane ticket bareback into the waves. It was all right here in the palm of her hand, as it had always been. The world lay at her feet, ready to explore, halfway down the hill in that cramped and rundown flat. She smiled, her neck poking forward under the weight of the straps like an etiolated plant making a bid for the sun: she was going home.

The front door opened with that strange shoosh shooshing noise and…

'Hello.' No reply. No peep over the banister.

She pelted up the stairs two at a time and placed the haversack carefully in a corner of the bedroom. No one was there. The bed was newly made, the curtains wide. He must be in the sitting room, she thought, engrossed in the TV magazine or hiding somewhere for a practical joke. She laughed at the ridiculousness of him and crept across the carpeted hallway ready to surprise him.

But no one was there – the blue magnetic butterfly sat cold and alone on the heater, no gas fire's pretend embers lit.

'David?' she called querulously. Where *was* he?

His coat was hanging from the hatstand, his money belt there on the chair. He couldn't have gone anywhere.

The kitchen was cold and bare: the dishes freshly washed and stacked, no smell of dinner cooking in the oven to go with the new-bought bread and scone; everything packed up and swept away – the marmalade jar, crumbs of toast. A little morsel of cheese sat ready and waiting to entice the mice. Humane Dead Cert it had said on the box… Marly's head went suddenly quiet and cold like a whisper or a feather or a listening snowflake, though outside the sun still glittered like a great golden bauble, a revolving disco light. The time it took to step to the bathroom went lightning quick yet oh so slow.... She tapped the wooden door with the gentlest of taps, fearful lest she disturb him – it opened with that strange shoosh shooshing noise and…

He lay quite still in red-coloured water, his eyes tight closed.
    'David?' she uttered, pale and perplexed, half hidden by the door. 'My love?'

No smile. No laugh. No reply.

At times of great physical or mental agony, the mind detaches from the body apparently. The body carries on and the mind goes off on holiday or follows a few steps behind like a dozy sidekick or little old familiar. And so it was with Marly: her legs hastened her over to David, her fingertips felt the temperature of the water, his pulse, opened the little window, unplugged the bath, bandaged up the gash that went from elbow to wrist in pure white liniment. Her arms threw towels around his cold wet dripping body, pulled him roughly and breathlessly over into what she thought was the recovery position. Her voice calmly and efficiently summoned an ambulance to 120 East Hill.... Her heart bonged and pranged on xylophone ribs...

And all the while her body did these things her mind kept up a little chatter of its own, a flare of hope:
    *No doubt some practical joke ho ho... putting ketchup in the bath... ketchup on his arms and legs, ketchup on his face and toes. He just couldn't live without ketchup. What what! What a lot of ketchup the gods must need for their daily bread…. He'll be back in the early hours, crawling drawling brawling his way back home, if I sit quite still and quiet as a mouse. He'll turn up again like a little bad old penny ho ho.*

Her body darted about the flat, this way and that, searching for clues: a note, a sign, perhaps a goodbye… and her hands fluttered in front of her, uselessly waving the air like flowers or frantically sponging the blood from the walls, the knife, a marbled eyelid, the tip of his nose…

*Oh Rudolph the red-nosed reindeer*
*Had a very shiny nose*
*And if you ever saw him*
*You would even say it glows.*
*All of the other reindeer*
*Used to laugh and call him names*
*They wouldn't let poor Rudolph*
*Join in any reindeer games.*
*Then one foggy Christmas Eve*
*Santa came to say*
*'Rudolph with your nose so bright*
*Won't you guide my sleigh tonight?'*
*Then all the reindeer loved him*
*And they shouted out with glee*
*'Rudolph the red-nosed reindeer*
*You'll go down in history.*
*You'll go down in his sto ry.'*

When everything was spruce and neat and clean she stopped and waited. She waited as the great golden bauble spun behind a cloud and the rain began. In films the ambulance always comes in a jiffy but in real life it takes an eternity. She sat beside the bath and gripped his hand, her breath breathing warm life over him; and it seemed to her that her own life had come full circle and she was back at the beginning of some endless, hopeless journey; that some unlawful throw of the dice had sent her sliding to the bottom of the snake again. The rain pattered down on the roof like little footsteps or shouts of protest, soft insistent protests; and she was glad because he loved the rain – with or without an umbrella – it reminded him of the hills and valleys of Wales. She sat and held his hand in the darkening room and waited for the ambulance. She sat quite still and quiet as a mouse, a whisper, a feather, a listening snowflake. She wished the ambulance would hurry up so that it could all be over and she might go to sleep again and wake up in a dream. Marly felt quite sure at that moment that for the rest of her life there would only be dreams.

Dearest David

I'm glad we had that argument and glad you made me see how close I came to losing you. I don't want to lose you. I've dealt so long with the evil in my head (and I don't think evil's too strong a word) that when you came along I put it onto you and into the world and wondered why it came back. I treated you like shit and then wondered why you started behaving like shit. And then, when you started behaving like shit I felt justified in treating you like shit... and, feeling guilty when you hurt yourself, I hated you more and treated you worse.

But I always loved you. I think I loved you from the first moment I saw you in your Tony Hancock t-shirt with your wide shy tender smile, your funny jokes and the letter you sent me so full of the things I wanted to be told. You, the mathematician, so good at letter writing. You, the mathematician, so imaginative. How far I thought I was above you when we first met and how soon I came to see that I didn't even come up to your knees. How real you are and alive, my rock, my velveteen rabbit! And how I love you for that! You have no need of a Terry to guide you, as I do, seeing your way so clearly (all those carrots you had as a child!), surefooted as a cat through the quagmires that bog me down.

And how you've helped me. Never think for a moment you didn't help me. If it weren't for you I shouldn't still be here. You, with your patience, your understanding, your simple uncomplicated love; your humour that kept me from fits of distraction, your incredible, ingenious responses to my illness (your fairies, feathers and Quality Street spell, your 'gorgeous gorgeous gorgeous' refrain); not to mention your generosity for, as you rightly say, I have no financial capability – I sucked you dry, like a spider on a dark cloud, reeling you in, wrapping you up, leaving you bloodless. Weaving my silken lies (for, as you say, my whole life is built on a fabrication) to gain sympathy, love, respect... playing the victim when I was really the monster. And you, seeing through the sham, hypocrisy, dishonesty and pretension – what astonishing luck for me – you still loved me. I can't quite believe you loved me, for all that.

Yet how I took you for granted – believing it some natural right that you should love me, help me. Making your love unconditional yet mine so conditional. Making our relationship an unequal equation. You bore the brunt of it, taking it all in for my sake. I poured the crap out, believing myself to be sharing not destroying. Overwhelmed by my own misery, I never saw yours. (Please forgive me for that. I shall spend the rest of my life trying to make it up to you.) You faced my reality – how selflessly – never burdening me with your own. I live my life, you might say, on too many points of an Argand diagram while you, my love, are that famously fabulous Fibonacci flower, as Turing might have said. (Well he might have done!)

Terry says we see the rainbow for a while and then it's

gone. I must try to keep it in my mind's eye. Will you help me? I know I've made you ill but I can make you well again. We can both be well. We can both regenerate, can't we, like the flowers? Maybe we can see the end of the rainbow together, you and I, if you like. Please let's try.

I love you always,
Marly

## About the Author

Zillah Bethell lives in Wales with two children, two cats, one husband and an old piano.

# Acknowledgements

With thanks to Penny Thomas for her support, encouragement, and editing precision; DSB for his verbal inventiveness and Grade 8! and SPMB for her unfailing good humour.